GW00360197

Devil's Fire, Love's Revenge

WORDSWORTH ROMANCE

Devil's Fire, Love's Revenge

BARBARA PAUL

WORDSWORTH EDITIONS

The paper in this book is produced from pure wood
pulp, without the use of chlorine or any other substance
harmful to the environment. The energy used in its
production consists almost entirely of hydroelectricity
and heat generated from waste materials, thereby
conserving fossil fuels and contributing little to the
greenhouse effect.

This edition first published by Macdonald & Jane's Publishers Ltd

This edition published 1994 by
Wordsworth Editions Limited
Cumberland House, Crib Street, Ware,
Hertfordshire SG12 9ET

ISBN 1 85326 519 5

Printed and bound in Denmark by Nørhaven

Devil's Fire, Love's Revenge

Chapter One

Along the narrow country lane fringed by acid-pink willow-herb and bordered by low dry-stone walls went the horse and wagonette driven by a girl with whip and reins in her slim, capable hands, her velvet bonnet ribbons dancing madly over one shoulder, her full, striped skirt a flurry of wind-ruffled frills. It was a blustery morning after the previous night's rain, but shining, bright, and clear, the sky full of swallows and martins, a few seagulls careening on lazy wings. Racing clouds, riding high and billowy, dappled with a moving pattern of sunlight and shade the broad flanks of Howling Hill, which dominated the undulating landscape. The wind, blowing in vigorously across the Lancashire fells from the Irish Sea created the particularly draughty current that had given the hill its bleak name long since and brought with it the blended scents of watermint and wet earth, meadowsweet and crushed wild thyme.

With a little upward tilt of her chin Delia Gilmore bliss-fully inhaled the pot-pourri. A signpost went by when she turned the horse at the cross-roads, but she gave it no glance, being more than familiar with the route she was following. She was on the last lap to the house known as Halewood Hall, which graced dramatically the summit of the great hill. Twice a week for over a year she had made the short journey from the market town of Penghyll where she lived, and the little tasks she did at Halewood gave her an exhilarating sense of independence at a time when no young woman in her station of life was expected to do more than decoratively await the day when she would marry.

But it was a state of affairs not without its disadvantages too. First of all, there was the strange empathy she had with the house itself, which tore at her heart with its mellow-stone beauty and sometimes exerted on her a pressure of unknown secrets that caused her a disquiet she felt unable to discuss with anyone. Then there was the curiosity she encountered whenever people heard that she had an *entrée* to a place that had kept its gates locked against the world for a number of years. They tried to question her in devious ways, and even her closest friends were not above trying to trick information out of her, but she knew how to keep her own counsel and would no more have revealed the happenings at Halewood than her father, Dr Charles Gilmore, would have betrayed his patients' confidences.

Last, but by no means least, was Matthew Shaw's disapproval of her visits to the house. He hated Halewood. If he could possibly help it he would not mention it by name, and the only time he ever referred to it of his own free will was to ask her if she had decided to give up going there yet. She guessed he considered it an affront to his male dignity that his betrothed should even partly earn a living as a scribe and general factotum, no matter that it was in the capacity of friend to a titled personage, Lady Hart, who was virtually a recluse, but this piece of pompous silliness on his part was his only real fault and she felt the deepest affection for him, the man who had been her childhood sweetheart, and she knew how greatly he loved her.

With a slight frown she glanced down at her gloved left hand that was gripping the reins and tightened it into a fist, making the fine kid stretch over the pearl and ruby ring. Why then, when she had cared for Matthew for as long as she could remember and had no doubts that he would be all she wanted in a husband, did she avoid setting a date for their marriage? Could the reason be that which he had once

2

shouted at her in sudden exasperation? Had Halewood set up a barrier between them? Was it true that it had laid some kind of spell on her? She did not entirely disbelieve it. There were many kinds of enchantment. All she knew was that she wasn't ready to break her ties with it yet. Not until — what? She wasn't sure.

The horse, its satin rump dancing in the shafts, took the last bend in the lane. Ahead, set between dragon-headed pillars in a high stone wall, were the tall gates of Halewood. As usual she experienced that odd, ambivalent pang of the heart at the sight of the house beyond them. Giving the reins a tug, she slackened the horse's pace. The lodge-keeper had spotted her, but he was old and it took him a long time to move his arthritic joints to the gates, which he would unlock with a key fit for a castle fortress.

The horse, familiar with the routine, came to a placid halt facing the gates, and Delia sat looking directly through the veil of intricate iron-work to the beech-lined drive, which curved no less than half a dozen times before it opened out into the forecourt of the house that crested the hill. Out of the glory of the Elizabethan Renaissance had been created that edifice of great bay windows, elaborate carving, and giant pilasters. An archway in its glorious, symmetrical south front led to a vast inner courtyard around which the house formed a perfect quadrangle and therein lay the grand porch entrance with an impressive flight of twenty wide stone steps. On her work-a-day visits Delia used the less imposing, but no less splendidly built doorway in the rear of the building, which faced a spread of lawn and gave convenient access from the house to the stables and coach-houses.

Long ago in childhood she had woven tales about Halewood, for she had been able to see it from her attic bedroom window in the living quarters above the surgery in Penghyll's market square, and if her parents had not decided to move into a larger, grander house when the practice had expanded, she would have been able to see it still. It was years before she discovered it had its own stories to tell, more dramatic and tragic than anything she had ever invented. By that time she was growing up and her mother dead. And far away in a foreign country Edward Hart, the estranged only son of old Sir Harry of Halewood, had died too, and for the first time in three hundred years there was no heir that anyone had heard of to inherit the great house on the hill whenever the time should come.

Local people thought that was why Sir Harry had married again so late in life, bringing home from one of his rare visits to London a wife much younger than himself, a woman whom nobody had heard of or knew anything about, but if he had hoped for a child it was not to be. He had gone to his grave a year ago, leaving everything to his wife, Berenice, who had made one of her rare public appearances at the funeral, but the heavy black veil she wore gave no curious person a better chance to see her face than on any other occasion when she ventured out of the grounds in a closed carriage.

'Mornin' to thee, lass.' The lodge-keeper had come shuffling into sight, swaying with every difficult step, the key in his knotted hand.

'Good morning, Mr Newby,' Delia replied. 'What a lovely day.'

'E-eh, it is tha'.' The key screeched. The gates began to open.

The horse went trotting through. The lodge-keeper's wife gave the girl a wave from an upper window, which was returned generously. At nineteen Delia, friendly and out-going, possessed appealing looks, an intelligent mind, and a slim-waisted figure. Her face was finely moulded with a neat, straight nose and firm chin, her skin creamy, and her eyes, which were a clear, light grey, direct and straightforward in their looking, were shadowed to a deeper shade by the sweep

4

of dark lashes under arched brows. There was an unconscious sensuality about her mouth, which was full-lipped and red, for she was capable of enormous passion, but the knowledge of it was not yet hers, the rigid conventions governing a betrothment having kept her wholly chaste, and it would not have occurred to her that it might have been otherwise.

Although the beech trees bordering the drive created a wind-break to a certain degree, nothing ever kept at bay the gusts that swirled about the hill, causing branches, bushes, flowers, and grass to sway and dance in rhythm under its spasmodic onslaught. Only when thick mist came rolling in did the endless friction of the wind die into silence and then the whole countryside would lie oppressed by a grey canopy, leaving Halewood enclosed in stillness and shut away from the rest of the world.

Delia had just freed a hand to press her bonnet a little firmer on to her head after the wind had tugged sharply at it when a brougham approached round a curve in the drive, coming from the direction of the house. When it drew near she recognized the passenger inside as Mr Radleigh, a local lawyer, who attended to Lady Hart's legal affairs. He was sitting with a leather briefcase across his knees and he lifted his hat as he passed her. She wondered what important business had brought him to Halewood so early in the day.

She was soon to know. In an east wing room, which had been allotted to her as an office from the first day she had started work at the house, she hung away her bonnet and jacket in a cupboard and tidied her wind-blown, light brown hair before a looking-glass on the wall. She wore her hair parted in the middle, drawn smooth over the temples, which emphasized her high forehead, and dressed in long ringlets over her ears. Satisfied with her appearance, she set off for Berenice's apartments, which by tradition had been occupied by the mistress of Halewood ever since the house was first built.

The suite was on the same upper floor as the office, but in the parallel west wing, which gave Delia a daily choice of route to take to get there. She could either walk the corridor that spanned the archway in the south front, or she could traverse the portrait gallery, which stretched the length of the north wing that was still used by Berenice, who was following in the footsteps of generations of Halewood ladies before her, as a place to stroll for gentle exercise when the weather was bad and it was impossible to venture into the grounds. Usually Delia chose the corridor, for the gallery was a gloomy place on dark days, having no windows and being illumined by a vaulted roof of glass, which was entirely original. Unfortunately the charming distortions of the old glass were masked by a film of greenish dirt outside, for due to the inaccessibility of the roof for cleaning, a mammoth and hazardous task, it was left untouched from one year's end to another, and the strange underwater light that resulted gradually deepened in hue and made the gallery a place of mystery and shadows.

But today being bright and sunny, Delia went to the west wing by way of the gallery and ran the gauntlet of those rows of Halewood eyes, which arrogantly returned the gaze of anyone studying the portraits. More than once she had experienced a sense of unease when, lost in thought or con-templation of some task in hand, she had happened to glance idly to the left or right and found herself enmeshed in a cold Halewood stare that followed her relentlessly until the doors at the end of the gallery swung closed behind her.

Whenever Delia entered the small yellow drawing-room she never failed to appreciate its charm and lightness. Today, with the sun streaming in through the windows, it was like a golden bowl filled with light, a buttercup sheen to the silk-panelled walls, a reflecting glitter in the crystal droplets of wall-sconce and chandelier, and in the woven

carpet a pattern of tiger lilies and mimosa ma
spread of matching brilliance.

Berenice was fond of the room and used it or
lying against cushions on a sofa, wearing a gre
morning gown with sloped shoulders and fashionably
sleeves that came in tight at the wrist. Although a widow and
a matron she did not wear a cap, but preferred always to
drape a mantilla of filmy scallop-edged lace over her head,
crossing it under her chin to fall behind her over both shoulders. It gave her protection should she come across some
person whom she had no wish to acknowledge or address,
the merest incline of her head bringing the lace drifting
forward to shadow her features; in addition it helped keep in
place her burnished, red-gold hair, which she wore looped
over her ears up into a top-knot, for being gossamer fine it
would tumble at the slightest disorder of pins into a flaming
cascade down her extraordinarily beautiful face, the bones of
which stood out a little harder and more brilliantly than they
should have done, due to her thinness, for she ailed in the
North Country dampness and often declared she had never
been really well since coming to Halewood. Well-matched to
the magnificence of her hair and enhancing beyond measure
the perfection of her features was her flawless complexion,
pale indeed to be almost transparent, but the faintest hint of
applied rose colour gave a glow to the wide cheekbones.
Most striking of all were her eyes, velvet-dark as purple
pansies, but so lustrous that the light seemed to go from her
whole countenance whenever she closed her lids.

When Delia crossed the room to her, Berenice smiled in
greeting and gestured languidly towards the small table
hung with a lace cloth on which stood a silver chocolate pot,
shell-thin cups, and a gilded and painted dish of ratafias.

'Pour the coffee, Miss Gilmore. It's just been brought in
and it's fresh and hot. Mr Radleigh was here, but he
wouldn't take any refreshment.'

7

'...met him leaving when I was half-way up the drive,' ...ia answered, lifting the chocolate-pot.

'I sent for him. I'm going to sell Halewood.'

Berenice's words were so startling and unexpected that Delia almost overfilled the cup in front of her. 'Sell it? Sell Halewood? Oh, you can't!' Then seeing the slightly quizzical expression on the woman's face, she bit her lip apologetically. 'I'm sorry. It's no business of mine, but why? Please tell me why.'

Berenice took the cup that Delia handed to her and sipped at it. 'I thought you might have guessed that I've had the idea in my head for some time.'

Delia sat down on a brocade-upholstered chair, facing her. 'I've seen that you've not been happy,' she ventured tactfully.

Berenice gave a bitter little croak of a laugh, lifting her chin. 'I've loathed every minute I've had to spend under this roof. Do you know, I married Sir Harry for this house. Not his money or his title, but for Halewood. I thought to escape from a life that had brought me much misery and heartache. In my folly I saw Halewood as a refuge, a retreat, a place of peace. How wrong I was! It's a watching, hostile house. I'd have gone from it the day my husband died if that could have been possible, but naturally I had to wait for all the complicated affairs of his estate to be settled. Now at last I can dispose of Halewood and its contents and all the land that goes with it.'

'You mean you'll take none of the beautiful things in the house?' Delia gasped.

'I want nothing to remind me of my years here. Everything is to be sold.' Berenice put aside the half-drunk cup and leaned her head back against the cushions, the mantilla wafting into folds, a look of blissful anticipation on her features. 'I feel like a caged linnet watching the unlocking of its prison.'

8

It was on the tip of Delia's tongue to blurt out a warning not to tempt the house with such innocent optimism, but she told herself not to be foolish. This was the nineteenth century, the year of 1848, a time of enlightenment and great industrial progress. Not the dark ages. Yet the old belief that Halewood enveloped in an ancient curse all those bearing the name of Hart, either through birth or marriage, who had ever lived in it, was not to be lightly dismissed. Although she loved the house, her eye always delighting in its beauty, at times a sudden upsurge in the turbulence of its atmosphere could be alarming, although always to her it seemed as if the house sought to break free from the evil bonds that held it, and her first sharp fear of Halewood's sinister side had long since subsided into a wary caution.

'Where shall you go?' she asked.

'I fancy Italy. Mr Radleigh has my instructions. He's setting a foreign agent to find the kind of residence I have in mind and has recommended a London agent to take charge of the sale of Halewood. It has to be sold by public auction. That was a stipulation laid down in Sir Harry's will. Naturally he thought I'd live in it until the end of my days and it would be put up for sale after my demise. So it will go up at the Penghyll Assembly Rooms as soon as everything can be arranged. Mr Radleigh suggested an auction of the contents of the house where they stand, but that I'll not allow. Hordes of people are not coming to poke and pry in idle curiosity. Viewing the house itself shall be by appointment only, and after the auctioneer's gavel falls on Halewood I'll leave it looking exactly as it was when I first walked into it eight years ago. Only then will the removal men take over, and all the furniture, the pictures, and everything else will be boxed and crated and despatched to the best of the London salerooms. I want the contents of Halewood dispersed far and wide. Only thus do I see a lessening of the house's power to hurt and destroy. A superstitious whim, perhaps, but one

9

that I intend to follow through.'

'I wonder who will buy Halewood,' Delia said uneasily. She rose and went across to the mullioned window where she looked down into the inner court. In the centre of it lay a long, rectangular green sward surrounded by the flagged drive, unchanged since the architect wrote on a plan of the house in black ink: *Halewoode whereof ye first stone was layd 1569*.

'One of the *nouveaux riches*, I expect,' Berenice replied without interest. 'There are enough of them springing up out of Lancashire's boom. A cotton-mill owner, perhaps. Or a shipping magnate. Or maybe one of the mine-owning families will move in. Many of them are building, or have built, enormous red brick monstrosities to live in, I understand, but others prefer to watch out for the older and better properties, believing that it gives them a more acceptable status in society if they acquire the trappings of a past grander than their own.'

Delia did not turn, but there was a low note of anguish in her voice. 'Some of those properties get altered beyond recognition. Suppose Gothic towers were added to Halewood! Or the archway taken down and a new and horrible façade put in its place. It would be sacrilege!'

Berenice was unmoved. 'I do not care what happens to Halewood. I owe it nothing.'

Delia left the window and came slowly back to sink down on the edge of the chair she had vacated, her hands clasped tightly together in her lap. 'May I make a suggestion? It could be that you will think it impertinent of me, but it is something I feel I must say.'

Berenice raised her eyebrows with a slight smile. 'You sound very solemn. Speak freely. We've known each other for – is it more than a year since you were first carried into this house with your terrible leg injuries and I wouldn't allow you to be moved?'

'Eighteen months and two weeks, to be exact.' Delia

smiled, too. 'You were kindness itself to me. Papa said the Queen herself couldn't have been better nursed than, I was. And then when I started convalescing and took over writing letters for you – a task you detest – it led to my coming here twice a week to deal with your correspondence and anything else you wanted done. I've often wondered why, when you shun all company and live only for your books and your painting, you insisted on caring for me yourself, doing everything in your power to distract my mind from the pain I was enduring. You read to me for hours on end and brought your easel to my bedside, so that I could watch you paint. Then your patience was boundless in helping me to take my first steps in learning to walk again.'

Berenice answered reflectively, her smile a trifle wan, a look of tiredness across her eyes. 'I've known what it is to need encouragement. That's one of the reasons why I'll always be grateful to your father. He is a clever physician and has taken good care of me since I became his patient soon after coming to Halewood. Looking after you gave me a chance to show my appreciation in a practical way. Then there was the fact that you suffered your injury in the grounds of the house itself – even though Sir Harry did call you a trespasser, which was mightily unfair of him, considering the circumstances – and I felt duty-bound to try to undo some of the harm inflicted on you.' She paused, tapping the tip of her forefinger against the side of her mouth. 'No, I must be honest. It was more than that. It was an act of defiance against Halewood itself, which I blamed entirely for your misfortune. I decided if I could nurse you back to health and help you walk again – and there was a strong possibility at first that this might never be achieved without the permanent use of crutches or a stick – I would at least have achieved something of value during my barren years as the woman of Halewood.'

Delia caught her breath. 'You know that the local

townsfolk call you that?'

A cynically amused twist took over Berenice's lovely mouth. 'They only echo the words of those in a certain stratum of society who believe that Sir Harry married beneath him and regret that I've never given them an opportunity to snub me.'

Delia leaned forward in protest. 'How dare they even think it! Sir Harry wasn't fit to lace your shoe. He was vulgar and coarse-mannered and rougher than any navvy working on one of Matthew's railway lines. Oh!' She could have bitten off her tongue at having spoken out so frankly — albeit truthfully — against her listener's late husband, and she coloured deeply, the rose flooding up her neck and into her cheeks.

But Berenice was not offended. She shared Delia's opinion, and although she knew even better and with much bitter cause that gentlemen such as Sir Harry were greatly misnamed, she did not intend to reveal that.

'Well,' she said with a show of severity, 'having made that statement, what else is it that you wish to say to me? It can't be worse, that's for certain. Come along. Speak up. What suggestion was it that you wanted to make?'

With the flush still burning in her face Delia's words came in a rush. 'You remember the unopened letter we found in Sir Harry's desk when I was helping you go through his papers?'

'Yes. The one that turned out to be from his disinherited son, Edward, written from America.'

'If you remember, he had written specially to inform Sir Harry of the birth of his son, Aaron.'

'Well?'

'Mr Radleigh wrote to that grandson through the address on the letter and informed the young man of his grandfather's death as well as letting him know that there had been a second marriage leaving a widow.'

12

'Yes. The young man had the good manners to write me his condolences, which you acknowledged for me.'

Delia squared her shoulders firmly. 'I think Aaron Hart should be given fair notice of the sale of Halewood.'

'You don't imagine he would want to buy it?' Berenice exclaimed, throwing up her hands at the absurdity of the idea. 'Why should he? He was born in the New World and his roots are there. England is a foreign country to him. I doubt if he knows where Lancashire is on the map.'

'Whether he does or doesn't is beside the point. The fact remains that he has more right than anyone to Halewood. It should not go up for auction without his knowledge.'

Berenice sucked in her cheeks slightly, her eyes narrowing at Delia. 'Are you trying to say that he has more right to it than I?'

It was dangerous ground, but Delia plunged on. 'The fact that his father quarrelled with Sir Harry and was disinherited is no fault of his. Halewood is his natural birthright. Had Sir Harry ever opened that letter and known he had a grandson, his last will and testament might have been penned very differently.'

'You *are* impertinent, Miss Gilmore!' Berenice swung her feet to the floor and rose to her full height with an angry rustle of stiff petticoats. Her skirt swayed like a bell as she took a few paces one way and then the other, the ends of her mantilla floating out behind her. But after a minute or two she came to a halt, her indignation gone from her, and she acquiesced with a deep sigh. 'You've pointed out a hard fact to me, and it's not to be denied. The first letter you write for me today shall be to Mr Radleigh, telling him to inform the young man of the forthcoming sale.'

Delia did not relax. 'Allow me to write direct to Aaron Hart on your behalf. Every day counts with the post if he is to have sufficient time to consider the matter, to say nothing of travelling so great a distance should he decide to come and

13

make a bid for the house. Mr Radleigh can write with all the official data as soon as they are to hand.'

Berenice made a fluttering gesture as if to wave the whole topic away. 'Very well. Do as you please. Where is that letter of Edward's?'

'It's in my room in the east wing with all other correspondence that you wanted me to keep for you.'

'How old would Sir Harry's grandson be now?'

'If I remember rightly from the date of that letter, he'd be about twenty-six years old.' Delia dived into a pocket in her skirt and brought out a list she had made earlier at home. 'Before I write to him – and I want to catch the midday post – let me hear what else you wish me to do today. Have you decided on a pair of gloves out of the selection I ordered for you? And did you want me to settle the lace-maker's bill? It is somewhat overdue.'

The conversation stayed on such mundane subjects until Delia stood up to return to her study. Then Berenice referred to Aaron Hart again.

'There's one complication if he should make a decision to attend the auction. By all the rules of hospitality, and with his name and lineage, he should be accommodated at Halewood itself, but I neither want him here during my last days, nor do I wish to meet him. It could be both humiliating and embarrassing for him to stay in a common hostelry with everybody soon knowing who he was and that he had come to bid against all comers for a house that he should by rights have inherited. Have you any solution?'

The hint was obvious. 'Papa and I will gladly make him welcome at our home,' Delia answered sincerely, 'and if he has a wife and children to bring with him we can accommodate them as well.'

Berenice looked relieved. She was again lying on the sofa. 'Thank you. That's most kind. Then make the letter your own instead of preparing one for me to sign. Explain who you

14

are, why you are writing, and add your invitation at the same time.'

'I'll do that,' Delia said with a nod and left the room.

She sent a servant to the post with the letter ten minutes later. It would reach Liverpool that same night and the next day it should be in a mail-bag in the hold of a fast packet bound for the United States of America. Boston was Aaron Hart's city. Delia, about to return his letter of condolence to the box from which she had taken it to get his address, looked again at the name of the house where he lived. Lincolnshire Hall. That sounded quite grand.

Hadn't she read somewhere that Boston had received its name from the town of Boston in Lincolnshire, several of the English immigrants who founded the city having come from there? She must look it up. There was a lot she must look up. All she had learned in the past about the North American continent and its history needed refreshing. She would not have Aaron Hart find her ignorant about his country when he came.

With the letter still in her hands she went across to the terrestrial globe that stood in a corner of the room and sent it spinning slowly on it axis. Ah! There was Aaron's city. Boston. Rich in its own newly-moulded history, where on a fateful day British soldiers had fired on unarmed citizens in its streets and brought the American Revolution that much nearer. Her finger, pin-pointing it, rested on the wavy, blue rim of the sea into which the famous cargo of tea had been dumped with such angry defiance and such shattering results. All that had been over long, long before, when young Edward Hart had turned his back on his home among the grey, rain-swept fells of Lancashire and set his face towards a new life in a new country, vowing that the past was behind him for ever. Yet, in spite of bitterness and anger and filial enmity, would he have managed to instil in his son something of his inherent feelings for an ancestral home that had

15

been old when the Pilgrim Fathers had first set foot on American soil?

But that was something not to be known until a reply came from Aaron Hart. She glanced again at his letter and thought what a strong and positive hand he had. It was the writing of a man who knew what he wanted out of life. She hoped he would want Halewood, but she had no power to will him across the sea, no matter how she feared for the fate of the house in the hands of others with more brass – to use an old North Country term for money – than aesthetic values. Aaron Hart must make up his own mind. But oh! how she hoped he would come!

It was late afternoon when she arrived at Sycamore House on Victoria Avenue, which was situated in a quiet residential area of Penghyll. Ellen, the parlourmaid, opened the door to her and informed her that Mr Shaw had called to see her and was waiting in the drawing-room.

Hastily she shed bonnet, coat, and gloves. Never had she been more pleased to know that Matthew had come to see her. Never had she needed him more. With as much speed as she could muster she hurried to the drawing-room door, which stood ajar, and she paused on the threshold, savouring the sight of him, happy to remain unnoticed by him for a few moments until she chose to make her presence known.

He was leaning over a dissected puzzle, which lay spread out on an unfolded card-table, the light of the window behind him making a fair halo of his smooth, well-brushed hair, and he was trying to fit in one of the dozens of intricately cut wooden pieces that would eventually make up a picture of a pastoral scene. Even as she watched he clicked the piece down and, still unaware that she was there, he reached for another and tried again.

She took in every detail of his appearance. He was wearing a grey frock-coat that she had not seen before, its elegant style suiting his lean, long-limbed frame, the Paisley silk handkerchief, which flowed from a tail pocket, toned tastefully with his cravat; his profile was turned towards her, clear-cut as a monarch's head on a golden sovereign, his forehead broad, his prominent nose balanced by a strong chin, his mouth narrow-lipped and full of energy. Seeing how deeply he frowned over the puzzle, all her feelings for him swept over her in a warm and gentle wave. A month since she had last seen him. Far, far too long!

She moved forward with a little swaying swoop of her skirt. 'You look extremely busy!' she exclaimed teasingly, holding out her hands to him.

He raised his head with a start, broken out of his concentration, and his whole face lighted up at the sight of her. 'Delia! I didn't know you had returned!'

He came swiftly to her, taking her outstretched hands in his, and he drew her to him, kissing her lovingly on the mouth. There was a faint, familiar aroma about him of Macassar oil and starched linen and clean, young maleness, and she swayed against him, her eyes closed. His arms went about her and he kissed her more ardently, holding her close to him. When they drew apart, smiling at each other, she gave him a little reproachful tap of puzzlement on his chest with her forefinger.

'Why didn't you let me know you were coming? Not a word in your last letter! I would have left Halewood an hour ago if I'd known. Have you been waiting long?'

They had moved to the sofa while she had been speaking and they sat down beside each other.

'Not more than twenty minutes at the most, I suppose. I'd have driven to meet you if the parlourmaid hadn't reminded me that you sometimes leave Lady Hart early and do shopping for her in town.'

'Ellen was right to stop you. You could have missed me quite easily if that had been the case. I've such news! News that will please you, I know, although it will probably be two

17

or three weeks yet before it becomes public knowledge. But first of all I want to know why and how you managed to spring this surprise visit on me. The last I heard you were practically working round the clock to get the eastern end of the Manchester and Huddleston railway line finished ahead of time.'

He laughed, sitting back and crossing one leg over the other, his hand resting against her waist. 'So I have been – and the work went through faster than we dared hope. I've already been transferred to a new assignment – not a minor assistant engineer any longer, but promotion! I'm to be in charge of the construction of a new branch line that is to have its terminus at Penghyll.'

'Matthew! How wonderful!' She flung her arms about his neck and hugged him. 'Congratulations. It's what you've been hoping for. And to be at Penghyll itself.'

'I'll simply be visiting the district now and again while surveyors investigate suitable sites for the tracks, but after that I'll be permanently in this area until the line is finished.'

'Does that mean we'll be able to see each other really often?'

He clasped her hard to him, his face close to hers, his expression very serious and intense. 'Why not every day and every night, Delia? Let's get married. There's no need to wait any longer. We've been betrothed a long time – and before my ring was ever on your finger we both knew that one day you'd be my wife. I love you. If only you knew how much I love you.'

He bent his head and put his lips yearningly against her throat, sending a delicious little shiver through her, and tenderly she smoothed her finger-tips from his temple down to the line of his jaw. There was nothing to keep them from marrying. Halewood was to be sold, and no matter how she felt about the house there was nothing more she could do for it. In addition, her extremely pleasant little tasks there

18

would shortly come to an end and she would find time on her hands again. Why not use that time looking after Matthew? That was where her duty lay.

'Where would we live?' she whispered.

He knew it was the answer he had longed to hear. He raised his head, his expression adoring and jubilant. 'Dearest, you shall have any house that pleases you.'

The thought came unbidden to her mind. If only it could have been Halewood! Then she thrust it from her and let him sweep her into a joyful discussion of wedding plans. They talked of church and guests and the wedding breakfast, where they should live and whether the village of Miry-clough would be more convenient to his new assignment than the town of Pendlewick, both of which lay within a seven mile radius of Penghyll, but when they came to settle on the actual date for the ceremony she surprised him by saying she could not decide until she had seen Lady Hart again.

'Why ever not?' he asked, grinning in puzzlement. 'She'd never come to our wedding. Not unless it was held in Halewood itself with no other guests but her!'

She did not smile and he regretted his poor joke. That damnable house had been a bone of contention between them ever since she had recovered from her accident and started to go to work there, for paid employment was what it was, no matter how genteel the tasks she carried out. He hadn't been able to understand how her father could have allowed it. When he had tackled Dr. Gilmore about it the reply had been that it did Delia no harm to be useful and in his opinion his patient, Lady Hart, benefited greatly from having young company to cheer her isolation. So that had been that. But, Matthew thought grimly, as his wife Delia would have enough to do running their home and entertaining and sharing with him countless delights that would drive that place for ever from her heart.

Then he knew. It came to him why he loathed Halewood. In some extraordinary, indefinable way it had taken some part of her affections from him and instinctively he had been jealous of it without understanding why.

'Lady Hart will soon be leaving Halewood,' she explained, deep in her own thoughts and not noticing that he had given her an oddly self-conscious look. 'The house is going up for auction. That is the news I had for you. Of course it will take time for everything to be arranged, and I suppose the sale won't be for another two or three months, but I shall need the same amount of time to get my wedding dress made and my trousseau together, to say nothing of choosing everything for a home once we have found a house we like. We'll get married when Penghyll's annual Ball is over. By that time Halewood will be sold and the new owner settled in. My responsibilities there will all be discharged.'

'Then we're not to be married until late autumn or early winter by the sound of it,' he said, somewhat disgruntled. Now that he had pinned her down to a definite decision the burden of waiting even a short while longer seemed quite unendurable.

'What could be better?' Smiling, she leaned forward and put her cheek briefly against his in a velvet touch. 'It's such a wonderful time of year. There are still rowan berries on the trees and old man's beard on the hedges. If there's hard frost or early snow we'll draw the curtains tight against the night and sit together by the hearth with a cosy fire leaping up the chimney. There'll be time to talk about all the things we've never had time to talk about before, and I'll bake you blackberry-and-apple pies and gingerbread and the best plum cake you've ever tasted.'

Her words were affectionate and full of confidence. Having committed herself she would go forward with no aim other than to make him a good wife. That was her destiny. It was a path that had been set for her by circumstances, but one which she would tread lightly and with a glad heart. Why then did she not visualize it bathed in a rosy light? What was that little nagging doubt that she couldn't identify, but which was lurking somewhere at the back of her mind?

The sound of a carriage coming up the drive made her spring to her feet and dart to the window. 'It's Papa! Now we can tell him. He will be surprised.'

'And pleased, too, I hope,' Matthew said, coming to her side.

She looked up at him and was moved afresh by the devotion she saw in his eyes. If he loved her a little more than she loved him he should never know. It was a secret she would keep to herself to the end of her days. Nothing must hurt him. She would protect him, he who aimed to cherish her.

'Papa has always thought highly of you, as you well know,' she admonished lightly. 'Didn't he as much as say that when you asked formally for my hand? He's not likely to put up any obstacles at this late hour.'

Dr Gilmore entered soon afterwards. He was an erect, distinguished-looking man with shrewd eyes and a kindly mouth, his fairish hair brindled with grey. Through the open doors of the drawing-room he could see his daughter and her betrothed standing side by side waiting for him. As he went in to them he could tell by Delia's deep curtsey and Matthew's bow that they had something of importance to disclose. It wasn't hard to guess what it would be.

21

Chapter Two

With the wedding date settled there were many new demands on Delia's time, but she continued to go twice a week to Halewood, fitting in appointments at the dressmaker's or the milliner's in between. Looking at houses with Matthew, which changed from a pleasure to a chore as disappointment followed disappointment, also took up many more hours than she had anticipated. At first they had set out together with high hopes each time, but that soon dwindled. The houses were either too large or too small, faced a busy turnpike, distant slag heaps, or the high wheels of a coal mine. Some were awkward and inconvenient, others smelt of dry-rot. One in a Georgian terrace, gracious enough in appearance, proved to be overrun by rats. In the end it was she who came across the ideal residence and it was quite by chance while on her own.

She had gone that morning with Matthew to the village of Fellfoot where he was to keep an appointment with several important representatives of the Lancashire and Yorkshire Railway Company. There was to be a discussion on the findings of the Company's surveyors in that area. The siting of the new branch line was presenting difficulties, the expensive process of tunnelling being inevitable in such a hilly district, and the Company, wanting to keep down costs, had rejected one proposed route and were considering another.

Matthew had thought to be kept no more than a couple of hours at the most, but Delia, waiting in the chaise, came to the end of the novel she had brought with her and closed it, looking to see if there was any sign of his return. She sighed. She could see him with the little group of stovepipe-hatted men tramping along on the far side of the river, all holding maps and sheaves of papers that were fluttering in the wind. It did not seem that their business was anywhere near an end, judging by their animated conversation, which had every appearance of argument, and she decided to take a stroll through the village to pass the time.

She alighted from the chaise and set off leisurely along the main cobbled street, which was flanked by seventeenth-and-eighteenth-century houses, some of them quite large, a few with gardens in the rear, which were interspersed with several little shops where she lingered to look at the goods in the windows before wandering on again. A row of thatched cottages were clustered picturesquely together, and honey-suckle threaded the pointed railings of the nearby Norman church. She spent some time in the church, studying the ancient stained glass and the Jacobean three-decker pulpit and richly carved chancel screen. It was when she came out again that she saw in the side-lane a property for sale.

She opened the gate and went up the path. The house was built of greystone with a giant wistaria spreading gnarled branches over the porch and windows, the foliage hanging like green, tangled lace. She peered in the curtainless windows, cupping her hands against the glass to get a better view of the empty rooms, which were low-beamed, but well-proportioned, and the fireplaces were elegant. The house appealed to her in every way. If it proved to be as sound in structure as it appeared, she would suggest to Matthew that they look no further.

Holding up her skirt-hems she went down through the orchard and found that the river swirled right past the end of it. Even as she watched, a pair of wild duck rose in flight and she caught the flash of a kingfisher. That settled it. She would get hours of enjoyment from the river. But what was that in the grass on the opposite bank? It was a red-painted marker left by one of the railway company's surveyors! Her eyes searched along and she saw another. Her heart sank. She had thought to find quiet in Wistaria Lodge, for she had already named it in her own mind, but the tranquillity of it would be shattered by a railway line with locomotives rushing by belching black smoke over everything. Soot would lie on the leaves and the grass and darken the clear water.

How far did those markers go? Slowly she left the garden and found her way to a tow-path that ambled past cottage gardens to a bridge where the village extended to a number of picturesque, low-browed little dwellings on the other side of the river. The ominous red markers disappeared into the midst of them.

When Matthew returned, he found her waiting in her seat in the chaise, and he apologized somewhat abstractedly for being longer than he had expected, his mind very much on other things. But he did suggest they lunched at the inn before leaving Fellfoot.

The other railway gentlemen were there before them, but there was a table for two in an alcove. After ordering, Matthew busied himself with jotting down notes on some official-looking papers.

'Those markers,' she said tentatively, knowing he did not want to be disturbed, but unable to keep silent. 'If the tracks are laid on the other side of the river half the cottages by the bridge will have to come down.'

'Not half of them,' he replied, not looking up. 'All of them would have to go.'

'Where would all the occupants be housed?' she demanded, aghast.

He shrugged, still writing. 'That's not the concern of the railway company. It has been ascertained that the owner is willing to sell the land and the property. The tenants are his responsibility.'

'But if he gets a good price will he guarantee to rehouse those villagers?' she persisted.

'He'll get a good price – the value of land soars once it's known a railway company is interested, but there'll be no obligations put upon him. That's impossible anyway. It does happen sometimes in a farming community that the squire or landowner will see to it that other accommodation is made available, but in this case it's most likely that the villagers will have to shift for themselves as people have had to in other parts of the country.'

'That's montrous!'

He looked up from his writing then, mildly amused and slightly irritated by her vehemence, but she knew him well enough to know he was not so indifferent to the plight of those turfed out in the name of progress as he chose to appear.

'Don't get too upset about it,' he advised her with a half-smile. 'This surveyed route is proving no more popular with the Powers-That-Be than the first one. They will probably consider half a dozen more sitings before they reach a decision.'

Hope lifted in her. It sounded as though the cottages would be reprieved and the house by the river would remain steeped in quietude. 'I saw a house, Matthew,' she confided, her eyes sparkling. 'A pretty house – right by the river – and opposite those nasty markers. It's empty and it's for sale.'

He grinned at her and put his hand over hers on the table. 'Then we'll find out who has the key and look it over. I think there's a fair chance that Fellfoot will be by-passed by the railway.'

He liked the house as much as she. By the end of the week he was able to tell her definitely that the markers had been removed from Fellfoot and they could go ahead and buy the house. Not until everything was signed and sealed did she venture up into the attic by way of a precarious ladder,

25

although she had visited the house almost daily and the painters and carpenters were at work in every room.

'You forgot to tell me there's a window up here!' she called out to Matthew, who had inspected every inch of the house before buying it.

He appeared at the top of the ladder, resting his elbows on the attic floor while he waited to assist her down again. 'There's a good view. You can see for miles.'

She ran to the window, rubbed away the dust and looked out. Then her heart missed a beat. She could see Halewood on its hill. The sun, shining on its windows, caused it to blink at her like a watchful, golden eye.

She was somewhat subdued on the way home afterwards, but Matthew did not notice. When he left her at the gate she nodded absently when he reminded her he would be calling for her at seven o'clock, for they were to dine that evening with his grandparents, who had brought him up and with whom he was staying again for the time being.

'Is there anything wrong, my dear?' her father asked her later. He had come across her sitting with a book of world history, open at pages dealing with early colonial America, but she gazed unseeingly into space, her expression serious and preoccupied.

She turned with a little start and smiled at him. 'No, Papa. How could there be? It's just that – well, today I found I could see Halewood from the attic window of Wistaria Lodge. It reminded me of when I used to look out at it when I was a child, not knowing then that it was to put such a physical mark on me.' Briefly she indicated the folds of her skirt that hid the leg that had once been injured. 'It gave me the strangest feeling to view it again from a similar distance, although from the south this time instead of at a north-west angle.'

Dr Gilmore sat down in his favourite chair with a sigh of relaxation. He linked his hands across his waistcoat and set his feet on a footstool, folding them neatly at the ankles. He had had a long day, travelling a considerable distance to see an old patient in an outlying district, and afterwards in his surgery, which was always busy, he had dealt with a large number of poorer and less fortunately placed patients to whom he gave as much consideration and care as to those able to pay lavishly for attention. He had dealt with his partner's patients as well when the younger man had answered an emergency call to a man crushed under some machinery in a workshop, needing an amputation to set him free.

Until a few years ago when he had first taken on a partner, Dr Gilmore had felt able to take everything in his stride, but now at the age of sixty-three, although to all appearances a well-preserved and still remarkably young-looking man, he was not as fit as he might be, and he thought, not for the first time, that he would be glad to see Delia safely married and settled. There had been a period when he suspected she was having second thoughts about marrying Matthew, but he had said nothing, and whatever uncertainty she had been experiencing appeared to have passed. He approved the match. No prospective son-in-law was ever faultless, but young Matthew Shaw would be as good as any and considerably better than most, having advanced quite swiftly in his chosen career, as well as being due to inherit handsomely from elderly grandparents. What was more, he had seen the lad grow up and knew him to be a good-living young man.

'Halewood is such a landmark,' he commented, taking his watch out of his waistcoat pocket and checking its time with the clock on the mantel, 'that it's not surprising that you can see it from Fellfoot.' He closed the watch with a snap and replaced it. 'How is the work on your house progressing? Is it nearly finished?'

She nodded. 'The workmen should be out by the end of the month. You must come and see it again, Papa. All the paintwork is white and I've chosen the most delicate wall-papers. The garden has improved beyond recognition, too. A local gardener and his boy have worked hard on it, and they are to come weekly to keep it in order – '

She looked towards the door. The parlourmaid had entered with the afternoon post on a silver salver. But the letter brought in was not for the doctor. As it was held out to her she saw that it had come from America.

'Thank you, Ellen,' she said, taking it. When she had read it through she lowered it to her lap and raised a shining face. 'Aaron Hart is coming! He accepts our invitation with the most heartfelt thanks. I had prepared him in my letter for a communication from Mr Radleigh and he waited until receiving it before replying, knowing that only then would he be able to make definite plans. He has all the details of the sale, plus the highest figure that Halewood can be expected to fetch, which has been based on recent sales of similar properties in other parts of the country. Mr Radleigh has done everything to make him familiar with the situation.'

'Well, well. So Edward's son is to make a bid for the property, is he? I can understand his reluctance to let the family home pass into other hands, but he'll have to make sure he employs a trustworthy bailiff to manage the estate for him, or else it could be disastrous. He can hardly keep an eye on things for himself without visiting twice a year at least.'

'He's going to do more than visit!' She spoke excitedly. 'He's selling up everything he owns in Massachusetts and writes that he is about to take the biggest step of his life. He intends to live at Halewood!'

'Without having even seen the place! My word! A reckless young fellow indeed!' Dr Gilmore shook his head soberly. 'He's a Hart right enough. They always have let their emotions and their tempers run away with them. Has he a wife? How will she take to being uprooted, eh?'

'He's not married.'

'Just as well in the circumstances. Nevertheless, he must be a gentleman of some substance to be able to afford such a venture.'

'I'm not sure. The tone of his letter suggests he is all but scraping the barrel.'

'Then his action is even more foolhardy than I at first supposed. What will he do if some rich mine-owner's wife has set her heart on living there and makes her husband promise to get it for her? The price could soar beyond Aaron Hart's purse.'

'Don't say that!' she cried with a frantic intensity. 'I don't want even to think such a thing could happen!'

Dr Gilmore raised his eyebrows. 'There's no need to get so upset. I'm sure Mr Radleigh has prepared him for such a contingency, and even Lancashire's new-moneyed class will not go beyond the realms of common-sense and value for brass. However, I still think it would have been wiser if he had allowed Mr Radleigh to appoint a representative to bid for him. It would have saved him an unnecessary journey if the price should go against him.'

She had calmed down again. 'Obviously he wants to see the home of his ancestors – whether it becomes his or not.' While speaking she abstractedly folded the letter again, and she ran her finger and thumb along the length of it in a little sliding movement. 'Why did his father quarrel with Sir Harry?'

'There are plenty of versions of what happened in circulation,' Dr Gilmore answered with a slight smile. 'Have you heard none of them?'

'Indeed I have.' She hesitated. 'It is most generally supposed that father and son quarrelled over – a woman.'

'Then I suggest you leave the matter there and trouble your head no more about it.'

She realized he had no intention of discussing the unsavoury scandal with her, but she could not resist questioning him further. 'Were you well acquainted with Edward?'

'I never met him. He had left for the New World before I moved to Penghyll. As my predecessor had been physician to Halewood I was asked to carry on in his place and I attended Sir Harry from that time forth.'

'Was the first Lady Hart alive then?'

'No, she wasn't. She died while still young, which was the reason why Sir Harry had no other children.'

'Did he ever talk about Edward to you?'

'Never. From the moment Edward left home Sir Harry considered himself childless, cutting off all connection with his son as when a man lops a branch from a tree, not caring whether it ends up as firewood or rots where it falls, he himself having no further use for it.'

'Why then did he keep that unopened letter from Edward in his desk?' she queried.

'Knowing Sir Harry, I'd say that it gave him a certain perverse satisfaction to know that Edward sought to offer an olive branch by contacting him and he was casting him off anew, not once, but every day that the letter lay with its unbroken seal in his desk.'

'How cruel! Edward could have been in dire straits! Dying, for all Sir Harry knew. If only he had read that letter!' She thumped a fist on her knee. 'How different everything would have been for Aaron Hart.'

'In what way?'

She looked surprised that he should ask. 'Halewood would have been left to him. Sir Harry would have divided his fortune between his second wife and his grandson, which would have enabled both of them to live in comfort for the rest of their days — Aaron at the house and Lady Hart, if she'd a mind to it, could have gone on living there or anywhere else she cared to settle. As it is, she's decided to reside in Florence.'

Dr Gilmore gave his head a shake. 'I must disagree with you there. It's my opinion that it would have made no difference at all if Sir Harry had known he had a grandson. The Harts have always been a proud, unforgiving family, and Sir Harry was a true Hart in that respect. He was a stubborn, cantankerous man who could be extremely difficult – as you saw for yourself on more than one occasion before he died of that attack of apoplexy – and I'm convinced he would have considered the bequeathing of Halewood to any child of Edward's as a gesture of reconciliation, which was a move he would never have made, not even if he had been told that his estranged son was dead and gone.'

'You really believe that?' She looked sadly incredulous. Then she added on a sigh: 'What a sorry business it all is.'

'I agree, Delia. I feel heartily sorry for the young man in question. If he has the true Hart pride – and, as I pointed out, a stiff-necked tribe they've always been – he'll not take kindly to the humiliating position in which he finds himself. I'm extremely glad that we're able to do something to ease the way by offering hospitality. When exactly does he expect to arrive?'

She flicked open the letter. 'He wrote this a few days before sailing on an American packet of the Black Ball Line, which is due to dock – er – let me see – oh, yes! A week today. Will the ship be on time, do you think?'

'I don't see why not. These United States vessels keep remarkably good schedules. They have tip-top captains, you know. American insurance companies want to know a captain's character before they insure a vessel these days.'

She had become momentarily motionless and withdrawn, not paying attention to what he was saying. 'Having the date of Aaron Hart's arrival makes me realize how much nearer my marriage has become,' she said in a small voice. Then deliberately she assumed a look of gaiety. 'What a hubbub

31

he will find in this house when Aunt Rachel brings Melissa to stay for the Penghyll Ball. At least we can guarantee he'll have plenty of entertainment.'

Dr Gilmore looked depressed. 'I was hoping Rachel might decide not to come this year. Surely she can find enough suitors for Melissa in London.'

Delia rose and drew up a footstool beside him. 'Papa! You should be pleased that your only sister thinks highly enough of Lancashire gentry to want her daughter to marry one of them. Aunt Rachel marked out years ago the eldest Whinlatter boy with all he'll inherit.'

'That Penghyll Ball is nothing but a marriage market with all the mothers bringing their daughters from miles around and parading them like heifers at a cattle auction!'

Delia laughed and shook his arm affectionately. 'I suppose it is, but what better way for girls in country districts to meet all the eligible bachelors of half the county in one fell swoop. After all, it's the start of all the winter festivities, and the girl who wins a beau at the Penghyll Ball is certain of invitations everywhere, to say nothing of winning a husband for herself by the time spring comes again.'

'I feel sorry for any young man who marries that minx my unfortunate sister has produced,' he said with a shake of his head.

'You're too hard on Melissa,' Delia protested lightly. 'Admittedly she is rather like a whirlwind sweeping through the house when she comes to stay, but you must remember Uncle Henry is very strict with her and the freedom she can coax from her mother when they're out of his sight quite goes to her head, I'm afraid.'

'My sister is a fool,' he stated crisply, 'and Henry – even if he is a Member of the Commons – is an arrogant dunderhead. Melissa, being an only child, has been alternately browbeaten by her father, who's treated her harshly for not being the son he wanted, and spoiled by her mother, who is too weak and silly to cope sensibly with any situation. Melissa has been full of sly tricks to get her own way or avoid trouble since she was first laid in a cradle. You must admit she's been unkind many a time to you. I'm not blind, y'know. If Matthew had been a more susceptible young man she'd have taken him away from you without the slightest twinge of conscience – not because she wanted him for herself, but simply to score over you and chalk up another conquest to amuse her until it was time to leave again.'

'Now that's only your opinion, Papa,' Delia stated firmly, 'and it could be unjust. I know Melissa likes to flirt, but so do most girls. Anyway, I like having Aunt Rachel to stay – it's a treat for her to get away from Uncle Henry, too – and she wouldn't come if she didn't bring Melissa.'

'Hmm. Well, all I ask is that if they do come this year you'll keep them both out of my way as much as possible and grant similar consideration to Mr Hart. He certainly won't want to be bothered by Melissa's frivolousness and inane chatter.'

Delia lowered her eyes and looked away from him to hide a smile. Most young men responded to Melissa like flowers to the sun. She didn't think Aaron would find Melissa's company a burden. Quite the reverse, in fact. But that, of course, remained to be seen.

33

Chapter Three

Delia turned up the lamplight in the guest-room. She wanted to make sure that everything was ready for Aaron and that nothing had been overlooked. Approvingly she noted that there were plenty of towels on the wooden rail by the wash-stand, soap in the dish on its starched mat, and a lace-edged linen square keeping dust-free the cold water in the rose-patterned ewer, which stood in its matching washbowl. Moving to the bed she smoothed out a crease in the spread and stooped to twitch a valence-fold into place.

Would the young American be resting his head on that pillow the next night or the night after? His ship should have docked at Liverpool by now, but the journey to Penghyll was an awkward one, necessitating several changes of trains, transport by coach and horses where no railway link existed, and a final stretch of road that he would have to cover in any vehicle he could find that was available for private hire. When the branch line was built to Penghyll it would make travelling much easier, but that day was still distant, nothing having been settled yet by the Lancashire and Yorkshire Railway Company, and in the meantime Aaron Hart would have to make his own way as best he could.

She turned out the lamplight and went from the room, closing the door behind her. At a leisurely pace she went to the head of the stairs and started down the flight. It was a wild evening and the wind was howling round the house, making it cosy to be indoors and out of the heavy autumn rain. Half-way down where the staircase bent at right-angles she stopped and held back the curtain to look out on the drenched garden. A gasp escaped her. A hackney cab was entering the gates from the lamplit street beyond, baggage piled on its roof. Instantly she guessed the identity of the passenger within the cab. Aaron Hart had arrived!

She hastened down the rest of the flight, thoughts racing through her mind. Her father was out! Nothing special had been planned for dinner! She would have to receive him on her own! If only Matthew were here, but he'd had to go out of town for a few days again and wouldn't be back for a week. She flung out a hand, cupped the newel post, and swung herself with a swirl of petticoats from the last stair.

A quick look in the glass on the wall above the hall table was an anxious check on her appearance. She gave a swift touch to her hair and smoothed down the plaid silk of her bodice. Turning, she hastened to the coloured glass doors of the vestibule, pressed down both handles, and went through to the entrance, her heels clacking on the black and white tiles. But when she shot back the bolt of the oaken door and reached up to set her fingers on the latch to lift it, a feeling of approaching destiny not unmixed with foreboding attacked her with such force that all power to move seemed to leave her. The premonition was intensely physical, sharp and articulate, stretching the skin over her cheekbones and giving them a burnished look, the cords in her young throat tightening convulsively. It had been her intention to fling the door wide and let the light stream out in welcome, but that was forgotten. She knew as surely as if she had been told that Aaron Hart's shadow was about to fall as darkly across her life as that of the great house he had come to make his own.

Outside in the rain-damp air the clop of hooves drew nearer, the wheels of the hackney cab spitting aside the gravel of the drive. She stood as though transfixed, only the rapid rise and fall of her chest indicating the turmoil of her emotions. Listening intently, she could picture the horse taking the curve of the driveway that encircled the lawn in front of the house, which Aaron Hart would be able to see from the dank, leather-upholstered interior of the hackney cab as a black, rectangular shape with tall chimneys and a slate roof, the fanlight above the entrance a spread of jewel colours, the drawing-room windows with their closed curtains glowing crimson. The tall trees, which made a windbreak at the side of the house, would be a wild tumble of tossing branches against the scudding sky.

Wheels scrunched as the cab came to a halt, and the sound of voices told her that the passenger had alighted. The rattle of the bell-pull was followed by a jingle of the bell far away in the depths of the house, and Delia started violently when it was followed unexpectedly by the sudden thunder of the brass knocker, which made the whole door vibrate under her fingers, but still she did not open it. Outside, the squeak of a shoe's sole on the stone steps told that Aaron Hart had swung back after announcing his arrival to supervise the unloading of his boxes.

Behind her in the long hall there came hurrying footsteps from the kitchen regions, accompanied by the pristine rustle of a newly tied apron. Delia spoke, not turning her head.

'Mr Hart has arrived from America, Ellen. See that the groom knows which guest-room has been prepared when he carries the visitor's boxes up the back stairs. Also inform Cook of the gentleman's arrival at the same time and ask her to serve the best dinner possible under the circumstances.'

'Er – yes, Miss. But – er – t'door?'

'There's no need for you to wait. I'll admit Mr Hart.'

Ellen's face became sulky and she dawdled, not departing, resentful at being dismissed from a duty that would have enabled her to catch a first glimpse of the visitor whom the whole household had been awaiting with interested anticipation. She thought it surprising that the front door had been reached before her arrival, for she had moved sharply

36

when the bell rang. What was more, her inquisitive nature was aroused. Her mistress's face was hidden from her, but there was something odd in the way she was standing, with shoulders slumped and her head slightly bowed, her attitude almost defensive, and she was making no move to pull on the latch-hook.

'Is it stuck again?' Ellen optimistically took a step forward, thinking her help might be needed. It did happen sometimes that the wooden panels of the door became swollen and difficult to open when the rain pelted ceaselessly for days and weeks on end, beating in to turn the lanes to liquid mud and crown the summit of the fells with leaden clouds that never lifted.

'No!' Delia straightened up and recovered herself with effort. 'Go and do as I told you.'

Ellen had no choice but to obey, which she did with little grace, flouncing off down the passageway. Delia tightened her grip on the latch, slowly exerting pressure until it went upwards with a click. Unaware that she was holding her breath, she wrenched the door open in one swift movement, a cold draught sweeping in on her. She had expected to find Aaron Hart returned to the steps and facing her, but the moment of meeting had yet to come.

He was paying the cabbie his fare, his broad-shouldered back towards her while he dived into his pocket for more change and brought out a fistful of sovereigns and silver coins, which he sorted out on the palm of his hand. Two pieces of baggage had been unloaded and set down on the ground beside him, a large trunk bearing a steam-packet label and a portmanteau of good leather, which was much scuffed by long journeying.

There was a purposeful air about him, a powerful litheness to his tapered body, his clothes well-cut and having the sheen of good cloth. She could not see what his features were like, his face being turned towards the cabbie, but under the

37

tall stovepipe hat, which added to his already considerable height, his hair was blue-black, thick and vigorous, curly as a bearskin rug.

The dread was ebbing from her, but her heart was still thudding and her mouth felt dry. He did not look alarming; indeed, there was every reason to suppose that when he turned around he would prove to be extremely personable, and she was beginning to wonder how and why she had allowed herself to be foolishly overcome by his arrival.

The cabbie accepted the fare, which appeared to have been crowned by a large tip, judging by his pleased expression and the flourish with which he touched his cap. 'Thank 'ee, sir. Good neet, sir.'

'Good night,' the newcomer replied in a deep voice that held an unmistakable Yankee intonation. He picked up the portmanteau, turning as he did so, and his gaze swept up and over the house before lowering to settle on her slender-waisted, bell-skirted silhouette in the doorway.

In those few seconds of his appraisal of her home she had looked on his face and gathered in an impression of it that she knew would stay with her until the end of her days. It was not a handsome face in the classic sense, lacking symmetry, but moulded strongly and the more arresting because of that. The wide brow glowered over the long, narrow eyes vizored by their lashes, and the nose was large, but wonderfully shaped with winged nostrils unmistakably aggressive, the rock-like chin a stubborn thrust, and the mouth, full-lipped and sensual, did not look as if it had smiled often or easily. Even in her innocence she knew she was meeting a man who would be a formidable adversary, a dangerous enemy, and without doubt a passionate lover, whose desires would reach out into the dark distances of which she knew nothing and did not dare to contemplate.

'How do you do, Mr Hart,' she said, relieved to hear no tremor in her voice. 'I'm Delia Gilmore.'

38

'I'm honoured to make your acquaintance, Miss Delia.'
He removed his hat and took firmly the hand she extended to
him. 'I hope my being unable to give the exact time of my
arrival has caused no inconvenience.'

'Not at all. Come in, do. My father is out until later, but in
his absence and on his behalf I bid you welcome to Lancashire and to our home.' She drew aside with a swish of her
skirt to let him enter, the gaslight casting a running gleam
over her shining hair, well aware of being scrutinized by that
steady gaze of his, but not, she thought, with anything more
specific than an alert and intelligent interest in all he was
seeing in this country that was entirely new to him.

'I thank you. Your kind words are much appreciated.' He
set down the portmanteau and his voice took on a clipped,
wry note. 'I believe my late grandfather would turn in his
grave if he knew that his disinherited son's son had come
home to roost.'

She caught the undertone of outrage and defiance in his
words. If he had the stiff, fierce pride of the Hart family – and there was every indication of it in his face and
bearing – the humiliation of having to bid publicly against
all comers for his own birthright would be harder for him to
endure than for the ordinary run of men, a savage, running
sore that might never heal. And what if he did not get it?
That did not bear thinking about! She took his hat from him
and put it on the hall seat.

'Did you have a good journey?' she enquired. He had
slipped off his travelling coat and she would have taken it
from him, but he would not let her wait on him further and
put it with his gloves over the arm of the seat.

'It was a rough passage, but the wind was with us all the
way and we docked ahead of time. I contacted Mr Radleigh's Liverpool representative as arranged and left him to
see to the crates in the hold. The most difficult part of the
whole journey from Boston has been getting from Liverpool

to Penghyll. When I got as far as the nearest railroad depot I took a cab to cover the rest of the way. I must say I'm exceedingly glad to get here at last.'

'I'm afraid the rough weather you spoke of has followed you to our doorstep. We barely saw the summer this year and autumn is proving wild and cold. Lancashire weather will be harder on you than anything you have known in the United States, I'm sure.' She went ahead of him and paused with her finger-tips against the drawing-room door, ready to open it when he reached her side.

He had observed with some surprise that she walked with a slight limp and wondered if her disability was permanent or if she had recently sprained her ankle. She was like a dainty, fragile little bird dragging an injured wing, but the carriage of her head and straightness of her back suggested that she was not without courage or determination and would reject pity for her condition out of hand. He found this combination of gentleness, timidity, and high spirits extraordinarily appealing, arousing as it did both a desire to protect and to challenge. He thought her quite lovely, this scrap of a girl with her neat, sparrow-brown head, long neck, and small breasts.

'I doubt whether the climate has much that is new to offer me,' he replied easily. 'I've lived through a tornado that tore a town into plank-wood and I've survived a flood. Should I expect worse than that?'

She smiled, inclining her head. 'I think not. I just wanted to prepare you.'

He glanced again at the hall before following her into the drawing-room. The house was much as he had expected it to be, large and comfortable, not unlike the residence of any small-town but prosperous physician back in the United States. Obviously he had caught the household unprepared, Dr Gilmore being out and Delia herself somewhat taut and tense beneath her polite façade. Had they thought he would

40

dally in Liverpool, seeing the sights or some such nonsense? He had not travelled all these miles to waste time when Halewood was so near. If it had not been too dark to see anything he would have gone to get his first glimpse of it before arriving at Dr Gilmore's door. As it was, he could hardly wait till morning.

The drawing-room was warm and inviting, a multi-coloured Turkey carpet on the floor, the furniture rosewood, and the lamplight cast a pleasing glow over the apple-green upholstered sofa and the embroidered tapestry cushions on the fringed chairs. Opposite to the fireplace a pair of white-painted doors had been folded back to reveal an adjoining music room graced by a piano and a gilded harp. Delia invited him to take a comfortable-looking chair by the fire.

'Do you play?' he asked, gesturing towards the music room as he seated himself.

'A little,' she replied.

'I look foward to hearing you.'

'May I offer you some refreshment?' she asked, crossing to a cabinet embellished with marquetry. 'A glass of claret perhaps? Or would you prefer Madeira?'

He chose the claret. She took a crystal decanter from a shelf and poured it for him. When she gave it to him he saw that her hand shook slightly. Wanting to put her at her ease, he waited until she had seated herself on the scroll-ended sofa and then raised his glass to her.

'To you, Miss Delia – and to Halewood.'

She put her hand to her throat. It was an involuntary reaction to being linked with the house, but he did not notice. 'I – I hope you will be happy there.'

He held his glass as though studying the colour of it before putting it down on the small table at the side of his chair. 'I haven't come seeking happiness. According to my father, there is no place on earth where one is less likely to find it. Legend has long held and been believed that there is a curse

41

on the Harts of Halewood.'

She was astounded at his words. 'Why then have you made up your mind to live in it?'

He gave an easy little shrug. 'I grew up believing that one day it would be mine. My father talked to me about Halewood from the time I was first able to understand that somewhere far across the sea there was a house that one day would belong to me. He fed me tales of its bloodthirsty past that excited my imagination – my poor mother couldn't bear to listen to them. How much was myth and how much the truth I've no idea, but all the adventure I ever dreamed about as a boy was linked to a place I'd never seen.'

'Did it never occur to your father that Sir Harry might marry again?'

'I don't think so, but even if it had he would have lost no sleep over it, for in matters of inheritance the only son of the eldest son is – or should be! – secure. Even if the second Lady Hart had had a dozen boys not one of them would have had an hereditary right to come between the house and me. That I should be cut off with my father was a possibility that occurred to neither of us.'

'I did explain that Sir Harry never opened the letter giving him the news that he had a grandson.'

'Yet my father was careful to make sure it was received into my grandfather's own hands.' His lip curved wryly. 'Not wanting to risk such an important piece of information in the post, he entrusted the letter to a church minister visiting England, who delivered it to Halewood himself. Had Sir Harry returned the letter unopened to Boston my father would have understood that all was not as it should be. As it was, he took for granted that it was read and that my grandfather harboured no ill will against me.' He gave a long sigh. 'I know it was homesickness as much as alcohol that killed my exiled parent, one cause aggravating the other. Through me he dreamed vicariously of returning to

Halewood, and it was a longing that kept him from making a new life of any worth in a new land.'

'Would you have preferred to grow up in ignorance of Halewood's existence?' she questioned with interest.

'Indeed, no! My childhood, as I explained, was the richer for it, and there is such a sense of belonging to Halewood inherent in me that I'm convinced I should have found it out had the name of the place never been spoken in my hearing.' He turned to a point gaining pre-eminence in his mind. 'I have much to thank you for. By notifying me in good time of the present Lady Hart's intention to sell you gave me fair chance to arrange my affairs and get here for the auction.'

She glanced down at her hands folded in her lap. 'Lady Hart instructed me to write.'

He leaned forward, looking directly at her, one elbow resting on his knee. 'I still believe you had much to do with it.' Then he sat back again, crossing one long leg over the other. 'Do you enjoy the time you spend at Halewood?'

She pondered before she answered. Mostly she was as happy there as she could be, but it was the curious rapport she had with the house that was often deeply disturbing, and she always avoided going near the sward in the courtyard for reasons of her own she had never discussed with anyone.

'It's been wonderful working in such splendid surround-ings,' she answered carefully, 'and Lady Hart has always been most kind to me.'

'Tell me how you spend your time there. Where do you deal with correspondence? In which room were you when you wrote to me?'

He listened with rapt attention while she answered him as fully as she could. Finally she asked him another question in turn. 'How can you be sure that you will settle down in this part of the world?'

'Why shouldn't I? I've come home.'

It was a statement of fact that he appeared to think

43

brooked no argument, but she wondered how much he knew about the husbandry of land and livestock, for Halewood was more than just a property to live in; the estate stretched out to encompass the homes of tenants and acres of good farmland. 'It was the second time he had referred to his arrival as a home-coming. Home to roost, he had said before. Yet was it so strange that he should think of Lancashire in such a way? After all, his roots went far back into local soil. Perhaps to the time when the Vikings had swept inland in their longboats out of the mists of the Irish Sea. Or even before that.

'Wasn't it hard to leave Boston and all that was familiar to you?' she wondered aloud.

He considered before he answered, taking a sip of claret and putting the glass down again. 'Hard? No, I can't say it was hard. You must remember that I've always had my sights set on this side of the ocean. Naturally I'll miss many of my old friends, but most of them expect to take vacations in Europe at some time, and they'll visit me. I should have liked to keep my mother's old home, which my maternal grandparents left in trust for me to prevent my father getting hold of it in their daughter's lifetime and selling it with everything else he could lay hands on for his gaming and drinking and his – well, his other extravagances. It became mine when I was sixteen. I lost both parents the same year.'

'What was your house like?'

'It was small compared with Halewood, with no more than a dozen rooms, but it was graciously designed and – in my opinion – one of the most interesting old houses in the Boston area. But' – here he let his hands rise and fall '– it had to go with its land and all else I possessed in that field to help finance my venture here in Lancashire. I've burned my boats. There'll be no looking back over the shoulder for me.'

'Did you run the estate yourself?'

'I did. I figure there'll be no great difficulty in running

44

Halewood on more or less the same lines.'

'You'll have no slave labour here,' she pointed out innocently.

His brows snapped into a deep frown. 'I'm aware of that, Miss Delia. I'll have you know that only free men have ever laboured for me, and those I employ in this country in my house and on my land will receive fair wages for their toil and see their wives and children properly fed and clothed, safe from the squalor and misery that I've glimpsed from train and cab window since landing in Liverpool. I can assure you that slavery will eventually be abolished in the United States as it has been here long since and in the British colonies. Attitudes are changing towards the slave-trade. Not so many Americans are as far behind the times as you appear to imagine.'

She saw she had annoyed him. For a man who professed to have left the country of his birth without regrets he was highly sensitive to even the most veiled criticism of it. In future she would guard her words more carefully. But words were easy to guard. The heart was more vunerable.

'I'm sure you would like to see your room before supper,' she said, rising and going across to pull the bell-rope.

'Thank you.' He emptied his glass and stood up, but his gaze had dropped to her left hand. 'You're betrothed, I see. Who is the fortunate man?'

She looked down at the ring on her finger as if she had forgotten it existed. 'His name is Matthew Shaw. He's a civil engineer at present with the Lancashire and Yorkshire Railway Company. His work takes him far afield.' She turned, hearing the door open. Ellen stood there, her eyes, wide with curiosity, going straight to the visitor in an unblinking stare. 'Show Mr Hart to his room, Ellen. Has a fire been lit there?'

'Yes, miss. This way, sir, if you please.'

45

On her own again, Delia stared at her reflection in the looking-glass above the mantel. Slowly she put up her hands and rested her fingers against her cheeks. She did not look any different, but something was happening to her over which she had no control. No matter that her mind cried out against it, every nerve and fibre of her was being attracted to Aaron as though to a magnet. Never before had she experienced such a violent onslaught upon her senses. She had not known that such an urge could exist in the female form and she was frightened and shamed by it. This wild stirring was alien to her and somehow she must crush it down and forget that it ever threatened her.

Dr Gilmore returned shortly before dinner. Aaron came downstairs soon afterwards, carrying gifts that he had unpacked from his baggage. He presented the doctor with an antique tobacco jar inlaid with silver, and Delia unwrapped a white silk shawl delicately embroidered with roses in every shade from palest pink to deepest crimson and trimmed with a heavy fringe.

'It's beautiful!' she exclaimed, swirling it into place about her shoulders and looking down to admire it. 'Such exquisite handiwork!'

'I'm happy the shawl pleases you. It was bought in Boston, but is Spanish in origin. However, I've another gift for you, Miss Delia, which is of Massachusetts and nowhere else.'

He handed it to her. It was a book of very fine prints of Boston, showing the city streets, individual houses and gardens, the harbour and quayside, and historical scenes from the past. One print showed his own home and from what she could see of it there was no doubt it was a charming residence of character and elegance.

'I've never received two more delightful gifts,' she said sincerely, holding the book to her. 'I shall treasure them.'

She kept the shawl looped around her during dinner. Her

father and Aaron found much to talk about, which enabled her to sit quietly listening for most of the time. But in the drawing-room afterwards Aaron made a point of addressing himself more to her, and several times she caught his gaze resting keenly on her for a reason she could not comprehend. It made her pulse quicken and her colour come and go. It was with a sense of overwhelming relief that she was at last able to slip away to bed, leaving Aaron answering questions from her father about President James K. Polk's handling of the affairs of the brash young nation on the other side of the wide Atlantic Ocean.

Chapter Four

It was barely six o'clock when Delia emerged fully dressed
from her bedroom to go downstairs, having spent a restless
night, getting little sleep, and she was thankful to be up and
about.

'Good morning, Annie,' she said to the housemaid polish-
ing the landing on hands and knees.

'Good morning, miss.'

She carried on down the stairs and to her astonishment
she found that Aaron, who was dressed to go out, had
stopped at the vestibule door at the sound of her voice and he
came back to the foot of the flight to meet her.

'Mr Hart!' she exclaimed. 'You're an early riser, indeed.'

'I'm heading for Halewood!' His whole face was alight
and eager, and he reached out and caught both her hands in
his. 'Come with me! I can wait no longer to see it.'

Her first instinct was to cry out a refusal, but following
hard upon it was a rebellious longing to be with him at such a
momentous moment in his life.

'You won't be able to view the place,' she felt forced to
point out. 'That's to be by appointment only, and yours is on
Monday next.'

'It's the exterior I'll be content to see for the time being.
The rest can wait. Put on your coat and bonnet and come.'

She laughed shyly, carried away by his enthusiasm. 'I'll
come!'

'Good!' He pressed her hands hard and went hurrying out
into the fierce, wind-blown morning.

Before returning to her room to get her outdoor clothes she hurried to the kitchen and told the cook to pack some food into a basket, having decided she could not let a guest take off on an expedition that might mean a couple of hours or more before he could sit down to breakfast.

She was fastening the tiny buttons of her gloves in the hall when he darted back into the house for her, having hurried the sleepy groom into harnessing two horses into the shafts of one of the vehicles in the coach-house.

'What have you there?' he asked, seeing her pick up a wicker basket with a double-hinged lid.

'A snack for you to eat on the way.'

'That's most kind of you. Later, perhaps. Are you ready?'

He took the basket from her and hastened her outside. He had chosen the phaeton, which was built for speed, and when he had helped her into the seat he took his place beside her, whip and reins in his hands. Then they were off, bowling down the drive and out into the quiet, residential avenue, deserted except for a milkman with a hand-cart.

She gave him directions, explaining that they would go through the centre of town where she would point out buildings of interest. He had not been able to see much of Penghyll in the darkness of the previous evening, but as they drove along at a spanking pace it was revealed to him as a busy, thriving market town, a deal more prosperous than it had been in his father's day.

It was built of mellow stone with dark slate roofs and was as yet unsullied by the grime of industry that had blackened whole areas of Liverpool and other places that he had glimpsed from the train windows on his journey the previous day. Its streets were cobbled, some with pumps providing a public source of water for the humbler dwellings, and there was a number of quite grand-looking municipal buildings, which Delia pointed out in turn as being the Town Hall, the Courthouse, and the Corn Exchange. When they entered the

49

market square they drove past the white-washed eighteenth-century frontage of The Red Lion Hotel in order that Delia could show him the next house, which was her father's surgery, and directly opposite, on the far side of the square, adorned with Doric columns and a tall flight of stone steps, were the recently completed Assembly Rooms in which, Delia told him, the auction of Halewood would take place, some posters announcing the sale adorning its walls.

In the square itself the market was already in full swing with stalls and awnings erected and people milling about. From wagons and carts garden produce was being unloaded, as well as fowls in crates, pots, pans, rag rugs, rush baskets, bales of cloth, and furniture, all of it being borne away and set in place for the day's selling. The sticky-sweet aroma of gingerbread and brandy-snaps mingled with the more pungent odours of leather, raw meat, strong cheese, and new clogs.

He noticed that, amidst all the bustle, there were plenty of signs of the abject poverty that existed side by side with high wealth in this cotton-, coal-, and ship-booming county in the North-west of England, most of the people being poorly clothed, the women bleakly attired with grey shawls over their heads, and many of the ragged urchins running barefoot. The more well-to-do shoppers and the discerning housewives had yet to appear, but affluence was there in the presence of a number of business men and landowners in loud check coats, money jingling in their pockets, who were laughing and talking together as they converged on the inns in the vicinity of the square where drinking was already in progress and pints were being pulled.

They left the square, passing down narrow streets lined by tall, small-windowed buildings and the rhythmic clacking of looms, and Aaron thought of the mill-girl whom his father had lusted after and his grandfather had seduced, bringing about a quarrel of such magnitude between the two of them

50

that only by the merest chance had it stopped short of patricide. Indeed, when Edward Hart had been thrown bodily out of Halewood by servants at their master's orders it had not been known for certain whether Sir Harry would survive the violence received at his son's hands.

Delia's soft voice interrupted his train of thought. 'Turn left when you come to the next corner.'

They passed a church, a few mean terraces, where women were scrubbing their doorsteps in a foam of suds, and then the street petered out into a lane. Soon Penghyll was behind them and grazing cattle and small farmsteads were spread out around them. When the countryside became more deserted the wind, sweeping down the clough between the rolling hills, beat into their faces, sharp and cold, and not far away a flock of hardy fell-sheep flowed through a broken gap in one of the low stone walls as though driven through it by the invisible buffeting that never ceased. Delia huddled closer into the travelling rug that covered her, not liking the feel of the weather, for she had caught the first faint rumble of thunder over the hills and the sky was pressing down.

'What a strange light,' Aaron commented with curiosity, observing the odd, almost eerie glow caused by the storm clouds diffusing the daylight. It was like looking at the scenery through pale green bottle glass. In the distance lightning flickered and thunder rolled again.

They were approaching a crossroads. The road they were following led straight ahead, but to left and right there were narrow, water-logged lanes. Delia indicated which turning he should take and with muddy splashing the wheels shot along in the wake of the horses which he was keeping to a fast and steady speed, and all the time he kept his eyes strained ahead to catch the first glimpse of the gates to the estate, which he knew to be less than a mile away. To a rapid thudding of hooves the last curve in the lane was taken and ahead he saw them, flanked by great, dragon-topped pillars,

51

but they were closed against him. Impatiently he urged the horses to a swifter pace and they covered the remaining distance in record time.

He had forgotten the girl at his side. Yanking the horses to a slithering halt he leapt out and almost hurled himself at the gates. Gripping the cold iron bars he looked through at his ancestral home for the first time, fixing his hungry gaze on the mansion topping the rise of the hill, its shape curiously clear-cut against the dark, bruised sky.

It was as though the ink-sketch that his father had once made had taken on form and colour, but the impact on his senses was beyond anything he could have imagined. Its magnificence stunned him. His longing to possess the house, to know himself master of it, was akin to frantic desire at the height of passion. A fiery adoration went out from him towards Halewood. Suddenly he could not bear that the gates were locked against him. He shook them in a fury of frustration and shouted towards the lodge on the other side.

'Open up! Open up!'

The lodge was occupied, a thread of smoke rising from the chimney, but although the curtains at the windows twitched nobody came to do his bidding. He roared his demand again, crashing a clenched fist against the gates and making them rattle.

'Damn you, lodge-keeper! Open up, I say! Bring your keys and let me in!'

When no response was forthcoming he took a few steps back and stared wildly upwards and about at the gates and spike-topped walls to see if they were climbable, but they had been constructed to keep out intruders and there was no easy way to overcome the formidable barrier presented.

A touch on his sleeve made him turn sharply. Delia had alighted from the phaeton and her face within the frame of her bonnet-brim was strained and tight, her cheeks hollow.

'It's useless, Aaron. You won't be let in. Even if I

52

asked – and the lodge-keeper knows me well – Lady Hart's orders can't be flouted.'

He was trembling in every limb and he almost cast her hand from him, but there was something in the look she was giving him, eyes luminous with unshed tears, and in the whole drawn-bow tautness of her slim figure that he found peculiarly touching, impossible to reject.

'Why should they not?' he demanded fiercely. 'I have every right to be admitted.'

'It doesn't matter who you are or why you're here,' she insisted tensely. 'Apart from myself, Lady Hart receives few people other than my father, her priest, and her lawyer. Strangers are never welcome at Halewood and never were in Sir Harry's time either. He was suspicious of everyone, but that is not in Lady Hart's nature. I believe she cut herself off from her past life when she married Sir Harry and wants never to meet anyone from it again, whether by chance or design. At the present time when hosts of idle sightseers are wanting to get into the grounds of Halewood on the pretext of wishing to purchase the place she is being even stricter about who is to be admitted, and nobody – not even you – can gain admittance except when expected at an appointed hour. If you stay on this spot all day you'll never get the gates opened up for you.'

His brows had drawn into a frown, but he gave a reluctant nod. 'I'm letting my eagerness run away with me,' he conceded. But although she had succeeded in cooling his temper somewhat, his anger at the injustice of the situation did not abate. Reaching out, he put an arm about her narrow shoulders and jerked her with him in one swift movement to the gates, so that they both stood pressed against them and the angle at which he was holding her forced her to look towards Halewood.

'That's the house where I should have been born, Delia,' his voice grated harshly. 'That's where I'm going to live for

53

the rest of my life and where I intend to die – and my children after me.'

She made a faint sound that was a dry sob in her throat. His arm tightened about her and he half-lifted her off her feet, feeling the need to put some seal on the vow he made, and crushing her between the gates and his own hard body he bent his tall head swiftly and took her defenceless mouth with his in a kiss of such ferocity that it sought the very heart of her.

He released her more gently than when he had snatched her to him, lowering her back on her feet, but continuing to support her. She stared at him dumbly. Overhead a curlew cried, winging its way across the morning sky. There was a drowning warmth in his gaze fixed on her and slowly he brought up his hand to touch her face with his finger-tips. Almost in tender reassurance as if he believed her to be afraid of him. She could have been some tiny, injured bird, stunned with fright. She heard herself speak, her voice oddly tremulous.

'Come away from the gates now. Please.'

He obeyed after one last sharp and resolute look towards the house over his shoulder, taking her by the elbow at the same time and leading her back to the carriage. Where he had not spoken on the last lap of the way to Halewood he talked volubly as he drove back, his mood completely changed, his exultation in the house taking over. He told her he knew of the different rooms there and how he had had all his own books indexed and crated before leaving Boston in readiness for when they would fill some of the emptied shelves in the great library.

'Halewood will be in a barren state when the present owner has departed and all the contents gone. I'll go to the London sale-room and buy whatever I can afford of them there, which will ensure that some of the houses's own furnishings don't fall into other hands.' He gave a quiet, good-humoured laugh. 'At least they'll help to stop my rattling about in forty empty rooms like a solitary pea in a pod.'

'Don't you mind that the best of everything will be going from Halewood?' Delia asked, speaking for the first time since they had left the gates behind them.

He shot a look at her, his eyes glinting behind their lashes. 'I mind. Make no mistake about that. I mind that portraits and furniture, porcelain and sculpture, tapestries and family silver were left to a woman who considers them only in the light of their monetary value. But I have the house!' He seemed to forget that the business of the sale had yet to be gone through. 'Halewood itself is mine. That's all that really matters.'

'Shall you close up a wing or two for the time being?'

'I guess I'll have to. Fortunately I should be able to furnish all the rooms I'll need for my immediate use with the furniture and goods I had shipped over with me, which are being stored in a Liverpool warehouse until such time as I'm ready to have them removed. Most of the furniture is French – family pieces from my mother's side that I didn't care to sell.'

They had reached the crossroads, but instead of turning left on to the road that would take them into town he drove straight across, making for the lane on the other side, which took a rambling route through wilder moorland and over a hill.

'You're going the wrong way!' she exclaimed.

'I know, but I thought we'd stop somewhere out in this beautiful countryside and eat that picnic you brought along.'

'There's going to be a storm!' she protested faintly. The purple clouds were pressing down on all the hilltops and there was a faint rumbling that seemed to come from all around them.

He waved her argument aside with a curling flick of his

whip. 'The rain's holding off. We'll find some trees to give us shelter if it should start before we've finished the picnic.' Jubilantly he tilted his face into the bitter wind. 'This is true Halewood weather! My father mentioned often enough the damp, icy atmosphere of the bedrooms and the draughts that sweep permanently down the corridors.'

She looked at him wonderingly. 'Is nothing able to put you off the house?'

Unexpectedly he grinned at her. 'Nothing! Enough fuel will banish the cold, and draughts can be stopped up. I intend to bring the house up to a high degree of comfort that's probably unknown in these parts.'

'It's a very old house. It could prove more difficult to make it comfortable than you anticipate.'

'You have reservations about Halewood, haven't you, Delia?'

The directness of the question caught her off guard. She glanced at him and away again, recovering herself. 'The name of the hill on which it stands is chilling enough,' she said evasively. 'It is known locally as the Howling Hill.'

'So I learned from my father. But how could such a hill be called anything else? The howling of the wind never leaves the house in winter and at other times of the year the sighing never leaves the chimneys. It was probably one of my distant ancestors who named it the Howling Hill.'

'There are other theories,' she replied, looking ahead at the winding road.

'What are they?'

'This district was notorious for its witches in days gone by. Some say a witch put a spell on the hill to prevent it from ever knowing the gentleness of summer again. That's why the house suffers.'

'That I don't believe.' There was amusement in his tone.

She did not say whether or not she shared his opinion. She was simply stating the facts. 'My father has done a lot of

56

research into the history of this district. It's his hobby. He holds to the theory that a dwelling-place on the same site in centuries gone by was known by a Norse name that meant a wolves' den. Hence it was a short step to the hill's present name.'

'I remember hearing something about that. It's as good an explanation as any in my opinion.' He pulled on the reins, bringing the horses to a halt, for he had spotted a copse of rowan trees forming a natural wind-break. 'We'll have our picnic over there.'

He carried the basket and the tartan travelling-rug from the phaeton, walking with her across to the trees. Gorse grew thick on all sides and the heather went down with a rustle under their feet and sprang up again behind them. Everything was astir in the wind, all foliage restless, the berry-laden branches genuflecting dementedly before the ceaseless buffeting. Resilient cobwebs, wet with dew and strung like swaying gossamer sails between the stouter blades of grass, collapsed before them, small scraps clinging to the light grey check cloth of his trousers and to her deep blue skirt folds. She glanced skywards, wondering how long it would be before the storm broke. The light was fast fading as if the day was dying almost before it had been born, the weird, greenish glow having surrendered to an oppressive gloom, which steeped the undulating landscape in darkening shades.

A felled tree-trunk made a seat for them and he spread the rug over it for her. She lifted the lid of the basket and took out a folded, starched white napkin, which contained some slices of cold partridge, chicken, ham, and tongue. In another were oatcakes and some newly-baked rolls, which had been delivered from the bakery at the first light of day, and a container of tea that had been wrapped around with a special piece of flannel for insulation and was still warm.

She did not feel hungry, but he settled down to enjoy the

food, the fresh air and the outing having stimulated his appetite. He sat with his elbows on his knees, taking hearty bites from the pieces of meat, which he held between the fingers of both hands. His high-crowned, round-topped hat was tilted slightly forward over his eyes and he let his gaze wander over the wide stretches of heather and the hump-backed slopes of the surrounding landscape, an expression of vast contentment on his face.

'What else do you know about the Vikings who came to Halewood?' he enquired with interest, reaching down to pick up the cup that was lodged conveniently on a jutting slab of limestone and taking a sip of the lukewarm tea.

'Only that they must have arrived with their fellow Norsemen in the dragon-headed longboats that invaded the estuaries, coming first to plunder and then to settle. The Norwegian Vikings penetrated inland along the rivers, and those who took over land in these parts probably came part of the way up the ribble. The warriors and sea-rovers became farmers and landsmen – and the names they gave their settlements are with us today. Anything with *wick* is a derivation of *vik*, which means an inlet in Norwegian, such as Salwick and Urswick, and there are countless other examples. We call our hills the *fells* because the old Norsemen called them *fjells*. My father can list hundreds of place-names that are Norse in origin. That's how he knows the summit of Howling Hill boasted one of them.'

Aaron stood up and stepped briskly away from the copse to stand amid the waving grass, looking towards Halewood, which he could just discern in the distance, his hands set low on his hips, coat-tails whipping in the buffeting wind.

'Now I know why there are stone dragons on the gate-pillars! They're links with those longships. It could be that my forebear who set them up for all to see was as proud as I am of Halewood's past glories!'

A great crack of thunder followed hard on a blue flash of

58

lightning that greeted his words, and the first heavy drops of rain began to fall. Delia sprang up and scrabbled at the picnic things, snatching them up to thrust them into the basket. He made no move to help her, apparently oblivious to the rain, his expression rapt, enchanted, set towards the house as though he were gazing at a woman he loved.

Delia paused in what she was doing, straightening up to stare at him, a linen napkin trailing in her hand, and suddenly the chilling sense of foreboding, which had assailed her upon the moment of his arrival the night before, returned to wrench through her as searingly as if she had been pierced by one of the shafts of lightning darting across the sky. On his own admittance he did not look for happiness at Halewood. He was prepared for the shadows that lurked there. But would he know how to defend himself from the strife and hate and bitterness that had accumulated there over the centuries? The Halewood curse he had called it. One title for it was as good as another for the tricks that fate played. She herself had not been left unmarked by her contact with the house, but as a parent forgives a child that strikes out in the throes of a tantrum she bore it no malice. But how would he fare? Alone. A helpless fury surged up in her, the reason for it completely escaping her at this moment of tempestuous stress. She was angry with him, with Halewood, and mostly with herself.

She hurled aside the napkin and dashed across to him. Seizing him by the arm she jerked him round to face her, catching him off guard. His eyes expanded in baffled astonishment at the rage and anguish tearing at her face.

'Glories! What glories?' she exclaimed tormentedly, echoing his words. 'Brothers have fought and killed each other for possession of Halewood! Women have been wed into the family against their will for the riches they could bring to that handsome house! It has split asunder father and son! You talked to me of the Halewood curse! There *is* a curse on it! Some awful, indefinable curse that hits out without warning! No one is safe from it. Least of all you – unless you discover how to free that poor, suffering house from it and set a new future for yourself and your children after you.'

He grabbed her by the arms and held her hard, thrusting his face towards hers. 'What's behind all this? What haven't you told me?'

The rain was lashing them, running down their faces, making strands of their hair stick wetly to forehead and cheek, the curled brim of his hat collecting the drips that ran in rivulets from the crown and becoming awash like a roof-gutter. When she did not answer him at once, biting deep into her lower lip, he shook her in his impatience, determined to have the truth out of her.

She reacted instantly, tearing herself away from him with elbows awhirl. Again the thunder rumbled deafeningly and the horses whinnied in fright, jerking their heads violently. Having withdrawn a couple of paces from him she stood with her arms against her sides and her hands pressed flat against her skirt, her attitude defiant and defensive.

'Something happened to me eighteen months ago at Halewood. This!'

With a single movement she hoisted aside her stiffened petticoats and extended her left foot in a froth of lace. Then he saw why she limped. Her leg above the ankle was cruelly scarred. There was no mistaking the cause of such lacerations.

'You were caught in a trap?' he exclaimed on a note of appalled disbelief.

'Correct!' She threw down her skirt-hems, which fell swishing into place. 'Sir Harry had man-traps all over the grounds to keep out poachers and other intruders. A clever surgeon saved my leg, but it was a long time before I learned to walk again.' She cupped her elbows in her hands, flinging herself into a half-turn from him, chin jutting. 'I only tell you this to warn you to be on your guard at Halewood. Anything can happen there.'

'No,' he stated stonily. 'There's more to it than that. You haven't told me everything.'

She shot him an angry glance. 'What do you mean?'

'What were you doing in the grounds of Halewood in the first place?'

'Trespassing! That was Sir Harry's judgement!' She gave a jerky, intensely unhappy laugh, and without another word she bolted past him, making for the phaeton, but she did not get back into the vehicle. Instead, she went to the horses and spoke soothingly to them as they flared their nostrils and tossed their heads in alarm at another clap of thunder.

Aaron watched her. He did not know if it was rain or tears on her face. When she moved to pat the rivulet-streaked neck of the horse nearest to her he saw that her eyes were closed tightly as though she were struggling to regain control of herself. He turned and went back to the copse, rescuing the linen napkin from a bush before packing all that was left of the picnic into the basket. Swinging it in his hand he walked across to the phaeton where she had taken her seat. In silence he stashed the basket aboard, climbed in, and took up reins and whip. At his signal the horses plunged forward, eager to get home to a dry stable.

'How did the accident occur?' he questioned. It was as though there had been no break in their conversation, except that she was calmer now with a dignified air of resignation.

'Through unlucky chance. Up to that time I used to go riding a lot out from Penghyll into the surrounding district. As much as the riding itself I loved feeling at one with the open air and the countryside. Sometimes Matthew or a friend or two came with me, but usually I was alone. I liked best to ride across the moorland not far from the boundaries of Halewood. There's always much to see when one comes along quietly without talking. Gambolling hares. A pheasant strutting. Leverets chasing around in circles. And so many birds – my father taught me to name most of them from a dipper's bib to a kingfisher when I was still a child. I went riding in all seasons, when there was heather as far as the eye could see or snow on the ground. The only days I had to watch out for were those when the weather threatened to be really treacherous, but a light rain never stopped me, although it's probably the reason why I rode alone more often than not. I was on my own the day it – happened.'

She paused. The drops were thudding relentlessly on the carriage hood above their heads and although they were no longer exposed to the torrential downpour he noticed in a glance that she looked pinched and colder than she had previously; whether it was due to her soaked condition or what she was about to tell him he could not be sure. He thought it was the latter.

'On this particular day there was some low-lying mist when I set out,' she went on, 'but there often is in these parts and I thought nothing of it. Later, however, it thickened without warning when I was far from home, closing down as swiftly as if a grey blanket had been flung over everything. Then my horse stumbled, almost threw me, and went lame. Visibility was no more than a few yards, but I reached the lane and it was only a short distance to Halewood. I knew well enough that visitors were never welcome there, but I thought that, under the circumstances and considering I was daughter to Sir Harry's physician, I could expect help to be forthcoming and a carriage and a groom provided to drive me home. The gates were open when they finally loomed up before me, and I remember glancing up at those stone dragons with their curling tongues on the pillars and thinking that was how the figureheads of the Viking ships must have looked coming in to the coast, with the sea-mist swirling about them. I led the horse through the gates, but I hadn't gone more than a hundred yards when the mist became so dense that I could only tell I was still on the drive by the uphill slope of it and the gravel underfoot. When the ground levelled out again I knew I couldn't be far from the house, but then for no apparent reason my horse took fright and was impossible to control. I tried to hang on to his bridle, but he swung away and I lost my grip and fell to my knees while he was swallowed up in seconds by the mist. I discovered I was kneeling on grass!'

'You'd gone under the archway without seeing it and entered the inner courtyard,' he exclaimed. 'I know it's made up of green sward surrounded by a flagged drive.'

'That's exactly what had happened,' she said. 'Even if I hadn't been struggling with the horse I wouldn't have noticed the archway, because of the mist, but I remembered how the hooves had clacked noisily and guessed it had been on flagstones. It was then that the nightmare began.' She clutched a fold of the rug over her knees. 'I got to my feet and decided to walk with hands outstretched until I stepped on the flagstones again and reached a wall. I intended to feel my way along to a door or a window and knock to try to get attention from a servant. If the worst came to the worst I was prepared to open a window and climb in. But I'd lost all sense of direction and I suppose I walked in circles on the grass – and suddenly I knew I was no longer alone.'

'What do you mean?'

'There was – something else with me in the mist. A – a presence that I couldn't see. A powerful, dreadful presence that was all around me, near enough to be almost tangible. I snatched back my hands, terrrified that I might touch whatever it was that pressed in on me, and the atmosphere had become icy cold. Demands were being made on me that I couldn't understand. A yearning that was angry, frantic and terrifying was getting through to me. That's when I gave way to panic. I ran – blindly. I could have gone crashing into a wall of the house or into any other obstacle, but I had

63

no thought in my head but to get away from – whatever it was there in the heart of Halewood. By some miracle I must have passed back under the archway and I ran on and on in that blanket of fog, conscious of going downhill and knowing it meant Halewood was rising away behind me. When I was almost out of breath, trees began to loom up on all sides and I knew I had stumbled into woodland within the grounds. I was slowing down, my breath rasping in the silence, when a sudden, awful clash of iron jaws threw me into excruciating pain and I fell headlong, my leg caught in that fiendish trap! Whether I fainted with shock or hit my head I don't know, but I didn't recover consciousness until long after a gamekeeper had found me and I'd been carried into Halewood. Lady Hart nursed me herself until I was able to walk again. It was she who paid the fees for a surgeon, expert in such matters, to attend me – not Sir Harry.'

His expression was grim. 'Halewood has much to answer for. It shall make amends.'

She showed surprise. 'I didn't expect you to say that.'

He frowned. 'I'm not sure I understand you.'

'I was certain you'd suggest that the mist had played tricks with my imagination – or that I lost my head foolishly and it was really all my own fault. Things I've told myself many times.'

'That's what you expected, is it?' He shook his head. 'My father fed me with tales of things said to have been heard and seen at Halewood. A house so old must bear heavily the conflicts of the past. The very walls are surely permeated with all the living and dying that has taken place within them – and you yourself reminded me that it has known violent times. Who's to say you didn't brush against a manifestation of some ancient, long-forgotten tragedy that came seeping out to you?'

She considered what he had said and waited until he had overtaken a lumbering horse and wagon before she spoke

64

again. 'There's something else.'

'Yes?'

'I've always been convinced that my running into the trap wasn't by chance.' She made a quick, emphatic little gesture. 'I don't mean that spectral hands dragged it in my path or anything foolish like that. I'm simply convinced that the house didn't intend that I should leave it that day.'

'I don't disbelieve that at all,' he said.

She was grateful for his patient listening, his matter-of-fact acceptance of all she had confided to him. 'I've never told anyone else about that eerie experience – or my feelings about it,' she admitted. 'Everybody thinks I simply lost my way in the grounds. You're the only one to share my secret.'

'Not even Matthew knows?'

'Not even Matthew,' she repeated.

'Why have you kept it to yourself?'

'I wanted to forget it. Never to have anyone remind me of it. Instead it has haunted me ever since, and I never enter Halewood without feeling that the request demanded of me – whatever it was – has yet to be fulfilled. So you see, instead of putting that experience behind me I've stayed linked to it – a kind of prisoner through my own silence.'

'Not any more.'

'What do you mean?'

'You're released. You've told me about it.'

'So I have.' She gave a faint half-smile. 'I wish I could say I feel liberated and free, but I can't. Instead I've involved you.'

'I welcome that.' He turned his head and their eyes met, binding her to him in a look that brought her to the edge of a precipice. She knew with every nerve and fibre in her body that he was about to say something tender and endearing that would drive a wedge between her and Matthew for ever. 'Delia – '

She made a little fluttering movement with her hands as if

65

she would have clapped both of them across his mouth to hold back his words. But in the same instant the sky cracked with such violence that the whole atmosphere seemed to shudder, and this time the horses in blind, eye-rolling terror bolted, the phaeton careening after them. Delia clung on with all her strength, gasping as each jolt made the vehicle totter anew, and it took every bit of Aaron's exceptional skill to wheel the horses on to the soggy moorland where eventually they slowed their frantic pace and came to a halt, steam rising from them. She relaxed back in the seat, quite breathless.

'No harm done,' Aaron said with a laugh, exhilarated by his mastery of the reins, and he turned the horses homewards.

Delia put her hand across her racing heart. The moment of danger, greater than the possibility of being thrown from the phaeton was – for the time being – past. But she had another fear to add to it, which sprang from her own turbulent emotions. She understood the reason why she had given way to anger. It had come from the frustration of denying a wildness of love and desire that had filled her heart and possessed her trembling body even more powerfully than before. If only he had not kissed her at the gates! He had unleashed from the deepest fount of her being a sweet and passionate madness that must be crushed down without question or consideration. But how – oh, how? – to do it!

Chapter Five

Aaron set off for Halewood on Monday morning. His appointment was for eleven o'clock, and as far as Delia knew and was able to tell him, nobody else would be viewing the house that day. With a sense of occasion he had decided to be driven in style, and he sat back in the elegant hired carriage with his gloved hands folded together over the gold top of his cane, which he held propped at an angle. He had dressed with care in a double-breasted frock-coat and trousers of grey broadcloth, his fold-over cravat fastened with a pearl-headed pin, his tall silk hat set at the slightest angle.

He had the intense satisfaction of seeing the gates of Halewood being opened for him when his carriage drew near. He was not to be kept waiting like a pauper at the gates this time! Remembering what Delia had said, he looked at the approaching dragons on the gate-pillars and it seemed to him those gaping, fork-tongued mouths were set in a grin of welcome. He smiled to himself at his flight of fancy and then forgot it as the carriage swept through the gates and far on the rise of the hill Halewood awaited him, its Elizabethan splendour glorious in the pale morning sun.

Taking notice of the grounds slipping past beyond the beech-trees, which stood sentinel-like along either side of the drive, he caught the silvery gleam of a lake and spreads of lush woodland. Nearer the house, terraced gardens rose to meet the open balustrade that bordered the forecourt, the parapet embellished with stone dragons similar to those at the gates, some moss-stained, others half-choked by ivy. But oh! the house! The mullioned windows winked at him in golden colours that became lost in shades of violet, olive, and sapphire when the carriage took a fine sweep and passed under the richly ornamented archway into the courtyard where it followed the inner flagged drive, which bordered the sward and came to a halt with timed perfection. Aaron found himself exactly level with the entrance, which was a superbly carved porch that ran clear through two storeys. The groom, leaping down from the back of the carriage, opened the door for him with a flourish, lowering the step at the same time. Just then the great main door of Halewood itself was flung wide for him by a footman.

Aaron alighted without haste and stood observing his surroundings while he savoured every moment of his homecoming. It was in this courtyard that Delia became frightened in the mist, but he had no time to think of that now, his gaze dwelling appreciatively on all he saw. He felt at one with it as if his own life's blood flowed within the arteries of its walls. Now he knew that all else he had ever known was alien to him and here on this isolated hilltop in a bleak corner of England his roots were snaking down to mingle with those that had been lying there for a thousand years.

'Good day, Mr Hart. How do you do. My name is Marsden. I'm agent to Lady Hart and in charge of all matters concerning the sale.'

Aaron turned to face the man who had emerged from the house, and saw he was dapper in appearance, hair slicked down from a centre parting, coat-tails swinging.

'Good day,' Aaron replied. 'I understand that I'm to view at leisure and that no one else is coming today.'

'That is correct, sir. Should you wish me to accompany you I will gladly do so, but her Ladyship thought you would prefer to go round on your own.'

'That's most considerate of her.'

'She wishes you to wander freely around Halewood. Only

her own apartments are sacrosanct.'

Aaron's face tightened at the snub. So the woman would not see him! It was a deliberate forestalling of any wish he might have expressed to pay her his compliments in person. Was it possible that it troubled her that she, who had lived a mere handful of years at Halewood, should be offering his rightful inheritance in the open market to all comers? In spite of Delia's praises of her he thought not. Delia in her innocence had mistaken an idle woman's whim to play nurse as evidence of a bountiful nature, but he held a different opinion of Berenice Hart. To have married his old rake of a grandfather was enough evidence to show she was avaricious and without principles. No woman of gentle breeding could have given herself to Sir Harry, whose first wife – his own unfortunate grandmother – had been married for her fortune and driven to an early grave through the misery and humiliation she had suffered because of her husband's countless cruelties and infidelities.

The agent was waiting for him to enter the house, but Aaron was determined not to be hurried. He let his gaze sweep over the inner courtyard and the enclosing walls once more before making a move to the entrance. Then his sharp eye caught a shimmer of movement in an upper window in the west wing as someone drew back out of sight. Ah! Berenice wanted to see what he was like, but he was not to be permitted to look upon her.

Passing through the porch he entered the oak-ceilinged hall with its grand stone staircase, the walls hung with tapestries and ancient arms, the pikes arranged in vast fans, the muskets slotted at a level, and the swords crossed. Marsden picked up a printed plan lying on a chest by the foot of the stairs and held it out to him with some other literature.

'This will enable you to find your way about, Mr Hart. Luncheon will be served for you in the dining-hall at one o'clock. When you have seen all you wish of the house, you

69

may want to inspect the stables and the coach-house and the grounds. A steward will be waiting to show you round and answer any queries that might arise. If time runs out he will either ride with you tomorrow – or arrange for a carriage if you prefer it – to take you to see over the rest of the land and tenanted property that makes up the estate of Halewood. Is there anything you would like to ask me now?'

'Yes, there is one point. I understand that everything in the house is to be sold in London. I would be willing to make an offer for anything I see today that I feel should not be removed from Halewood.'

The agent's face remained bland. 'I have already been instructed by her ladyship to reject any such offers.'

Aaron clenched the papers in his hand until they crackled, but he set his jaw and gave a curt nod, not trusting himself to speak. All that had been collected and treasured by his family throughout the centuries was to become nothing more than a job lot in a saleroom, no matter how grand a reputation the saleroom enjoyed, no matter how distinguished the buyers who gathered there.

'Is there anything else, sir?'

Fiercely irritated by the agent's obsequiousness, smarting under the injustice of the situation, Aaron answered on a staccato note. 'No. I'll start with the library.'

'Yes, sir. This way, if you please.'

The agent went in front of him to show him through. Then he was alone in the great library, which was at least a hundred feet in length with a spiral staircase on either side of him rising to meet the gallery that gave access to the books on the upper shelves, which reached to the ceiling. His feet made no sound on the Aubusson carpet and although brass-grilled glass doors protected the hundreds of volumes, all had been unlocked to enable him to pick out at random any book that caught his interest.

He could have spent hours there, but he had the rest of the

house to see and he moved on through more double doors at the far end of the library into a small drawing-room, which had been converted into a billiard room. From there he went on into other finely-proportioned rooms where almost all the ceilings were of wood with magnificently carved bosses. He was studying a time-darkened portrait of Queen Elizabeth, whose munificence had allowed his ancestor, Raoul Hart, to build the house, when a footman came to lead him to the dining-hall where luncheon awaited him.

Under a canopy of stone vaulting he took his place in a high-backed chair at a long table that would have seated thirty in comfort. The food served to him was excellent and the wines superb, but it was a lonely meal. He wished Delia was with him. He had been on the point of asking her to accompany him at breakfast, but – almost as if she divined his thought – she had mentioned that she had an appointment at the dressmaker's and would her father drop her off there when he set out on his rounds.

'Didn't you tell me last time that your dress for the Penghyll Ball was finished?' Dr Gilmore remarked mildly.

'So it is, and hanging upstairs ready to wear. Today I'm to have the second fitting of my wedding gown. There may have to be another. It must be quite perfect. Everything about my wedding must be quite perfect.'

She had made her declaration a trifle too vehemently. There had been an undercurrent of defiance in her voice directed towards – no, not her father – himself. He had watched her steadily and although she kept her attention on the plate before her she had shown she was aware of his gaze by the way her colour came and went.

He had wanted to speak his mind to her. Wanted to say that she might as well drop the farce of so much wedding talk because she knew – and he knew – that she would not be able to go through with it. It was sheer pretence on her part to make out she was prepared to go to the altar to marry

71

another man.

He loved her utterly. He didn't know exactly when he had fallen in love with her, but he believed it was that moment when he turned from the hackney cab at his arrival and he had seen her standing there. He'd been conscious of a curious fusion of spirits, as though something within himself had gone out to her, and when she had drawn back into the lamplight and he had looked fully on her lovely face for the first time he had known it was not only for Halewood he had come to England. Everything about her enchanted him. The way her face glowed when she laughed, her chin tilted upwards, both eyes closed in merriment. And those contented, fully absorbed looks that held her face in tranquil repose when she was reading something that interested her or was engaged in some small domestic task, such as the arranging of flowers, which gave her particular pleasure. In anger? Ah, he'd seen her wrathful and in despair on the day of the storm, and he knew that in passion she would blaze like a beacon under his touch, fiery in desire, tender in love.

But since that stormy day she was assiduously careful never to be alone with him. This in itself was an acknowledgement of awareness, although perhaps she didn't realize it. By her own admission she believed Halewood had laid claim to her, and through belonging to Halewood she belonged to him. That, apart from anything else, sealed her fate.

Sitting there in the dining-hall he was not quite sure when he became aware of being watched, but he gradually sensed something more than the impersonal gaze of the footmen who were waiting on him. Raising his head he looked towards the minstrels' gallery and there, staring down at him with a look of sullen hatred in his eyes, was a boy aged about eight years, a handsome child with chestnut curly hair, thick brows, and a stubborn mouth. Even as Aaron lowered the piece of pear he had been about to eat.

72

taken aback by the extraordinary ferocity of that youthful glare, the boy darted back from the carved balustrade and vanished. Somewhere in the distance a door slammed.

It was an incident of no importance, but Aaron had never seen such enmity on a child's face before and he found it impossible to dismiss the encounter without some thought. No doubt the boy was one of the gardener's children who had slipped in to take a look at a prospective buyer of the property which provided one parent – and probably both – with a livelihood, and their talk of the uncertainty of their future had aroused fear and dislike in the child. It was the only possible explanation.

He finished the pear, put down his crackling napkin, and rose from the table. Refusing coffee he left the dining-room and continued his inspection of the house.

In his late grandfather's bedroom he stood by the great fourposter bed where the Hart brides had been bedded, their children born, and the heads of the house – at least those who hadn't died elsewhere by violence or treachery – had drawn their last breath. Turning on his heel, he went across to the window and released a long sigh of satisfaction at the view. This would be his room. In this room he would make Delia his own.

There was a door half-hidden by a draped curtain leading off the room. He knew that it led to Berenice's apartments. When she had left the house, stripping those rooms bare, he would leave them as they were until Delia had time to choose her own décor, select her own furniture, and stamp her own delightful personality on that traditionally feminine sector of Halewood.

Leaving the bedroom he entered the portrait gallery, strolling from painting to painting, halting before each one to study the visages of his ancestors, which looked down on him. The men hard-eyed, hard-mouthed, who had fought bloody battles down the centuries, sometimes in the service

73

of the throne, sometimes against it, and always with each other. As Delia had said, brother against brother, father against son, uncle against nephew, but never before — until his own grandfather had struck the name of the rightful heir from his will — had a Hart failed to inherit Halewood. Aaron looked long on the face of Sir Harry, which had been painted when he had been no more than thirty, but debauchery had aged the arrogant features even then and gluttony had swollen the bulge of the waistcoat buttons.

An empty space showed where the portrait of Edward Hart had hung. Well, it was no matter. There was one in the boxes being stored at Liverpool, which had been painted by an American artist of no mean repute, and it should take its rightful place in the gallery even though the rest of the portraits would have been taken away. Aaron's jaw tightened. He'd start his own dynasty. In time to come his children and his children's children would look down from these walls at their descendants.

He had reached the end of the gallery and he turned to study portraits of the Hart women that lined the wall on the opposite side to their menfolk. Again Delia's words came back to him and he was forced to admit that those faces framed in caps and curls and standing ruffs lacked gaiety or spirit. There was one exception, a defiant-looking woman with a mocking glint in her eye. This was Alice Hart. He knew what happened to her. She had been burned as a witch shortly before the famous trial of other Lancashire witches in 1612 when another gentlewoman with the same Christian name had also been condemned to death, the law against witchcraft taking no account of a woman's station in life.

Wandering on from the gallery he came to a corridor where embrasured windows looked out on a flat section of roof, which was flagged and set with wrought-iron seats. Then he saw her. Berenice! She must have been taking a stroll on the terrace, for she was coming from the far end.

making her way back towards the house, her face veiled from his direct gaze by the filmy lace mantilla she wore draped over her head against the chilly outdoor air, the day having long since clouded over. But the breeze was strong as it blew across the terrace and suddenly the mantilla was lifted, wafting down on to her shoulders. As she sought to retrieve it she saw him through the panes of the mullioned window and her eyes met his.

He had been surprised to see how tall she was, not reaching his height, but tall nevertheless. Although older than he was by a number of years, she was still an incredibly beautiful woman, and even as he stared at her she drew the lace back to shield her face. Making a conventional pretence of not having seen him, she went out of his sight through a recessed door that led into another part of the wing.

It had happened in a matter of seconds, but he had seen enough both to partly confirm and partly disprove his original conception of her. As he had expected, she was unmistakably a woman of the world, but she had none of the hardness and greed stamped on her features that were the hallmark of such females. Instead, she had retained a glacial hauteur as if her true self were locked away within her, safe from all sordidness, no matter how much she might have been physically abused. Therein lay her mystery, her eternal allure with its promise held out of passionate depths lying secret and undiscovered and unconquered. In all she possessed a sexual magnetism that must have been hers since she first grew to young womanhood with all the misfortunes attendant to the path in life she had decided to follow through choice or force of circumstances.

His curiosity satisfied as to the appearance of the widow of Halewood, he gave her no more thought and wandered on again. He was unable to pass a single piece of antique furniture without halting to feast his eyes on it, straining his memory to recall anything his father might have said about it. The fine old clocks particularly affected him, for he had a weakness for clocks and it gave him pain to think they were to be removed from the gracious rooms where they had langourously ticked away time for a century or more. He also took careful note of repairs needed and damp patches where the roof leaked, and he tested with the pressure of his foot the many places where the floor sagged. He could see himself up to his ears in debt and a poor man at Halewood until all the restoration work was done and the house made truly habitable.

He was coming from one of the upper drawing-rooms when he saw the boy again. The child was standing under an archway at the head of a short flight of half a dozen stairs, his whole stance defiant, fists clenched, feet set stoutly apart.

'Go away!' The youthful voice rang out. 'You don't belong here!'

Aaron was more curious than annoyed. 'Who are you? What's your name?'

The boy ignored the questions. 'This is my house! Halewood is mine! Go away and never come back! I order you to leave!'

Aaron's tolerance went before such a show of ill manners. He was about to rebuke the child when a sudden suspicion darted into his mind. 'What grounds have you for such a claim?' he demanded grimly, wondering why – if this should be a son of Sir Harry's old age – he had not been forewarned about him by Delia or the lawyer or even Dr Gilmore himself. 'My name is Hart. Can you match that?'

Tears burst from the boy's eyes, although not a muscle of his angry little face acknowledged the drops that ran down his cheeks as with dignity he chose to ignore the unmanly weakness that had overtaken him. 'No, I can't!' he retorted furiously. 'I'm Roland Alexander Newman, but Lady Hart is my mama, and I've always been told that one day Halewood would be mine.'

'Then I regret you've had to suffer a disappointment which – although you couldn't begin to comprehend the circumstances – is similar to mine. I also expected to have Halewood bequeathed to me. Nevertheless your rudeness of manner can't be overlooked. I suggest you behave in a gentlemanly way and say you're sorry.'

'Never!' The boy raised both taut fists and shook them. 'I'll see you damned first!' Then, to Aaron's shocked surprise, the boy spat contemptuously at him. An instant later, perhaps realizing the enormity of his misbehaviour, the boy had turned and gone bolting through the nearest door, banging it shut behind him.

Aaron, reaching the door after him, half-expected to find the key turned or the boy's youthful strength attempting to keep it closed to avoid expected retribution, but it opened easily and he found himself in a silk-panelled ante-room with an archway hung with velvet drapes in the same soft shade of apple green, which led into a drawing-room beyond. Even as he held back the drapes to pass through he realized he had entered Berenice's private apartments. There was no sign of the boy, who could have disappeared through some double doors into the rooms beyond, but Berenice herself sat in a high-backed chair, her feet on a foot-stool, some embroidery in one hand, a needle with scarlet silken thread poised in mid-air in the other.

'Mr Hart!' Her exclamation was chilly, reminding him in no uncertain way that he was an unwelcome intruder, but at the same time he had the extraordinary impression that she was not so averse to his unannounced entry as she would have him believe. He saw she was as beautiful at close quarters as she had been when viewed at a distance through the window, although he was able to see now that there was an almost transparent pallor to her skin, which suggested extreme tiredness, and tiny lines etched her forehead and magnificent eyes.

77

'I ask your pardon, ma'am, for bursting in here in such a fashion,' he said, watching her closely, 'but I was in hot pursuit of your insolent son, who had the audacity to order me out of Halewood.'

'I'm sorry indeed.' She showed distress and put aside her embroidery, throwing a harassed glance towards the door, not realizing that she was giving away the escape route that the child had taken. As she stood up, some of the rainbow skeins tumbled from her lap and clung to the cinnamon velvet folds of her skirt like a fall of twisted flower petals. 'He ran through with such haste I thought he was playing some game. He shall be punished, I promise you.'

'What did you have in mind?'

'I'm not sure.' Her hands were agitated. 'He's never been beaten. I couldn't bear to have him beaten and I've never allowed it. But he does deserve some punishment.'

'I wasn't thinking in terms of any chastisement for the child,' he said, seeing that he had her at a complete disadvantage, for his disclosure of her son's waywardness had made it impossible for her to dismiss him – however politely – from her presence without making some amends.

'What do you suggest?' she asked helplessly.

He thought her singularly inept at managing her own offspring. No doubt the boy had been left to the care of nurses and tutors, she seeing him for no more than an hour or two a day. 'I'd be satisfied with an apology from Roland,' he said crisply. 'If you can extract that from him I think it will teach him a well-deserved lesson in respect and courtesy towards his elders.'

She sat down again and almost absently removed her silver thimble and put it with her embroidery. 'He'd never do that, I know,' she confessed unhappily. 'No matter what happened to him. He thinks Halewood should be his.'

'He made that perfectly clear,' Aaron remarked wryly, reaching out for the back of a light rosewood chair, which he

78

swung into position near her, for she had indicated that he should sit down. He settled himself comfortably, and under his lashes he studied her, missing nothing. The pretty lobes of her ears adorned with jet droplets. The milky curve of her throat. The deep fullness of her breasts straining against the seams of her high-necked, lace-collared bodice. The well of her velvet lap where her right hand twisted the rings on the third finger of her left, causing a sparkle of diamonds and emeralds. The tip of a neat, soft leather shoe showing under her skirt hems, plain with a narrow silk bow. Discreet. Her whole appearance that of a lady, except to the discerning masculine eye. She had come a long way from her days of scarlet slippers with brass heels. Where on earth had old Sir Harry found her? In some better-class bordello?

She knew the query in his mind. There was nothing she did not know about the thoughts of men. She had long since learnt that poise, refinement, gentleness of manners and voice, all natural to her, could never camouflage her origins or the profession she had followed through wretched, unhappy years. She had deliberately contrived the conception of her only child in a last throw to keep the protection and affection of a man who was tiring of her, but it had been in vain. She had not loved the man, but she had been terribly afraid of the future. She would always be grateful to Sir Harry for taking it into his head to marry her instead of acquiring her. She had since realized that his whim had been evil in its intent, for he had used her as an instrument to outwit his own son and deprive his grandson of a rightful inheritance, but he had given her a wedding ring and his name, and although Halewood had failed to be the home she had imagined it would be, she had gained independence and need never again call any man her master.

'I can't understand why Roland should feel so strongly about Halewood,' she said in bafflement. 'He's spent scarcely any time here. Sir Harry had no wish that the son of my first husband should grow up at Halewood.' She knew that the lie about Roland's legitimacy would not be believed by the young American, but he would be well-mannered enough to bow to her pretence.

'Why was that?'

She had expected the question. 'Sir Harry was old and irascible. He didn't want the sound of a tiny baby crying in the house, and so Roland was fostered out from the start of our marriage. I used to visit him sometimes, but Sir Harry would never allow me to have him to stay. In all Roland's eight years he's spent no more than a few hours at a stretch here now and again, and one of the conditions imposed on me by Sir Harry was that I'd keep the child out of his sight. He had no liking for children at all. It was only a few nights ago that Roland slept under this roof for the first time, and he'll be staying with me now until I leave for Florence where I shall make a home for him at last.'

'How did he get the idea that one day Halewood would be his?'

She linked her hands and lifted them up and down in a restless manner. 'I blame myself. I used to talk to him of the home we'd have together one day, and I suppose he imagined it would be Halewood.'

'Now you are going to take that dream from him.'

She gave him a disturbed sideways glance. 'One house can be the same as another to a little boy as long as he can look upon it as home. I refuse to believe that Halewood has any special hold on him yet, but it soon would have if I let him grow up here. That's why I'm taking him as far away from Lancashire as I can get.' Her voice took on the rising note of vehemence. 'If good fortune is with me I'll see him reach manhood in the Italian sun among people who have never heard of this accursed place!'

His face did not change expression and he continued to watch her. 'I'd no idea you disliked Halewood to such an extent. Delia never mentioned it.'

She relaxed almost imperceptibly against the chair. 'Naturally she wouldn't. Delia is a highly-principled young woman. She would never betray a confidence or break her word. Her friendship has done much to ease the hours of loneliness for me in these bleak surroundings. Her father has also been a good friend to me as well as being my medical adviser. I shall miss them both when I leave.' Then she seemed to recollect her duties as the hostess of Halewood. 'Perhaps you would care for some tea, Mr Hart?'

He accepted her offer and she rang for it to be brought. When he watched her pour the tea from the silver Georgian teapot into the rose and gilt porcelain cups he realized that he was looking at other heirlooms that he would never see again. Over the tea, the tiny cucumber sandwiches, and the rich fruit cake she questioned him about America, and he talked at some length, for she parried all further questions about herself, and he understood that she had said more to him through the confusion over her son's ill-mannered behaviour than she would have done if they had met in any other way. He found it sharply interesting that for a few brief minutes he had caught off guard this woman of delicate beauty who had married Sir Harry for the most mercenary of reasons. Yet he did not begrudge her one penny of his grandfather's fortune. Far from it. He was only glad that she was selling Halewood, or else the opportunity to own it might never have become his.

He rose to leave. Already it was dusk outside and the lamps in the room had been lit. He decided to put directly to her the request that the agent had refused on her behalf.

'There's one thing I feel I must ask you, Lady Hart. I understand that the contents of Halewood are to be sold, lock, stock, and barrel, by auction. There are many pieces that have been in the house since it was built. I'd welcome the chance to purchase them individually if you would get a

81

valuer to set a price on them.'

The long, deep look she gave him held out no hope, and yet she took her time before replying; her gaze seemed to search his features in a curiously guarded way.

'My decision has been made. There can be no changing the arrangements at this late hour. Everything must go to the highest bidder.'

There was nothing more to be said. He hid his disappointment in a bow, murmuring some conventional thanks for the hospitality received that day.

She gave him her hand. 'Good day, Mr Hart.'

It was starting to drizzle when he went out to his carriage. He had had a final word with the agent to say he would be back in the morning to view the remainder of the house and go over the land and other properties. When the agent pointed out that his private time of viewing was at an end and there would be other would-be purchasers in the house and grounds on the morrow, Aaron gave a shrug of irritated resignation.

Sitting back in the corner seat, his thoughts leapt with anticipation towards Delia, who would be waiting for him at her home, and his spirits lifted. He did not know that Berenice stood at one of the windows watching his carriage out of sight. Only when she could no longer see the flicker of its lamps did she let the curtain fall back into place.

Chapter Six

When Aaron arrived back at Sycamore House Delia failed to meet him as he had expected, and somewhere upstairs there was the sound of female voices and the tap of heels. He frowned, handing his hat, cane, and gloves to Ellen who had admitted him.

'There appears to be new company in the house.'

'Yes, sir. Dr Gilmore's sister, Mrs Barton, and her daughter, Miss Melissa, arrived this afternoon from London. I understand Mr Barton was unable to accompany them this time due to being a candidate in a forthcoming borough election.'

Aaron's frown deepened. Delia had said something about guests coming to stay for the Penghyll Ball, but he hadn't paid much attention. Now he felt exasperated that he had lost all chance of a talk before dinner with Delia on her own. It would have been his only real opportunity in any case, for after dinner Dr Gilmore liked to engage him in a game of chess or backgammon while Delia amused herself playing the piano, stitching some petit point, or writing yet another letter to Matthew. Usually there was some conversation with her, but it was always inconsequential, and she made a point of going to bed before he and her father finished the game, giving him no chance to be alone with her.

Now, with strangers in the house making demands on her attention, he would have even less chance of ensnaring some of her time to himself than before, and he had much to achieve in the short period left to him before the appointed wedding day. At the very least he must wring from her a postponement of the ceremony, which might be all she would be prepared to commit herself to for the time being.

He made his way up the stairs in the direction of his own room, and he had reached the landing when Delia came from the one in which there had been much female chatter. Her face lit up when she saw him and she clasped her hands together.

'How did it go?' she enquired eagerly. 'Were you pleased with Halewood? Did everything come up to your expectations?'

'Beyond measure,' he said smiling. 'In spite of its urgent need of repairs. I was looking forward to talking it all over with you, but I hear that you have guests.' He nodded towards the room from which she had come.

Her forehead creased slightly. 'Aunt Rachel brought Melissa up from London today instead of next week, because she herself can't stay for the Penghyll Ball this year. With all the business of the election, Uncle Henry naturally wants his wife at home.' She took a step forward, intending to pass him, but he halted her with his hand on her wrist.

'I don't want to discuss Halewood with you in front of strangers. When may we talk alone?'

She was anxious to get down to the kitchen where there were domestic difficulties to solve and she made him the first promise that came into her head. 'This evening – after everybody else has gone to bed – I'll meet you downstairs in the music room.'

'I'll be there,' he said, releasing her.

As Delia went on down to the kitchen she wondered uneasily how she would manage to cope with Melissa on her own. She had been able to tell from the first moment of seeing her aunt and cousin on the doorstep that there was some trouble in the air, for Melissa's face had been mutinous and Aunt Rachel had looked strained and tired. They had not

84

been in the house more than ten minutes when Aunt Rachel had seized the chance to disclose the situation out of Melissa's hearing.

It was not an unusual state of affairs. Melissa had become infatuated with a most unsuitable young man. Uncle Henry had put an end to it, but he and Aunt Rachel had thought it best to get the girl away from London and into fresh surroundings where there would be no chance of further meetings, accidental or contrived. Aunt Rachel said enough to make Delia feel that there was some justification for their wishing to get Melissa away from the young man in question, but she wasn't sure that bundling Melissa ignominiously to Lancashire against her will had been the right action. Absence made the heart grow fonder, and there was nothing like parental opposition to make young love blaze. She must only hope that Melissa would accept her temporary banishment more graciously as time went by. In the meantime, she had to make sure that Cook in the kitchen had received enough extra meat from the butcher to extend the main dish for dinner that evening.

Dr Gilmore received the news that his sister and his niece had arrived with a noticeable lack of enthusiasm, and when he made a wry grimace Delia reproved him with a little admonitory shake of her head. He smiled, his eyes twinkling, and she was hard put to stop her lips slipping into a reciprocal smile, but she managed it by pretending to remain severe and went bustling off to see after the new arrivals once more. He knew she would keep them at bay long enough for him to unwind from the tensions of the day, but as yet she did not suspect the constricting pains in his chest that had begun to afflict him almost daily.

Rubbing his chest with his fist he went through his study and unlocked with a key from his pocket the little dispensary that led off it. Although the dispensary was not much bigger than a cupboard, the main one being at his surgery, he found

85

it useful to have on hand everything he might need for an emergency call or for domestic accidents, such as occurred in the kitchen from time to time, servants being singularly careless with the sharp blades of knives and scalding liquids. Taking down from a shelf the bottle of physic he had dispensed for himself for his own use, he poured out a measure and drank it down. Knowing it took a little time to have effect he sat down in a study chair, set his feet on a stool, and dozed for half an hour, undisturbed by the comings and goings in the rest of the house. When he bestirred himself he felt much better, the opiate having taken effect, and he straightened his cravat, flicked down his stiff cuffs, and went at a leisurely pace into the drawing-room where he found Aaron reading a newspaper. It was folded up at his approach and together they discussed matters of the day until Delia came with the two newly-arrived guests through the open double doors.

Rachel Barton, a once-pretty, harassed-looking woman, came forward in a whisper of lavender shot-silk to embrace her brother lightly with a stream of complaints in greeting. 'Charles! What a journey to get here! I declare the roads to Penghyll get worse every year. Delia tells me there's to be a railway branch line very shortly – and not before time. Think yourself fortunate to see your only sister as often as you do. Travelling without Henry made everything twice as difficult. I declare I'll never be able to do it again – '

Dr Gilmore checked the moaning flow with introductions. After some general conversation, Melissa was left with Aaron as the other three moved to sit down in grouped chairs. She looked about her and sank down into one half of a comfortably upholstered sociable, indicating that he sit beside her. She thought him handsome and because of that it was as natural for her to coquet with him as it was for her to breathe, but at the same time her innermost mood was at danger level. Before coming downstairs she had quarrelled again with her mother, a more than daily occurrence over the past weeks, and there was a pent-up savagery in her that sprang from a helpless rage at having been compelled to leave London when she least desired it.

'So you're from America, Mr Hart,' she said flutingly, baring her small, pearly teeth into a smile that brought dimples into play. 'From which place exactly, may I ask?'

'Boston, Massachusetts.'

'I declare!' She lifted her hands and put them together, prayer-like. 'Mama complains of the journey from London, but you've come from far across the sea. Tell me, do! What is it like to enter surroundings of a civilized and cultured nature for the first time?'

He eyed her with a sidelong glance, irritated and far from intrigued by her jibing attitude towards him, which – although sexually provocative – was damnably rude and patronizing. He thought it lamentable that, with her seductive looks, she should have all the makings of a snobbish shrew. Without doubt her features, framed as they were with a luxuriance of dark gold hair dressed in long ringlets that lay gracefully against her neck, would have been considered quite perfect by any fashionable artist of the day. Here was the smooth, rounded forehead, the slightly long but exquisitely narrow nose, the mouth that was rosebud, and the alabaster complexion. Her china-blue eyes with their deep lids and curling lashes added to her look of ultimate feminine docility, but he noted the steel behind her glance and the stubborn set to her hard little jaw.

He answered her question evenly. 'I've been accustomed to a similar environment since birth. Boston is a fine city, not a frontier encampment.'

'Indeed? But, of course, I was forgetting. You had an English father and he would have made sure you had a gentleman's education in the most barbaric of settings.' She gave a little tinkling laugh and tapped his arm lightly with

87

her fingers, finding it balm to her own searing emotions to do battle with him. On the other side of the room her mother sent a relieved glance in her direction, thinking that Melissa was responding in her customary flirtatious way to any young man she met of better than average looks, and she hoped it was a sign that she had found a new diversion to distract her from her former foolishness and there would be no more rebelliousness or trouble. Delia also concluded that Aaron and her cousin were getting on well and was thankful for it.

'I find it regrettable,' Aaron was saying laconically, 'that such ignorance exists about the land I've left behind. The progress made *since* the War of Independence has been outstanding.'

The point went home. Melissa flushed, but in her dangerous mood she found his retaliation exciting. She was carrying on a deadly flirtation with him and enjoying every barbed word of it. Tilting her head on one side, she studied him deliberately with a narrow smile on her lips. 'You're reminding me that you were born a foreigner. Pride centred in another country – and one that in the living memory of my parents' generation took up arms against our Canadian colonies – will not go down well here.'

He had no intention of disclosing to her his awareness of completely belonging to Halewood, and he answered her on an impersonal note. 'It's possible to harbour loyal and affectionate feelings towards the land of one's birth as well as one's land of adoption. America is made up mostly of such people.'

'But this is England! If you're going to be a true Squire of Halewood you must forget you ever knew another land.'

'That I could never do.'

She shrugged her pretty shoulders nonchalantly at advice rejected and leaned towards him, resting her elbow on the polished mahogany arm between them. What plans have you made? Do you intend to shut yourself away in that dreary old house or are you going to make it come alive again?'

He was saved from answering by the arrival of Matthew. Delia, who had expected him, sprang up and went forward to slip her arm through his and bring him into the centre of the room. He knew Melissa and her mother from many years back, but Aaron, who had risen from the sociable, he was meeting for the first time. There was no friendliness in Matthew's eyes, although normally he was agreeable and amiable to most people he met, but he felt that this American stranger from across the sea represented a further intrusion into Delia's life – and his, for that matter – by Halewood, and once again he experienced the sensation of jealousy. More and more he disliked her having interests that he could not or did not wish to share.

'I'm told you're a railroad engineer,' Aaron remarked as an opening. 'Before I left the States there was already talk of the not too distant day when a railroad will stretch from the Atlantic to the Pacific coast.'

They were on a topic that interested each as much as the other and from that point conversation flowed freely between them. It was not until dinner was over and the three ladies had left the gentlemen to their port that Matthew himself brought up the subject of Halewood.

'I understand you're hoping to purchase your family's ancestral home,' he said through a haze of cigar smoke, leaning back in his chair.

'I trust I'll be able to meet the highest figure it reaches at the auction,' Aaron replied, refilling his glass from the decanter before passing it on.

Dr Gilmore took it from him. 'Delia said you were well satisfied with all you saw.'

Matthew paid no attention to the answer that Aaron gave the doctor, but sat forward and leaned both arms on the

89

table in front of him. 'I think Halewood should be pulled down.'

'Come, come,' Dr Gilmore said reprovingly. 'It's a splendid example of Elizabethan architecture.'

'It was – but now it has fallen to rack and ruin,' Matthew persisted.

'You're mistaken,' Aaron argued good-humouredly. 'It's structurally sound and there's nothing that new roofing and the skill of local craftsmen can't put right.'

'But the cost – and for what?' Matthew went on. 'Why not build a new house on part of the land? It will set you back less in pocket in the end.'

'I think your suggestion is crazy,' Aaron stated bluntly, losing patience.

'I agree with Mr Hart, Matthew,' Dr Gilmore said. 'It's the family home he's come all these miles for. What pleasure would there be for him – even if he built the grandest house in England – to look out and see a barren hill-top where once Halewood stood as a landmark for miles around.'

'Then let him leave it to crumble and fall where it stands. It will save him the expense of having to erect pseudo-Italian ruins or some other absurd edifice in his gardens to follow the popular fashion for such follies.'

'I find your remark offensive,' Aaron said quietly, his eyes narrowed.

There was silence in the room. Matthew's jaw tightened, and he was conscious that he had allowed his suppressed enmity to come to the surface. 'That wasn't my intention,' he blustered truthfully. 'I apologize to you – and to our host, I only meant to proffer good advice.'

Aaron inclined his head with a complete lack of animosity, but he had seen that Matthew resented him and guessed that there could only be one cause. 'I accept your apology,' he said simply.

'Yes, indeed,' Dr Gilmore agreed. 'We'll let the subject of

Halewood rest there. In any case, it's high time we joined the ladies.'

Delia thought the evening went well. When it ended she picked up the Spanish shawl and put it about her shoulders to go with Matthew to the door and on to the porch. Being a fine night he had walked to Sycamore House and would be walking home again.

'Has Aaron Hart unlimited funds?' he asked thoughtfully as if it were a question that had been on his mind. 'I mean, is he a really rich man?'

'Not at all. At least, judging from all he's said to me I gather he had some difficulty in raising the sum needed. Why do you ask?'

'Oh, I'm curious. That's all. Let's not talk about him any longer.' He took her by the shoulders and smiled down into her face. 'It won't be long to wait now before this kind of good night parting for us is no more.'

She stiffened slightly and looked away from him. Reminders of the forthcoming wedding day were no longer welcome. Time was passing too quickly. She longed for it to stand still.

'Delia?' he enquired fondly, lowering his head to try to read her expression. 'Is anything the matter?'

She couldn't lie to him, but she couldn't hurt him either. Better to say nothing. Better to seek the comfort of his arms as a protection against herself, for she was her own worst enemy. Impulsively she moved nearer to him and buried her face against his shoulder.

'Dear little sweetheart,' he whispered, his arms enfolding her, his hands caressing her back and arms through the slippery silkiness of the shawl. 'You looked lovely this evening. I could hardly take my eyes from you.' The fringe slipped over his fingers. 'This shawl. I haven't seen you wear it before.' He chuckled softly. 'Did you buy it new for the Penghyll Ball and then find you couldn't wait to put it on?'·

How well he knew her, she thought despairingly. Always

91

she had adored new clothes. In childhood, when a new and pretty hair-ribbon had been purchased, she'd had to wear it from the market, unable to wait until she got home. Yet in a way he did not know her at all. It was a stranger he held in his arms. Guilt and misery swept through her.

'Aaron brought it for me from America,' she said, drawing back from him and gathering the shawl about her. She was shivering. 'It's cold out here. I must go in.'

He looked displeased. 'I'm not sure you should have accepted such a gift – or that he should have offered it.'

Because he had put her own original doubts into words she answered him with a gust of heated impatience. 'It's a beautiful shawl and was given as a token of appreciation for my being responsible for letting him know about the sale of Halewood. You can't object to that!'

He knew she was right and he was being unreasonable. He sought to make amends in kissing her, but her response lacked warmth, which he blamed on their difference of opinion over the shawl.

He went over the incident carefully in his mind as he walked briskly homewards. It would all be forgotten when they met again. Delia had never harboured a grudge in her life. On the remarkably few occasions when they had had words, even in their childhood, she had always been the first to end the quarrel with a kiss and a hug and a gentle entreaty for all to be at peace between them again. Nevertheless, it wasn't like her to be so quick to shut the door without waving him on his way. He'd take her flowers tomorrow. A posy. And the prettiest shawl he could find. Then the Spanish one could be put away and never thought of again.

In her bedroom Delia was sitting with her elbows on the dressing-table, her head in her hands. Somehow she must exert all her will-power to drive Aaron from her heart. She could not go back on her promise to marry Matthew. The pledge had been made and must not be broken for a wild and senseless longing that she refused to define as love. Love was gentle and tender and undemanding, self-sacrificing and loyal and faithful. Like the feeling between Matthew and herself. How ironic it was that she had been given the responsibility of persuading Melissa out of an unsuitable infatuation when she herself was similarly afflicted and knew no cure for it.

A tap came at the door. Hastily she straightened up and turned her head towards the door. 'Come in.'

It was Melissa who entered, a be-ribboned peignoir over her nightgown, a candle in her hand. She looked surprised to see Delia still in her gown with her hair untouched. Her own was brushed into a glimmering flow down her back.

'I thought you'd be in bed,' she said. 'I want to talk.'

It made Delia realize how long she must have been sitting motionless at the dressing-table. She was also thankful for Melissa's intrusion, which gave her a legitimate excuse not to go downstairs yet to the music room where Aaron would be awaiting her.

'I've been – day-dreaming,' she said with a vague gesture of her hands. 'Do sit down. I'm sure I can guess what it is you want to talk about.'

Melissa set down the candle. Then, with a choking sob, she flew across to Delia, where she dropped to her knees, flung her arms across Delia's lap and burst into a storm of weeping. 'I can't bear it! I'll die without him! I love him and he loves me. No girl ever had a more cruel father or a less understanding mother.'

Delia had seen Melissa fall in and out of love with as many as three young men in the same number of weeks on previous visits to Penghyll, and if Aunt Rachel was to be believed it was not an uncommon occurrence at home, but never had she seen her cousin more distressed, more heartbroken. Was it possible that this time Melissa was genuinely in love?

'Why not tell me the whole story?' she asked compassionately. 'All I know is that you met a young man named Richard Dibley, whom your parents regard as a scoundrel and a fortune-hunter, and – from what I've been told – not without reason.'

Melissa raised eyes swimming with tears. 'They don't know him as I do. All they can think about is that a stupid old great-aunt on my father's side of the family left a few thousand pounds in trust for me to inherit when I marry. Richard doesn't care about the money. Neither do I. We could be happy together in a garret.'

Delia doubted it. Melissa had been brought up in the lap of luxury, and although she would have learnt how to run a house and manage servants, it was doubtful whether she could cope with living in poverty, no matter how idyllic their love, for very long. Richard, too, appeared to have expensive tastes. According to Aunt Rachel, he spent his days escaping his creditors while Uncle Henry, who had had him watched and followed, knew that he frequented gaming clubs and certain other notorious night spots in London where gentlemen did not go for cultural entertainment, but this information had been divulged to Delia's unwilling ears in confidence and it was obvious that Melissa knew nothing of that side of Richard's life.

'How did you meet?' she asked, reaching over to slide open a dressing-table drawer and take out a clean handkerchief, which she unfolded and gave to Melissa, who appeared to have come without one.

'At Caroline Hewett's coming-out ball.' The words came muffled by the handkerchief and torn with gulping sobs. 'He would have danced every dance with me if my programme had not been already almost full. But I fell in love with him before our first waltz together had ended and he felt the same about me. Unfortunately Mama was already looking down her nose. She upbraided me all the way home saying that I should have known that he was *the* Richard Dibley who'd

94

been involved in unsavoury scandal, and I should have refused to dance with him. But I didn't care! I knew then that he would never be received by either Papa or Mama, and he must have known it, too, because he had already made secret arrangements to meet me in the park next morning. Within a week he had proposed to me and I'd accepted.'

'How did you expect to be allowed to marry him?'

'I don't know. I didn't think. All I knew was that I couldn't live without him. After that we had so many perfect hours together. I used every kind of lie I could think of to escape chaperonage and meet him. We used to laugh at the tricks I'd played to get away, and he helped me to think up what to say next time.'

Delia suppressed a sigh. It was a familiar pattern of lies and deceit and trickery that Melissa had used all her life to get her own way, but this time it was on a dangerous level. The more Delia heard of Richard, the less she trusted him. It was probably not unknown that Melissa was an heiress and to a young man in desperate financial straits she could offer a solution to all his problems; more than that, marriage to the daughter of a respectable and distinguished Member of Parliament could do much to wipe out indiscretions of the past. Unfortunately for Richard, it also worked the other way, and Uncle Henry, jealous of his good name and that of his daughter, had made it clear enough that he would consider such an alliance tarnishing to say the least. Aunt Rachel, when talking about it all, had passed quickly over the scandal in which Richard had been involved, but unpaid gambling debts had been mentioned.

'How was your romance discovered?' Delia questioned.

Again the pretty, tear-wet face was raised, but it was a mask of bitterness with a sullen twist to the mouth. 'Somebody saw us and Papa got wind of it. Who it was or how it happened, I don't know. He called me into his study and demanded the truth.' Her eyes closed briefly on the fright and horror of the interview. 'For the first time in my life I stood up to him. I told him that, no matter what had happened in the past, Richard had mended his ways and was full of plans for a new beginning. When we were married he intended first to settle his debts and then we'd travel abroad for a while before returning to buy a house in London that suited us. After that, he'd invest in some business venture on the highest level, and everything would be quite wonderful.'

She drew a shuddering breath and bit her lip until it showed white. 'That was when Papa nearly exploded with rage, saying that I was too stupid to see that if it were not for my inheritance Richard wouldn't give me a second glance. But that's not true! I know I'm pretty and desirable – enough men have told me that, heaven knows! – and all Richard wants is to make me his own dear wife. But Papa forbade me ever to see him again.'

'Did you obey his order?'

'I had no choice. I was confined to the house and not allowed to go out without Mama. All my correspondence was checked and opened. Then, with the election coming up, Papa needed Mama to dance attendance on him and see that important guests were properly received, which meant she couldn't keep an eye on me all the time. That's when they decided between them that I'd learned my lesson and would never dare disobey them again. Oh, how I had to humble myself before Papa for that concession! I grovelled. It was humiliating! I'll hate him for it for the rest of my life. Then all I earned from it was temporary banishment to Lancashire to give me more time to think over how magnanimous he had been. Ugh!' Her whole body shuddered with aversion to her parent. 'Mama held out the Penghyll Ball like a carrot to a donkey – as if I cared about so provincial a social function any more! – and said that she knew I'd be welcome to stay on afterwards until your wedding, because I could help you

96

list the gifts you'd receive and all that. But it's banishment nevertheless!' The tears overflowed again. 'I can't live without Richard! She sobbed. 'What am I to do?'

Delia could tell it would take some time to soothe and quieten the girl sufficiently for her to be able to get some sleep that night. She must go downstairs and tell Aaron not to wait for her. It would be far too late before she managed to get Melissa back to her own room.

'You're uncomfortable there on the floor,' she said. 'Go and sit on the bed. I have to go downstairs for a few moments, but I'll be back at once.'

'Don't leave me!' Melissa clutched childishly and pettishly at her skirt.

Delia unplucked the girl's hands and helped her to her feet and across to the bed, where she collapsed forlornly, lying on her stomach, her face within the circle of her outflung arms. Delia had barely reached the door when Melissa raised herself to make a blubbering, self-pitying enquiry.

'Why *are* you leaving me alone like this?'

'Aaron was hoping to talk over Halewood with me. I'll be back almost at once.'

Melissa flung out an appealing hand. 'Don't tell him about Richard and me! I couldn't bear anyone to know how my parents have humiliated us and degraded our love for each other.'

Delia returned to the bed and spoke reassuringly. 'You should know I'd never repeat anything you've told me in this room or anywhere else where you might choose to speak to me in confidence.'

'Promise?'

'I promise.'

Melissa gave a satisfied nod and dropped her head to the coverlet again.

In the music-room Aaron turned when he heard Delia's step across the drawing-room floor and pleasure flashed into

97

his face when she appeared in the frame of the open doorway. She could see he had begun to be afraid she was not coming.

'I can't stop,' she said hastily before he could speak. 'Melissa is slightly indisposed, and so I'll be sitting with her for a while. I came to let you know. I didn't want you to think I'd forgotten.'

He gave a rueful smile, showing his disappointment, but accepted her statement without question. 'I'd many things to ask you, many things to tell you. I'm returning to Halewood tomorrow. Come with me.'

Regretfully she shook her head. 'There'll be too much to do here with Aunt Rachel and Melissa in the house. I have to organize everything to allow myself some free time to wait on Lady Hart the next day.' She took a step backwards to leave again. 'I must go.'

Swiftly he moved forward and blocked her way. 'You mustn't neglect one guest for the sake of two others,' he said, not entirely in jest.

Her eyes clouded. 'I know,' she said sincerely. 'I'm sorry.'

'Then we'll meet tomorrow night instead. There'll be twice as much to talk about.'

'Very well. Tomorrow. And now good night.'

She flew back up to her bedroom. Melissa, chilled by misery, had gathered about her the Spanish shawl that Delia had left on the bed, and was sitting up, dry sobs racking her, tears still trickling down her cheeks. Delia was moved by pity for the girl's undeniable distress. She sat down beside her.

'I know it seems hard,' she said with compassion, 'but such a liaison was doomed from the start. It would – '

Melissa interrupted her. 'I'm not giving him up. It's not over. I refuse to believe it. No matter what anyone says. Richard loves me. He really loves me. He said he did a thousand times.'

She collapsed heartbrokenly against Delia, who simply held her in comfort, thinking that perhaps to cry it all out

98

was the best possible remedy. Uncle Henry would never retract his decision once it was made. There was nothing to be done but to hope that Melissa would recover quickly from the whole affair. Normally her feelings were remarkably shallow, and it would be ill luck indeed if this should prove to be the first time they were otherwise. There was something desperate about Melissa's whole attitude that made Delia feel singularly uneasy, but she could not pin-point the reason why. It was against her nature to be suspicious, but when dealing with Melissa it was difficult not to be wary of whatever she might be plotting for the future.

Aunt Rachel departed in the morning. She was far less anxious than when she had arrived, having seen Aaron as the ideal person to distract Melissa from her languishings, and if anything should come of it she herself would be more than delighted and Henry would not hesitate to give his permission there. Mistress of Halewood! Personally she didn't believe the place was as sinister as everyone said it was. Probably all it needed was up-to-date plumbing and new curtains.

'Good-bye, my dear,' she said affectionately to Delia. 'I know Melissa will be in good hands here at Sycamore House. It will take a few days for her to get over that highly unfortunate little *contretemps* in London, but I believe it's going to be a case of "all's well that ends well." '

'Good-bye, Aunt,' Delia replied. 'Give my regards to Uncle Henry. I hope he wins the election.'

Her aunt looked surprised that Delia seemed to think the result might be in any doubt. 'He will, my dear,' she said with innocent seriousness. 'Nobody would dare defeat him.'

When the carriage had left Delia went back indoors. The house was quiet. Her father was on his rounds, Aaron had gone to Halewood, and Melissa was somewhere upstairs. With a little sigh she thought of the innumerable small tasks that awaited her attention. After checking the day's menus with Cook she must settle down to them.

She was seated at the desk in her father's study, writing out bills for his patients before dealing with the household accounts, when Melissa appeared, dressed in bonnet and sealskin cape, her hands in her muff. Relief that her mother had departed showed in her face, but she was pale with purple smudges under her eyes.

'I'm going for a walk,' she announced. 'It will be the first walk I've had on my own for ages. I can't tell you what it means to me to have regained my freedom.'

Delia smiled, hoping that this was a first indication that Melissa might be reconciling herself to the situation. Last night's storm of grief could have been the climax and the shutting of a door on the past. She tilted her head sympathetically, thinking that Melissa looked as if she had had little sleep.

'Some fresh air will do you good. You have no colour in your cheeks. Are you feeling well? I noticed you ate almost nothing at breakfast.'

Melissa hooded her eyes quickly. 'I'm perfectly well. I intend to go as far as the market square and look round the stalls and the shops. Should I meet you at the dressmaker's?'

'That's an excellent idea. It will save you coming back here first. The appointment is at noon. I gave the dressmaker the measurements you sent me long since, and your bridesmaid's gown is ready for a fitting.'

Delia was left alone with her ledgers. Melissa walked purposefully and with haste. At the first postbox she took a letter from her muff and pressed it impulsively to her lips before sending it on its way. It was addressed to Mr Richard Dibley. She had given him her whereabouts, told him all that had happened to prevent her getting in touch again before, and poured out her undying love.

As she continued on towards the market square she willed him to reply by return of post. Otherwise her future was too bleak to contemplate for any number of reasons. Not least among them was the first disturbing suspicions she was beginning to harbour about her physical state, although she took hope from the fact that she had never been really sure when to expect the times of inconvenience to come upon her, a truly regular pattern never having established itself. Resolutely she crushed doubt below the surface of her mind and let her spirits lighten at the sight of the bustling scene in the market square. Her mood was even more greatly restored when she met two daughters of a local family with whom she was acquainted from previous visits to Penghyll over the years and she accepted their invitation to drink a cup of chocolate with them in the ladies' drawing-room at the Red Lion Hotel.

When Delia arrived at the dressmaker's she found Melissa being fitted in the rose-silver gown, her expression dubious, although she had known what to expect, having been sent a fashion-plate and a piece of the fabric, but a minor adjustment had had to be made, it having proved a little tight at the waist, and Melissa seemed a trifle disconcerted by it, even though now it fitted her perfectly.

'I admit it suits me,' she conceded with a critical air, twirling before the full-length looking-glass and making the skirt flounces, which were caught up by clusters of silk roses, dip and float. Then she noticed that Delia had been helped into her bridal gown by two of the dressmaker's assistants and she stood back to make way before the looking-glass.

Delia viewed her reflection. For the first time she was wearing the veil and circlet of wax orange blossoms to get the full effect with her gown of white lace and satin that trailed into a train behind her. Thus would she look on her wedding day. She barely recognized herself. It was as though she were simply studying the appearance of a bride with whom she had only the briefest acquaintance. She had felt the same every time she'd had a fitting. There was no sense of excitement, no happy anticipation. She was completely cut off from that serious, white-cheeked, grey-eyed girl who faced her in the looking-glass. Then with a flash of revelation she understood the reason why. Never once had she truly believed she was going to wear that wedding gown! Not into church or anywhere else for that matter. It was a conviction that had laid hold on her from the start without her being aware of it. Now it had come to light and with it a terrible chill seemed to strike her, similiar to the sensation she had experienced on the day of the storm when she had gone with Aaron to get his first glimpse of Halewood. She swayed and dropped her face into her hands.

Only then did she realize that the others in the room had been talking to her all the time. Melissa leading the praise in how fine she looked. Now they were all concern and the dressmaker herself took charge.

'Nerves! Brides often get them,' she stated, putting an arm about Delia's shoulders and leading her towards a chair, and she gave orders to her assistants. 'Fetch the vinaigrette. Make some tea.'

'I'm all right. Really.' Delia murmured, but she willingly sank down in a chair and let her head come to rest on the back of it, thankful to feel the circlet and veil removed. The aroma of the vinaigrette cleared her head and brought her sitting upright, coughing and gasping.

Melissa smiled uncertainly at her. 'That's better. Your colour's coming back.'

Delia gave a self-conscious nod, feeling she had made a fool of herself. The dressmaker had been right. It was only nerves. Nevertheless she was glad she didn't have to put on the gown again until her wedding day.

The tea was brought, and Melissa had a cup with her while the two assistants bore away the dresses and veil. The dressmaker made notes about the wedding day, saying she would be at the house by ten o'clock to help Delia dress and

102

then would go on to the church to make sure the train was spread out correctly before she started up the aisle.

To Delia's relief, Melissa did not chatter in the carriage on the way home, but sat with her elbow on the armrest, chin in hand, looking out of the window in a subdued and thoughtful mood. Delia, whose head was aching, appreciated the chance to sit quietly, but she could not help wondering what it was that had caused her cousin's silence. Perhaps the bridesmaid's gown hadn't entirely pleased her after all, which was a pity, for she had looked exceedingly pretty in it.

After dinner that evening Dr Gilmore was called out to a confinement and Melissa went quite early to bed, which gave Delia and Aaron the opportunity to be alone together sooner than they had expected. He moved from the sofa opposite her and drew up a footstool to sit by her chair.

'At last a chance to talk on our own,' he said with supreme contentment, looking at her, his arms resting on his knees. 'I've now seen the whole of Halewood, its land, and its properties. What a grand house it is! The interior doesn't disappoint in any way. Those ceilings! The panelling! That great stone staircase with its moulded arches and grand columns!'

She gave him a warm, spontaneous smile, enjoying his pleasure. 'At least none of those things can be ripped out and auctioned with the contents of the house.'

He laughed quietly. 'I had the same thought. Have you ever seen the original plan of the house? I came across it, framed most unsuitably and without the protection of glass, in one of those dark little upper anterooms.'

'I'm glad you saw it. Who would have expected the ink to remain so black and clear after just on three hundred years?'

They talked on in the creamy-golden glow of lamp and firelight, their shadows flickering around them. Then he remembered he had not told her about meeting Berenice. 'I met Lady Hart, too, and had tea with her.'

103

She showed surprise. 'She received you!'

'Yes, she did – and I saw her again for a short while today. It was raining, but she came out in a cloak and hood to the stables where the steward was taking me through.'

'I'm amâzed. She never sees strangers and she led me to believe that you would be no exception.'

'Unfortunately for her, no matter what she'd intended, she had no choice but to speak to me yesterday.' He went on to tell her what had taken place. 'Her reason for seeing me this morning was to tell me that Roland had been sent to bed without supper as a punishment for his insolence to me. Apparently an apology was not to be had, and I let the whole affair rest there.'

'So Roland is with her for good now,' Delia said reflectively, looking into the fire. 'I first met him when I was an invalid at Halewood, and I've seen him since on the occasions he's been at the house.'

'How did you get on with him?'

'Quite well. He was never rude to me, but then I didn't represent a threat to him as your presence in the house must have done. I felt sorry for the boy. Lady Hart's idea of motherhood is to spoil him foolishly. Luckily he's had sensible foster parents, but the boy always wept bitterly when it was time to leave his mother.'

'Perhaps it was the house he didn't want to leave.'

She considered carefully before replying. 'In the light of what you told me about yesterday that is possible, but personally I think he felt rejected whenever he was sent away again.'

'You've given a great deal of thought to the boy's problems, haven't you?'

She nodded. 'I'm fond of children. I'd like them all to have the sort of upbringing that I've had. A good home, discipline tempered with kindness and understanding, and lots of parental love. I'm the only one among all the girls I know who's not afraid of her father. He's never ruled me with a rod of iron. Unlike several of my friends, I'd never be expected to marry a husband who'd been picked out for me.'

'Maybe you make your own mistakes.' His comment fell like a stone into the silence of the room, which was broken only by the leaping dance of the flames in the coal fire.

Her face had swung towards him, startled and confused. 'Are you suggesting I don't know my own mind as far as Matthew is concerned?'

'I'm suggesting you're not listening to your own heart.' He reached out for her hand, but when his fingers touched hers, she snatched her own away and placed them tremblingly against the base of her throat.

'I've known Matthew nearly all my life. I've loved him for as long as I can remember. Nothing can change that!'

'I agree nothing can or should change the fondness you feel for an old friend who was also your childhood sweetheart. But it's not love you feel for Matthew. Habit and obligation and a promise given before you and I met bind you to him.'

'That's not true!' She sprang up from her chair as though she would flee from the room, but he was up in the same instant and had caught her by both her arms and held her, his head lowered as he looked into her frantic face.

'What are you afraid of? Of me? Or yourself?'

She knew the answer to that. Her fear sprang from the wild and senseless passion that had temporarily overwhelmed her, but it was nothing more than a storm in the heart, a storm that would pass. It was not to be listened to, not to be considered, not to be allowed to disrupt the peaceful existence she had planned with Matthew, who would be a broken man if she went back on her promise now. He needed her. Aaron did not need her. He would have Halewood to fill his life.

'I hardly know you,' she whispered brokenly. 'You're a

stranger in my home. I can count the days you've been here on the fingers of both hands.'

'Time has nothing to do with it. It's something a man and woman know the moment they set eyes on each other. That sense of belonging. The miracle of discovering the other half of oneself. The knowledge that love is of the eye, mind, heart, and body, a combined force that cannot be denied. I knew when you opened the door to me on the night I arrived at this house that it had happened. I'd found you.'

'You mustn't say these things to me!' she cried.

He released her arms and cupped her face between tender hands, bringing his own so close to hers that his breath was warm on her lips. 'To whom should I say them if not to you? I love you, Delia. I love you, my dear.'

She could not move. She did not want to move, aware that this kiss would be entirely different from the time he had taken her lips with such fierceness at the gates of Halewood. Her eyes closed as his mouth, warm, moist, urgent, came softly down on hers and was exploratory at first, his lips discovering the shape of hers in a kiss that was many tiny kisses. Then his arms closed about her and with a surge of passion he caught her to him holding her in an embrace that encompassed all she had ever imagined a kiss of love might be, free of all restraint, released from all the confines of convention, given up to the joy of conquest and surrender.

Neither heard the clop of hooves on the drive. It was the sharp tap of a servant's heels going past the drawing-room down the hall to open the front door that brought her back to reality and she thrust herself from him. She stood breathing deeply and he half-lifted his arms to her in a gesture of appeal, knowing that momentarily he had lost her.

'No!' she said agitatedly, making a little movement of her hands as if to keep him from her. 'It can't be!'

There was the sound of her father's voice in the hall. She heard Ellen answer, no doubt taking his hat and medical bag

106

from him. Delia knew that he would be tired and he would come to sit for a while by the fire before going to bed. She had a few seconds left in which to withdraw so far from Aaron that he would never presume in such a way again.

'In two weeks' time Halewood will become yours at public auction. Seven days after that I go to church to marry a man to whom I've given my promise. Our fates are settled. We are destined to go in opposite directions. You must dismiss completely any hope that it can be otherwise!' The door opened and she turned quickly and with relief, greeting her father a little too effusively. 'You're back, Papa! Did all go well?'

'Mrs Milner gave birth to her fifth son and wept, I regret to say, because it was not a girl, but her husband was content.' He rubbed his chilled hands and held them to the warmth of the fire. 'A brandy would not go amiss after being out in the cold night. Pour one for our guest, my dear, and another for your extremely tired father.'

She did as he requested and then escaped to her room. There she shut the door and leaned against it for a few seconds with arms spread as if it were a barrier between her and Aaron. Then she went across to the bed and sat down at the foot of it, setting her hand against the post, her head bowed. Thoughts spun in her brain, her face reflecting her torment. If only she had met Aaron last year instead of this. If only she had never accepted without question that one day she would marry Matthew. If only she had never let him give her a betrothal ring. If only — if only —

She heard the two men come up to bed. Some little joke passed between them and they laughed before parting company. Their respective doors closed. Immediately she sprang to her feet and walked up and down in an attempt to subdue her restlessness of mind and spirit, her hands clenched together. She would forget that kiss, forget the way her bones had seemed to melt! Or, if she was never able to do that, she would thrust it away as a casual incident not to be thought about. When she and Matthew were married he would kiss her in that searing, intimate way and she would feel the same sharp flare of ecstatic longing. He would drive Aaron from her thoughts and from her heart!

She wrung her locked hands, giving emphasis to all she had resolved. If only their marriage could be tomorrow instead of three weeks away! She wanted to be safe with Matthew and given no more chance to lose all reason in Aaron's arms. How right she had been never to be alone with him since the day of the storm. Instinct had told her it would be dangerous, and then she had allowed it to happen. But not again! Never again! Then, like the bursting forth of a mountain spring, the tears spilled over and she buried her face in her hands.

At Halewood the next day Berenice talked of how she had met Aaron and of her subsequent meeting in the stables.

'He told me,' Delia said briefly, not wanting to talk about Aaron, but Berenice persisted.

'He seems quite spellbound over Halewood,' she declared incredulously. 'Not at all like his grandfather. Perhaps Sir Harry cared about the property in his younger days, but it's my belief he had come to hate Halewood towards the end of his life. It seems to happen to all who bear the Hart name and live under its roof.'

For the first time the idea occurred to Delia that Sir Harry might have thought to end the curse of Halewood on the Hart family by deliberately avoiding any knowledge of a legitimate heir. Thus he would spare his descendants from all he and his ancestors had suffered. Certainly such a supposition put the old man in a more compassionate light. Delia made up her mind to pass on her idea to Aaron. It was only right for him to have the chance to consider giving old Sir Harry the benefit of the doubt.

'I'll go and write these letters now,' she said, collecting up the notes she had made.

'When you bring them back for me to sign we'll take tea,' Berenice said, returning her attention to the embroidery she was working on. 'I'd like to know what you intend wearing to the Penghyll Ball.'

Making her way back along the north corridor to her east wing office Delia considered the prospect of the ball with a heavy heart. She would not be able to avoid dancing at least once with Aaron. How would she react to being in his arms once again, no matter that it would be less intimate an embrace. It was not to be thought about. Not now. Not yet.

109

Chapter Seven

On the morning of the Penghyll Ball the postman's knock resounded as Delia was about to go into the study. She paused, watching as Ellen answered it and came from the door with a letter and two packages.

'More wedding gifts, miss!' the parlourmaid exclaimed, her round face beaming.

'Yes, I'm sure you're right.' Delia expected the letter to be handed to her with the packages, but Ellen withheld it. Normally Delia would not have given the matter a second thought, but something slightly furtive about Ellen's action made her give the girl a second look.

'T'letter isn't for you, miss.' Ellen pressed it down out of sight in her pocket, making it crackle. 'It's for me. From my Ma.'

Delia inclined her head and went into the study to unwrap the gifts, wishing that she could receive the well-meant kindnesses without being assailed afresh by depression, each one a reminder of her rapidly approaching wedding day. There were silver teaspoons in one and a fine damask cloth in the other. She sat down to write letters of thanks and was sealing the second one when she heard Melissa return from the dressmaker's. Her cousin had decided on a last-minute alteration to the gown she had made up her mind to wear to the ball that evening.

Picking up both letters she took them with her into the hall, intending to have them sent to the post, but she came to a standstill in surprise. Melissa was whispering to Ellen, their heads together. There was the clink of money being put in the parlourmaid's hand. Melissa herself was holding the letter that Ellen had taken from her pocket. It was Melissa who noticed Delia first, and Ellen, following her gaze with a startled glance, flushed scarlet and went scurrying away in the direction of the baize-lined door.

Melissa waved the letter tauntingly at Delia. 'Have you guessed who it's from?'

'Yes. I believe so. It's from Richard Dibley, isn't it?'

Melissa nodded with a trilling little laugh and ripped open the letter to read it through. With a smiling sigh she came to the end of it and held it to her breast, her eyes twinkling triumphantly at Delia. 'I told you it couldn't be over between us. As soon as I was able to let him have my address he has been writing to me.'

'It's none of my business whether he writes to you or not,' Delia replied, 'although I think you're extremely unwise. But I do object most strongly that you should coerce Ellen into deceit. She felt compelled to tell me a lie. In most households she would be dismissed instantly.'

'I don't care what happens to the stupid girl,' Melissa retorted crossly. 'I paid her well for keeping her mouth shut and it's her own silly fault if she gets discovered. I didn't want Uncle Charles to find out that Richard and I were writing to each other, or else he would have stopped it.'

Delia gave a nod. 'You were right in supposing that. Papa would have done, I know. Aunt Rachel told him exactly why she and Uncle Henry wanted your romance with Richard to come to an end, and although normally he hasn't much patience with your parents, in this case his sympathies are entirely with them.'

'Are you going to tell him?'

'You know I won't,' Delia said with a sigh, 'but I beg you not to make any promises to Richard. Wait. Take your time. It might not be the kind of everlasting love that you think it

111

is. Let things ride for a while.'

Melissa had picked up again the dressmaker's box containing her ball gown, which she had rested on a chair, and her little mouth smirked maliciously, her eyes mocking. 'As you wish you had done?' she enquired, her tone silky. 'Not knowing that Aaron was to come upon the scene?'

Delia could not answer her, her whole face taut. Had all the emotional turmoil she'd been going through shown so obviously? With effort she managed to parry the question with another. 'Why do you say that?'

'Keeping away from or deliberately avoiding contact with a man is a sure sign of being attracted to him against your will. You won't even meet Aaron's glance if you can help it. His eyes go to you as soon as he comes into a room. He sits looking across the table at you. Did you think I hadn't noticed that you've stopped me leaving you alone with him on some pretence several times?' She stepped nearer and thrust her face forward. 'Well, I'm not like you, thank God! I'm prepared to risk everything for the man I want, and I wouldn't care who I walked over or knocked down to achieve my aim. Nothing on this earth is going to stop me marrying the man I love.'

With a flounce of petticoats she stalked away. Delia pressed the back of a trembling hand against her mouth. Nothing would have stopped her either if it had not been Matthew standing in her way. She could not trample him down, not he who had shown her so much love and kindness through all the years they had known each other. She thought of the dolls he'd mended for her, the time on a picnic when she'd got lost on the moors and he had hunted on his own far into the night, not knowing she'd been found by another child's nursemaid and taken home, and the way he had dried her tears and bandaged her cut head when she'd fallen from her pony. Then there was her first kiss. No one but Matthew could have kissed her with such sweetness, shy himself, and she moved to wonder by the enchantment of the moment. After that their relationship had developed and changed, reaching a different level.

Always love had bound them together, for she knew his faults as well as he knew hers and neither imagined the other to be perfect. Even when frustrated and angry he would use her as a verbal whipping-post, lashing out with hurtful words, which later he wanted her to forgive. She had forgiven and forgotten, for the causes of his temper had been brief and passing things of no real importance, nothing serious enough to sever their affection for each other and invariably brought about by some outside trouble or annoyance that had had nothing to do with her in the first place. No matter how she stacked up against him his jealousy, his possessiveness, his shortness of temper, none of it outweighed the other side of his character, which had shown itself in gentleness a thousand times, or the fact that she knew herself to be the pivot around which his life turned.

Wearily she went back into the study and rang the bell. As she had expected, Annie had been sent to answer it. 'Send Ellen to me, Annie,' she instructed.

'Yes, miss.' Annie's anxious expression showed that in the kitchen quarters it was already assumed that Ellen would be dismissed without further ado.

While waiting for the girl to appear, Delia rested her elbows on the desk and held her head between her hands. She would reprimand Ellen severely, but that was all. Ellen's two years of faithful service entitled her to a second chance. Second chances didn't often come to people. She would have liked one herself, but that could never be.

That evening, she was almost ready for the Penghyll Ball when Melissa came into the bedroom, wanting the back of her gown hooked up. It was iris blue tarlatan, which suited her colouring and the richness of her hair. Underneath she was well-laced, but she pressed her hands on to her waist as

Delia fastened one tiny hook after another.

'That stupid dressmaker!' Melissa grumbled. 'She hasn't altered the gown as I wished. I can hardly breathe. It's a pity Mama's lady's maid isn't here. She's French and *knows* how to sew. I miss her helping me dress. Mama always lends her to me for special occasions.'

In spite of her complaints Melissa was not in an ill temper. On the contrary, she was singularly high-spirited and, to Delia's mind, quite astonishingly excited about the ball they were to attend, considering she had no interest in any of the young men who would be there.

'How do I look?' she demanded, taking Delia's vacated place before the dressing-table's looking-glass to touch a ringlet into place. Pearl drops swung from her ears, and around her throat she wore a matching strand.

Delia paused in pinning a cameo brooch to the bodice of her cream *bouffante* gown, its stiffened underskirts holding out its rows of ribbon-edged frills. 'Do you want my candid opinion?' she asked.

Melissa met her eyes in the glass, a secret, anticipatory look on her face. 'Yes. What is it?'

'You look like a girl dressing to meet her lover.'

Melissa gave a squeal of delight and swung round on the stool. 'You've guessed!' she exclaimed delightedly. 'Richard is going to be at the Assembly Rooms this evening. I'm hoping he'll be there waiting for me when I arrive. Nobody knows him. Luckily Uncle Charles told me several days ago he wouldn't be attending the ball, and so I was able to go ahead and make plans with Richard for this night.'

Delia had not been looking forward to the ball, knowing that she must dance at least one dance with Aaron, uncertain how she would react to his nearness, and now she dreaded it even more. 'It's madness,' she said helplessly. 'Penghyll isn't London. Newcomers are always noticed. All the older ladies sitting round the room will ask each other whose guest he is and if anyone knows his name. Tomorrow, when my father goes on his rounds, at least half a dozen people will ask him who was the young man who danced with his niece '

Melissa laughed, the colour bright in her cheeks, and she leapt to her feet, flinging out her arms exuberantly as if she would embrace the whole world. 'I don't care! Nothing matters except this wonderful night of reunion that awaits me.'

Left alone, Delia draped about her shoulders the new shawl Matthew had given her, feeling obliged to wear it. She liked it less than the Spanish one, although it was of delicate lace, fine enough to pull through a wedding ring. Taking her fur-lined cloak from the mahogany wardrobe she looped it over her arm, knowing she would need its heavy warmth for protection against the truly bitter night with its buffeting wind, which held the peculiar intense iciness that presages snow.

She found that Matthew had arrived and had joined Aaron and Melissa in the drawing-room where her father was comfortably ensconced in his favourite chair by the roaring fire, a book on his knees and several others, all on the subject of local history, stacked on the small table beside him. Delia was struck afresh by the handsomeness of the two young men who were in love with her. Matthew's tawny fairness and Aaron's darker good looks were set off by the formal black of their evening clothes and the sharp whiteness of the high collars, the cravats neatly tied, the gleaming edge of cuffs, and the snowy gloves smooth and unwrinkled. Neither could take their eyes from her when she pirouetted for her father's benefit, making her wide skirt sway and billow.

'You look very fine indeed, my dear,' Dr Gilmore commented warmly.

'The Belle of Penghyll Ball, I'd say,' Matthew endorsed, proud of her and grinning hugely in his pleasure.

115

Aaron said nothing. He did not have to. His eyes boldly paid her a greater compliment and she pulled her glance from his glittering gaze, fussing with her cloak. Then he was there, taking it from her and putting it about her shoulders before Matthew could reach her. It was Melissa whom Matthew found himself waiting on.

'Enjoy yourselves,' Dr Gilmore said, settling himself even more comfortably against the cushioned back and arms of his chair, folding his hands across his waistcoat. 'I cannot say I wish I were coming with you, because it wouldn't be true. This is the best place for me this evening – by the fireside.'

'I hope you don't get called out,' Delia said, bending to kiss him on the cheek. She could tell he was looking forward to an evening on his own. They all bade him good night and went out to ride in the same carriage to the Assembly Rooms, the girls sitting side by side, the young men facing them. Melissa and Matthew did most of the talking. Once in the passing rays of a street lamp Delia looked towards Aaron and their eyes met and held until darkness took over the interior of the carriage again.

Their vehicle soon joined a stream of others crossing the market square, wheels rumbling over cobbles, horses snorting and harnesses jingling as the drivers manoeuvred into position to bring their passengers alongside the steps and pillars of the Assembly Rooms. As the two girls and their escorts alighted, the freezing air bit into their faces, and they hastened inside. After leaving their outdoor clothes, the four of them climbed the wide, curving staircase to the ballroom. It presented a spectacle of light and colour, garlands hanging from the ceiling, flowering pot plants ornamenting the dais where the musicians were playing, and the mirrored walls and polished floor reflected the glow of the new gas-lamp chandeliers and the swinging, bell-shaped skirts of the ladies rotating with their partners. All around the floor and

116

on the balcony above, others were seated on gilded chairs and sofas, the buzz of conversation blending with the music.

Melissa, after looking about quickly and in vain for Richard, made a rueful little grimace at Delia to confirm that he had not yet arrived, and then, to pass the time, she started renewing old acquaintanceships from her previous visits to Penghyll, including Tom Whinlatter, of whom Aunt Rachel had treasured such high hopes. Delia and Matthew were greeted on all sides by their friends and acquaintances, and Matthew presented Aaron, who found himself immediately in demand. To Delia it was obvious that to every mother there with a marriageable daughter – to say nothing of the daughters themselves – he was the catch of the Season, for word had long since spread around the district that Edward Hart's son was to be among the bidders for Halewood, and tales of his supposed wealth had been enormously exaggerated.

Delia danced most of the time with Matthew and saw Melissa take the floor in turn with a variety of attentive young men, all showing their delight at seeing her again, laughing with her as they swept her into waltz, mazurka, polka, and polonaise. She was alive with happiness, her face glowing, her curls swinging. No doubt each young man imagined that it was for him alone that she sparkled, not noticing how she kept an alert and constant watch for another, glancing towards the arched entrance whenever fresh arrivals appeared. Aaron had one pretty partner after another, blonde, brunette, and redhead, their top-knots and ringlets adorned with ribbons and flowers, each girl exuding the scent of violets or attar of roses, using every feminine art to attract, to intrigue, and to ensnare.

Delia danced several times with others to whom she had promised dances, but she was back with Matthew again and when there was a stir among those standing near the head of the staircase, and the suddenly aroused interest spread like a

117

ripple throughout the whole room. Delia, following the direction of the turning heads, gasped with amazement when she recognized the woman who had entered the ball-room.

'Matthew!' she exclaimed in disbelief. 'It's Lady Hart! She's never once attended any social function in the county in all the years she's lived at Halewood. This is the first time ever. We must go to her.'

Berenice had not chosen a sober gown suited to widow-hood, but one of rich red velvet that was severely elegant over its supporting petticoats, and around her throat she wore a necklace of garnets set in gold, which matched the earrings that flashed little sparks of crimson light as they swung from her ears. Over her face and head she wore a gilt-gauze, shoulder-length mantilla of gossamer fineness, which was fastened to her burnished hair with golden combs.

Aaron, having decided to dance no more until he could take the floor with Delia, turned his head and saw her poised there on the threshold. Compassion moved him. She had tried for one brief, glorious night to play the lady of the manor, her gown tasteful, her choice of jewellery correct, but to him – and surely to every man present with some knowledge of the world – there was a sharp-edged brilliance about her that was unmistakable. Without hesitation he decided to make an amendment to his decision not to dance again except with a certain partner.

He moved towards Berenice, a tall figure threading a passage through those clustered around the floor. When he reached her he closed heels together and bowed deeply. 'May I have the pleasure of this dance, Lady Hart?'

Relief showed in her eyes and he saw that she was as nervous as a young girl at a first ball and he wondered, remembering all that Delia had told him about her secluded way of life, why on earth she had ventured out into society at this late hour when her departure from Halewood was almost imminent.

'Thank you, Mr Hart.' She let him lead her on to the floor and looked up into his face as she glided with him in the dancing steps. 'I suppose everyone is much surprised to see me.'

'They are, I'm sure of that.' He was as much aware as she that all present were following their rotating progress down the floor.

'I saw how the word spread,' she confided, a tiny smile pulling at her mouth. 'Somebody at a window recognized my carriage even as I stepped from it and in so many seconds there was a crowd of faces staring down.'

'I guess few in this ballroom have ever set eyes on you before.'

'Only from a distance.' She acknowledged Delia as they passed in a bell-swing of their wide skirts.

'We had no idea you were coming,' he remarked. 'You gave Delia no hint.'

'There was no point. I might have changed my mind at the last moment.'

It was an insight into the torment of indecision she had gone through before eventually making the move to come. He could feel her trembling tautness as he held her. Around them the ballroom turned like a carousel, gas-lamps and mirrored walls and the other dancing couples blending together in rainbow lights and textures.

'I hope you'll enjoy the evening now that you're here,' he said.

She tilted her head. 'I don't intend to stay more than a few minutes. It was simply a whim to see one Penghyll Ball before leaving Halewood.'

'Surely you will stay to supper?'

'No, indeed. I should be forced to speak with the local dignitaries and their wives whom I have no desire to

119

acknowledge.'

He was not deceived. She was fearful of being snubbed. By ignoring them it was she who was doing the snubbing. Her brief but glorious appearance at the ball was in itself a derisive gesture. She was showing herself to them as though they were peasantry.

'Do you intend to live as secluded a life in Italy as you have at Halewood?' he enquired courteously.

'I trust so. I seek peace and solitude. In Florence a villa with a walled garden awaits me. I shall paint and read and bask in the sunshine. When I emerge it will only be to visit a gallery or go to church.'

'What of Roland? Should he not have young company?'

She raised disdainful eyebrows. 'I've no intention of mixing with the English emigrés there for his sake. He'll have lessons from a tutor to occupy him for most of the day. I'll buy him a pony. He can ride.'

'Would it not be better to leave him at school in England?'

'I want him to be with *me*,' she said with sudden tragic emphasis. 'Sir Harry kept me from him far too long.'

He saw there was the glint of tears in her eyes. Again the sharp curiosity about her rose in him. When had this sensitive, vulnerable woman first taken on that defensive outward shell that was like a proclaiming mark on her? When had she first stepped on to the mercenary path? What had been the circumstances? Who was the first man to have corrupted and debased her into a way of life that she must have followed until Sir Harry in his dotage had offered a means of escape? He would never know. Such women never talked about themselves. With her secrets she had come to Halewood and with them she would leave again.

The dance came to an end. Delia and Matthew were no more than two feet away and greetings were exchanged. 'Now I'm going,' Berenice said, and gently she waved aside Delia's protests. 'Mr Hart will explain why. Good night,

120

Delia. Good night, Mr Shaw.'

'I'll escort you to your carriage,' Aaron said.

Downstairs in the entrance hall the attendant, who must have been given instructions, was waiting with Berenice's sable cloak. Aaron took it and wrapped it about her shoulders. Then he walked with her down the steps to her waiting carriage. It had started to snow. Pale, silvery flakes that were settling like a mantle over the town. The groom had sprung forward to open the carriage door for her. She gave Aaron her hand.

'I think we shall not meet again, Mr Hart. I leave for Florence next week – the day before the auction. I wish you joy at Halewood. It brought none to me. But you love the house already and I never did. I pray that it will love you in return and soften its hard heart towards you. Good night – and good-bye.'

She stepped into the carriage. The groom slammed the door and jumped up behind, taking his place even as the carriage started to move, the horses with their breath steamy in the bitter night air obeying the flick of the coachman's whip. The wheels left dark tracks across the white square. Only when the carriage had vanished from sight did Aaron turn and go back into the warmth of the building.

The call had come for the supper-dance. Melissa hastened across the floor to speak to Delia, her face desperately anxious. 'Richard is late! He hasn't arrived yet.'

Delia tried to reassure her. 'Don't worry. It's difficult to judge exactly how long any journey will take and it's many miles from the nearest railway station, remember. If there's been snow, a drift across the road could hold up a coach or force the driver to follow a longer route. Delays can happen all the time.'

'What's that? Who's delayed?' Matthew asked, not having heard what was said.

Melissa shot Delia a warning glance and answered for her.

'My partner for the supper-dance.' she indicated the bare space on the little programme dangling from her wrist. 'I forgot to write it down.'

Almost everyone was dancing. 'We'll stay with you,' Delia said, seeing that Melissa was distraught. Matthew would assume that the reason was that she was reluctant to leave Melissa a wallflower for the supper-dance, which was every girl's nightmare.

'No need,' Aaron said, catching her words as he came up to them. 'Nobody should miss the supper-dance.' He did not turn to Melissa as she had expected, but took her firmly by the hand while he addressed Matthew. 'You, Matthew, can take Melissa on to the floor. I haven't had a chance to dance with Delia yet. This is my opportunity.'

He swept her into the waltz before she could make any protest, one white-gloved hand holding hers, the other placed firmly on her waist. He did not speak, but his eyes did not leave her as the dance took them round the floor. She felt compelled to break the silence of his stare.

'It won't be long now before you're back in these Assembly Rooms again,' she said lightly. 'But you'll be in the big hall downstairs, and an auctioneer will be on the rostrum.'

A smile touched his mouth. 'I'm counting on your coming to the auction with me. You'll bring me luck, I know.'

'I'll attend with pleasure.'

'It's right and proper that you should be there when it becomes mine. It is no longer only for myself that I want Halewood.'

She could not pretend not to understand his meaning. There could be no pretence between them ever again. She sometimes felt that if she willed it she and Aaron would be able to read each other's very thoughts. An awareness of the devastating consequences of such revelations made her keep a tight mental barrier of restraint whenever she was in his company.

'Don't make everything harder for me,' she implored unashamedly.

'I intend to give you no respite until you tell me once and for all you've finished with this masquerade that is deceiving neither of us,' he replied, giving emphasis to his words with a tightening of his hand on hers.

Her betrothal ring was cutting into her finger under his grip and she welcomed the pain, taking it as a fierce reminder of where her true path lay, but the tears that stung the back of her eyes did not come from that small agony. It was from the greater hurt she was inflicting on her own heart and his.

'It's too late,' she exclaimed despairingly.

'No, it's not!' He drew her closer to him than convention allowed. 'The wedding can be cancelled. Gifts returned. The chapter closed and another opened.'

The waltz was almost over. He spun her with slowly decreasing speed to the final notes of the music, and she found a way of answering him that could be no more to either of them than the tiny glow of a fading candle in a well of darkness.

'If Matthew should release me from my promise of his own free will, then I would listen to all you want to say to me. But the chance of that happening is too slight to be considered.' The dance had ended, and she dipped her curtsey in a sea of rippling frills.

'It will happen!' He did not release her fingers. 'It must happen! Without each other we shall both be destroyed.'

She felt herself whiten, hearing the terrible ring of truth in his words. His face, which she had adored in her heart from the moment of meeting, was set, the mouth firm, and his eyes held such love for her that she wanted only to hurl herself in his arms, forgetful of all else, engulfed beyond recall by the answering wave of passion that was sweeping through her. She was actually teetering on her toes, her arms half-raised, when Matthew's hands gripped her by the shoulders and spun her round towards him.

'Stop day-dreaming here! Everyone's going in to supper.' He was not smiling. He had been annoyed at Aaron's high-handedness in taking her away and leaving him with Melissa, for whom he had no liking, and now instead of joining the flow towards the supper-room Aaron had kept her on the floor in some serious conversation, which – to judge by her startled, almost shocked reaction to his own intervention – had been upsetting her.

'Are they?' she gasped vaguely. 'Where's Melissa?'

'Waiting for us. Come along.'

In the supper-room Melissa had more than her fair share of young men wanting to wait on her, but she was off-hand with all of them, taking no refreshment. 'What's the matter?' Matthew asked when she refused the custard-ice he had brought for her with the one he had fetched for Delia. He thought she seemed oddly detached and nervous when he had danced with her, and there was a pinched look about her mouth.

'Nothing's the matter!' she snapped back irritably. 'Except you stepped on my foot while we waltzed. I don't know that I can dance any more.' She sprang up from her chair like a released spring and swept away out of the supper-room.

Delia left her own untouched ice and followed after her. Melissa went hurrying down the stairway to the entrance hall. By the time Delia caught her up she was at a window, looking out at the square where a dusting of snow had fallen. She was quite frantic.

'He hasn't come. Oh, mercy, Delia! He should have arrived long ago. He must come! He must!'

'Give him time,' Delia urged persuasively, genuinely concerned for Melissa, whose voice had become shaky and high-pitched. She was obviously on the verge of hysteria.

'Remember what I said about the snowfall? See the layer that has come down since we arrived at the ball. It will be much thicker on the hill-roads, and they could be impassable.'

Melissa swung round to face Delia, her fists clenched together. 'Suppose he doesn't get here tonight or tomorrow or ever. Suppose something has happened to him. Something really dreadful! How shall I know? What shall I do?'

'If there was any kind of disaster anywhere along his route we should read about it in the newspapers tomorrow, and then we'd soon find out if Richard had been involved or not. But that's highly unlikely. I think you'll find that he's had to take shelter in an inn or hotel tonight.'

Melissa gnawed her lip. 'I wish I could believe that, but I can't. He should be here. He swore nothing should keep us apart a day longer. Only a catastrophe beyond anything imaginable would have stopped him coming to take me away at the hour we planned.'

'What do you mean?' Delia demanded in hushed tones.

Melissa did not answer her, for her attention had been caught by a hackney cab which had turned into the square. It was still some distance away, but it was the way the occupant, his face a misty oval, was peering through the cab window, conveying a sense of urgency, which succeeded in convincing her beyond a shadow of doubt that her time of anxious waiting was at an end.

'It's Richard!' she breathed, her whole face becoming radiant. 'He has come!' She grinned triumphantly at Delia, her eyes sparkling, her cheeks flushed with excitement and relief. 'Now I'll tell you the rest of my secret, but you mustn't say a word until tomorrow. Richard and I are planning to elope. We had planned to disappear while everyone was having supper. I'd not have been missed until you were all ready to leave in the early hours of the morning. But, as you said, Richard must have been delayed by the weather. He will have collected at the coaching-station a packed valise I smuggled out of the house yesterday. I'll send for the rest of my boxes as soon as we're safely abroad and married. Then Papa can do nothing to prevent my receiving my inheritance. Don't look so serious. Rejoice with me. I'm going to get my cloak and you get yours. I want you to come out to the hackney cab with me and wave me farewell. It's a pity you haven't any rice to throw.'

Giggling excitedly, she shot another glance at the approaching cab and hustled Delia with her into the ante-room to get their cloaks. Delia, fastening her clasp, was not adverse to meeting Richard. She would be able to judge him better for herself than from such diverse evidence as that which had been provided by Melissa and Aunt Rachel.

The cab came to a halt as the two cousins emerged from the building. Melissa ran down the steps followed at a slower pace by Delia, who was trying to pull up her hood. When she heard Melissa give a cry she lifted her head sharply and saw to her astonishment that her own father and a middle-aged man, a stranger to her, were alighting from the vehicle.

'Uncle Charles!' Melissa gasped hoarsely.

'Melissa,' he began, breathing heavily as though having difficulty in inhaling the ice-cold air, 'I have to tell you that Mr Dibley, who is in good health and has come to no harm, will not be arriving to fetch you. Allow me to present Mr Foley, who has been sent by your father's lawyers and will explain what has happened as soon as you have returned to Sycamore House with us.'

'Good evening, Miss Barton.' The man was thick-set and coarse-featured, plainly dressed in tweed travelling clothes.

Melissa stood as though transfixed, looking from one to the other, her eyes enormous in her blanched face. 'I want to know now!' she demanded harshly. 'Where is Richard? Why isn't he here?'

'Get into the cab, Melissa,' the doctor said. He would have

126

assisted her, but she drew back, throwing off his hand.

'No. It's a trick! Somehow you've found out that he's on his way to Penghyll and you're trying to get me away while there's time.'

Delia, who had come to her side, spoke up. 'Is that true, Papa?'

'No, my dear. Help me to persuade Melissa that we have only her good at heart. This is no place for her to receive the news that we have to tell.'

Delia turned to her cousin. 'I don't know what it can be, but take Papa's advice.' She was equally concerned for her father, whose face looked drawn, his colour patchy. She could imagine how his peaceful evening had been shattered by the arrival of this stranger out of the blue to tell him that his niece had planned an elopement and it was being stopped.

Melissa spoke through gritted teeth. 'I'm not moving a step until I know what's happened!'

Dr Gilmore rubbed an anxious hand across his forehead at her insistence, and although he ignored the nod from Mr Foley encouraging him to answer her, he did capitulate. 'Very well,' he said with regret. 'It is my sad and painful duty to tell you that you have trusted and believed a young villain who cares nothing for you. He has been watched and followed. When he purchased rail and Channel packet tickets from London to Calais it was not difficult for Mr Foley to deduce what he had in mind.'

Melissa turned like a fury on Mr Foley, her eyes blazing. 'So you're a spy! A despicable little spy sent out to snoop on your betters!'

Mr Foley's immobile face remained impassive. Abuse was nothing new to him, and he merely tilted his head attentively at the doctor, waiting to hear what he would say next.

Dr Gilmore was finding the whole affair upsetting and exceedingly distasteful, not least of all his brother-in-law's use of a paid spy or private detective as Mr Foley chose to call himself, and he tried to find the words to ease the blow that must befall his unfortunate niece, for he could not allow the unpleasant Mr Foley to be the bearer of the news. 'I have not enquired into Mr Foley's methods of investigation, nor do I intend to, but it suffices to say he was able to obtain sufficient information to discover the day that Mr Dibley intended to spirit you away from my present care into the unknown. Whereupon your father gave instructions that Mr Dibley be approached with an offer of financial reimbursement in return for signing a certain document.'

'Why? For what reason?' Still Melissa had not grasped the terrible fact that was only too clear to Delia.

'Your father realizes that to thwart this elopement attempt would not be enough in itself. Unless he kept you locked up, which was impossible, or kept you under constant surveillance indefinitely, there was nothing to stop another more cunningly planned elopement being attempted and perhaps carried out successfully.'

'He's right in thinking that!' Melissa retorted defiantly. 'Nothing shall – '

Dr Gilmore interrupted her. 'Hear me out, child. Mr Dibley left yesterday for a destination abroad that is not to be made known to you. He has agreed never to see you again.'

Melissa collapsed without a sound. Dr Gilmore and Mr Foley picked her up between them and lifted her into the cab. Delia would have gone with them, but her father bade her return to the ball.

'At all costs we must keep this affair quiet. There must be no scandal, Delia. Make some excuse to explain her absence to Matthew and Mr Hart. I'll tell you all the details later.'

Delia hurried back inside, to find Matthew looking for her.

'Wherever have you been?' he asked in amazement, seeing her in her snow-covered cloak.

'Melissa has gone home in a cab,' she answered as calmly

as she could.

'Hmm. Making a fuss about my stepping on her foot,' Matthew grumbled. 'I barely touched her toe. Come along. Let's go back to the dancing.'

They stayed until the early hours of the morning. Delia would have left long before had the decision been hers to make, but Matthew was enjoying himself, the fun having become faster and more furious, and she could not leave without him. She and Aaron danced several more times together, but they no longer talked except with their eyes, he saying such lovely things to her that at times she could not bear to receive his silent messages and danced in his arms with her eyes downcast.

She had grasped the consequences that would result if she did go through with the marriage to Matthew. As Aaron had warned, she would destroy not only her life and his, but Matthew's too. Sooner or later, no matter how she tried to disguise the fact from him, Matthew would discover that she had married him out of loyalty and affection and not love. Then he would not know how to cope with his anguish and misery. She, understanding him as she did, had no doubt as to the form his frustration would take. She, whom he would love no less, would become by her very presence in their home a constant thorn in his side and never again would there be harmony between them, his resentment increasing as the love he desired from her slipped ever from him.

The ball came to an end at last. She sensed that Aaron was as thankful as she that it was over. Matthew had offered two acquaintances a lift and the carriage was crowded. When it reached Sycamore House she was swift to bid him good night and hurry indoors where she went upstairs at once, leaving Aaron to enter after her and lock up the door.

Her father's bedroom door stood ajar and a candle flickered. She pushed it a little wider. 'Papa?' she whispered, uncertain whether he was awake.

129

He had taken to sleeping propped against his pillows in recent months and he rolled his head round towards her, lifting his hand, which had been pressed against his chest, to beckon her forward. 'Have you looked in at Melissa? I gave her a sleeping draught to calm her or else she wouldn't have closed her eyes this night.'

'Do you want me to check on her?'

'She'll be all right, but you can put your head round her door before you go to bed.'

'Why aren't *you* asleep?' she questioned with mock-reproof, sitting down on the edge of the bed.

'I have been, but I heard the carriage come up the drive.'

'Have you a pain?' she asked with a frown of concern, seeing how he rubbed his knuckles against his chest.

'A touch of dyspepsia. Nothing more.'

'Can I fetch you a drink of sugared water?'

'No, no. I've taken something for it. It will soon go off.'

'Where's Mr Foley?'

'He's putting up at a local hostelry for the night. We shall not see him again, thank God! Deucedly unpleasant fellow. He arrived saying that Melissa had planned to elope direct from the ball and we must get there and bring her away before she gave way to distress or hysteria when Dibley failed to arrive. My brother-in-law's chief consideration in all this has been his fear of scandal, which would ruin his chances in the election. His concern for his daughter has been of secondary importance, although there's no denying Melissa is well rid of the young scallywag. He would have brought her nothing but misery.'

'How was Richard Dibley persuaded to give up Melissa? Surely her inheritance was more than any sum Uncle Henry would offer?'

'But Dibley wasn't going to get his hands on her money. Henry has a couple of clever lawyers. It's a long and complicated will and they'd managed to pin-point some tiny clause

130

that could mean withholding payment through some counter-claim from Henry himself. A ridiculous situation, but it was enough to make Dibley realize that, even if he pressed on and eloped with Melissa, it could be a long wait before her money was finally in his hands. He accepted a cash settlement and agreed to go abroad for an indefinite period. He was glad to do it. Henry had been pulling other strings and there was the possibility of a charge of embezzlement and subsequent imprisonment. The young man's affections for Melissa just melted away. He made no stand at all.'

Delia let her shoulders rise and fall in a long, deep sigh. 'What a sad and sordid business. Poor Melissa. What happens now?'

'Henry and Rachel want her to stay on with us for a while. They're too busy with the election to cope with the gloom and tears that are bound to follow. I at least can keep a professional eye on her, but it's a lot to expect you to manage with the wedding on your mind.'

'I think it's best she stay with us,' she agreed, 'but as to my wedding – ' She fell silent. She wanted to talk to him about her dilemma, but this was not the time for it. He had had a most exhausting night with little sleep and it was almost morning. She rose from the bed. 'I'll look in at Melissa. Good night, Papa.'

Melissa was sleeping soundly, tears wet on her cheeks. Delia went into her own room. As she undressed and got ready for bed she thought what a full and fateful night it had been. Melissa had been jilted. Berenice had emerged from her self-induced isolation for a brief, bright, comet-like appearance. Aaron had made her face up to her love for him. And she herself was committed to finding a way of making Matthew see that marriage without her loving him would bring nothing but a tragic unhappiness that time could never ease.

She climbed into bed and slid down under the covers. In the servants' quarters there was already a stirring in preparation for a new day. Somewhere in the distance a cock crowed.

Chapter Eight

Delia seemed hardly to have closed her eyes before she was roused by someone shaking her shoulder. Ellen's voice came through to her. 'Wake up, miss! Something horrible's happened!'

Her first thought flew to Melissa and she bounced up in bed, thrusting back the hair from her eyes, her heart thumping. 'What is it?'

'Your father, miss!' Ellen's face was ashen. 'Annie took his shaving-water and couldn't get a reply. She opened t'door and found him lying face downward on the floor!'

Delia flung herself from the bed, and raced to her father's room and the anxious Annie drew back from the door to let her pass. She saw at once he must have fallen from the bed while reaching for a phial on the bedside table, for it lay by his hand, the liquid it had contained spilt into a pool. Dropping to her knees beside him, she felt for the pulse in his neck and found it was beating, although weak and irregular. He was alive! She looked over her shoulder at the two servant-girls.

'You, Annie, wake Mr Hart and fetch Cobby from the stables to help lift my father back into bed.' She snatched a blanket from the bed as she spoke and covered him. He was cold through his linen nightshirt and she had no idea how long he had been lying there. 'You, Ellen, send the coachman on horseback post-haste to my father's partner, Dr Pomfret. He's to come at once! Understand?'

'Yes, miss!' they chorused together and ran off on their

133

errands. She heard the pounding on Aaron's door and Annie's anxiety-pitched voice was answered by his deep tones. Seconds later he came hastening into the room, tying the cord of his dressing-gown, his feet as bare as hers.

'Is it a stroke?' he asked quickly in deep concern, going down on one knee beside the prostrate man and feeling immediately for the pulse in the limp wrist that he lifted from the floor.

'I think so. I don't know. I've sent for the doctor.'

'I'll get him back into bed.'

'The groom will be here in a minute to help you.' The words came shakily. Shock had set in and she was shivering. Aaron put a hand on her shoulder.

'Go and put on a robe. You'll take cold.'

'Not yet. I must see Papa into bed first.'

He reached for another blanket and folded it about her. She put her head on one side and rested her cheek against his hand as he did so, her eyes closing tightly. 'Thank God you're with me!' she whispered.

The groom came clattering up the stairs. Swiftly he lent a hand and together he and Aaron lifted the doctor back into bed. Only then did Delia realize her father was still conscious. He opened his eyes and looked at her, whispered something she could not catch, and gave a long groan of pain.

She sat by his bed, holding his hand between hers, and left him only to complete her morning toilette and put on the clothes that Ellen had brought her in his dressing-room where she could keep an eye on him through the half-open door. Slipping a last hairpin into her tresses she returned to the bedside and once more slid her fingers under her father's hand on the coverlet and held it. He lay perfectly still with his eyes closed, breathing with difficulty. She hoped that she was giving him comfort through contact as Aaron's presence in the room had been succour to her in her hour of need.

134

Dr Pomfret wasted no time in coming. He was a youngish man, brisk and capable in his manner, and he diagnosed a seizure of the heart. He did what he could for the patient, who was to have absolute quiet, and having administered a dose of laudanum to ease the pain, he gave Delia instructions about giving further doses.

'I'll be back later,' he said, picking up his bag, 'and in the meantime I'll send along a nurse whom I know to be clean, conscientious, and reliable.'

'But I want to look after my father myself!'

'Come, come, Miss Gilmore. We can't have you at the bedside twenty-four hours of the day, else I shall have a second patient in this house. Be advised by me. Your father needs constant and careful nursing, and if you're tired out you cannot give it. You want the best for him, don't you?'

'Indeed I do!'

'That's settled then.'

He left and she went back to stand by the bedside, pressing trembling finger-tips against her mouth. Aaron, after speaking to Dr Pomfret in the hall, returned to the room and she turned when he reached her, throwing herself in his arms and burying her face against his neck. He held her hard and tight in wordless sympathy.

When they drew apart he put up his hands and gently stroked her face down from cheekbones to chin. 'There's always hope,' he whispered. 'Your father is a strong man. He'll fight this attack if we do all we can to help him. Don't despair, my love. Don't despair.'

She gave a little nod, managed a glimmer of a smile in response to his encouragement, and went back to her chair at the bedside to take up her vigil again.

It was after midday when Melissa came to see her. Delia gave a start, ashamed that she had forgotten all about the unfortunate girl in the midst of her own troubles, and she was relieved to see that Melissa had not surrendered to tears

135

and apathy, but wore her hair neatly dressed and had on one of her prettiest afternoon gowns in striped blue merino. Her face, although pale, her still swollen lids bearing evidence of much weeping, was composed and set in hardness. It was easy to see she would not give her heart again with reckless abandon. All that was frivolous in her nature seemed to have been consumed in bitter resignation and all that was ruthless had turned to steel. Observing that she was about to speak, Delia put a finger to her lips and rose to draw her away from the bed and into the dressing-room.

'Papa mustn't be disturbed,' she whispered. 'How are you? Have you eaten?'

'I've spent the morning in my room, and I've eaten nothing, but I'm not hungry. Oh, don't worry about me. You've enough to think about with Uncle Charles. Is he very ill? Annie told me all about finding him.'

'Yes, he is.'

'I thought there was something the matter last night, although I was in such a state myself I could hardly think. He went into the dispensary to fetch me a special kind of medicine to calm me down, because I was quite beside myself, and I heard a crash. When he came back to the drawing-room there was powder all down his jacket. He held on to the back of the chair when he passed me the medicine and his hand shook more than mine – and I could hardly hold the glass, which rattled against my teeth. Then I went up to bed feeling strangely light-headed, almost tipsy. I remembered nothing more until this morning.'

Delia found herself trying not to blame Melissa for being the cause of her father's heart attack, but it was impossible not to take into account all the upsetting events of the previous night and stack them together. Determinedly she reminded herself that he must have been in poor health for a considerable while, and it could have happened at any time and anywhere.

'You must try to eat luncheon,' she said. 'Aaron will eat with you. I'm staying in the sickroom.'

Melissa looked disdainful. 'There's no need to suppose I'm going to pine away. I've no intention of doing that.' Then her voice became acid, her mouth tightening to control the tremulous lips. 'Richard was paid off, you know. My dear father paid him off. And do you know what was in the letter that my devoted parent had delivered to me by that hateful Mr Foley? He wrote that if ever I went against his wishes again he would turn me out and fight his claim to my great-aunt's money through to the High Court and make sure that not a penny of it came to me.'

'Oh, Melissa –' Delia said unhappily.

'Don't pity me!' Melissa flashed sharply, interrupting whatever she had been about to say. 'I won't be pitied! Never mention last night's affair to me again. Uncle Charles agreed to that last night when we talked after he had sent Mr Foley away. I'm putting Richard out of my mind. Will you agree to forget that he ever existed?'

'Of course I will.'

'It's a relief that I can stay on here. I feel I never want to see my home or my father again. Now I'm going to send a groom to collect my valise from the coach-station for me. After that I'll come and take a turn at the bedside if you like. I don't mind what I do to help. In any case, I'll be glad of a chance to sit and think.'

On her own again, Delia went over all that Melissa had said, and she frowned uncertainly. She could tell Melissa had spent the whole morning alone in her room coming to terms with the situation. It had not crushed her, which was admirable, but there was something odd about her abrupt severing of the past that seemed to spring more from desperation than from courage. She talked as if she had some other matter on her mind that she must plot to see through. Could she be planning some revenge against her father for putting

137

an end to the romance? That was unlikely, but what else could it be?

There came a moan from the bed. Delia sprang forward to lean over her patient and forgot about Melissa once more.

Nurse Baker arrived in mid-afternoon. She was not a stranger to Delia, who knew her from the times she had been called in to attend to some of the practice's more well-to-do patients. She was plump and straw-haired, neat in her appearance, and always wore while on duty a starched apron and a tiny cap that tied under her chin.

'What a sorry state of affairs this is,' she said, clucking her tongue as she smoothed the sheet over the patient. 'Now you take a rest while you can, Miss Gilmore. I'll call you if I think you should come – and I'd appreciate a tray of tea.'

Delia, after giving the order for the tea, which was to be the first of many such trays borne up to Nurse Baker, ignored the well-meaning advice to rest and went instead to check on the state of the dispensary, wondering what her father had broken to cause the crash that Melissa had heard. She was opening the locked door of the dispensary with her own key when Melissa, who had heard her, came drifting into the study.

'How is Uncle Charles?' she enquired listlessly.

'No change,' Delia replied with a suppressed and deeply anxious sigh. Then she stepped into the dispensary and gasped at the mess. A smashed jar lay on its side at her feet and the powder it had contained had spread out and settled dust-like over the entire black and white chequered floor. 'I must get Annie to come and clean up!'

As Delia pulled the bell-rope Melissa picked up a blue glass bottle that stood on the table and removed the stopper to sniff the contents. 'This is what I was given last night,' she remarked. 'I slept like a stone. Do you think I could have some more tonight? I don't want to lie awake.'

Delia took the bottle and set it back in a glass-fronted

cabinet where it belonged. 'I can't let you have that. I wouldn't know the dosage anyway.'

'It was about a tablespoon, I'd say.'

'*About* is not accurate enough with anything on these shelves. I'll ask Dr Pomfret to prescribe a sleeping draught for you.' To Delia's relief Melissa did not argue the point.

Annie was quick to fetch a bucket of soapy water and a cloth to clean up the mess. Delia stayed in the dispensary to wipe the powdery dust from flagons that she knew her father would not want the servants to touch. Melissa wandered out into the study and looked unseeingly along the bookshelves, fingering the collection of volumes of local history and folk-lore without really taking note of what she was doing, her thoughts turned inwards. She intended to get her hands on that bottle somehow – for use in what she deemed to be an emergency.

The audacity of what she had thought out that morning almost frightened her, but it had to be done. She had only to watch and pray – to the devil if needs be! – for the right opportunity and seize it when it came. She had nothing to lose and everything to gain. The whole scheme had come to her while she had wept, not shedding tears for her lost love or the dream that had been shattered, but only for herself. She, who could have had the pick of men, had made a fool of herself and been duped like any foolish servant girl. Had her humiliation become public knowledge in London among her friends and acquaintances she would not have been able to face it. Never had she thought to look upon the Pendle district of Lancashire as a haven. She envied Berenice, who was able to keep locked doors between herself and inquisitive intruders. No longer did she think of Halewood as a gloomy den, for in her present state of distress she saw it as a shining refuge.

Delia was locking the dispensary door and her voice broke in on Melissa's thoughts. 'That's Papa's favourite reading when he's not taken up with new writing on medical matters.'

'What?' Melissa turned towards her.

Delia, seeing her cousin's completely blank expression, indicated the leather and gilt-lettered spines along which Melissa had been running a finger. 'Those books are Papa's treasures.'

'Oh, are they?' Melissa remarked dully.

'He has files of his own notes on the research he has done throughout the years while he's been in practice in Penghyll,' Delia continued as they went from the study together. Then, seeing that there appeared to be no chance of arousing Melissa's interest in that subject or anything else, she parted from her at the foot of the stairs. 'I have to put the dispensary key away in my room, and after that I'll be sitting at Papa's bedside. Don't be alone. Aaron talked of taking a stroll about the town to look at some of the old buildings. Why not go with him?'

Melissa dipped her head, a closed look on her face, her eyes hooded. 'I think I will.' She went off to find him, her hard little mouth set in a thin, determined smile that Delia did not see.

Matthew came to the house that evening. He had been told of the doctor's heart attack by his grandparents. Delia received him in the study away from the drawing-room where Melissa had asked Aaron to play a game of chess with her.

'I came as soon as I heard,' he said, taking her in his arms. He was genuinely upset. He liked and respected Dr Gilmore, and there was another side of the matter which had to be discussed.

Delia moved away from him and sat in the swivel-chair by the desk. 'You realize what this means.' She picked up a quill-pen from its stand and played with it nervously. 'Our marriage can't take place on the date arranged.'

His face was intensely serious and disappointment lay like a dark shadow in the depths of his eyes. He perched his weight on the edge of the desk and looked down at her. 'I have to admit that was my first thought.'

Desolately she considered how she had yearned to avoid marrying Matthew on the appointed day, never dreaming that it would come about in such a way. Yet an unexpected gate offering ultimate escape had been opened for her and she had to use it. By a gentle path she must part from him. She would not have him hurt beyond hope of finding happiness ever again.

'Suppose,' she said, speaking slightly higher than a whisper, 'you should find in that extended time of waiting that perhaps we have waited too long for each other.'

'I don't understand.'

She lifted her head, the words almost choking her. 'Our boy-girl love has been the sweetest thing I've ever known, but we've changed, Matthew. We've grown up.'

A tender look suffused his face. 'Of course we have. And so has our love for each other.' He slid from the desk and came round to turn her in the swivel chair towards him, and he crouched down, his face on a level with hers. 'You've had a shock today and everything you're saying is tied up with last-minute nerves that you've been having.' He looked wise. 'You think I haven't noticed that you've been different towards me lately, but I have and I've known that it was nothing more than the fact that your days of girlhood have been drawing to an end. Now your father's illness has put an even greater strain on you. Nothing you could say to me under these circumstances can be counted or listened to.'

He leaned forward and put his head on her lap, gathering her legs and layers of skirt and petticoats within his arms. 'As soon as your father is on the road to recovery we'll fix another wedding day. It might be best if we counted on making it a small family affair with no outside guests, which would make it less of a strain for your father, and it would mean we needn't wait too long.'

'I don't want to consider another wedding day!' she protested, helpless before his refusal to listen to what she was trying to make him comprehend. To ride in the face of another's love was more paralysing than meeting anger, hurt or outrage. 'You must listen to me – '

'I'm listening, sweetheart,' he said soothingly, raising himself up and standing with feet apart, looking down at her. 'Naturally you can't think of anything at the present time except your father, but we must remember that he'd be the last one to want us to delay our marriage and the commencement of our life together any longer than necessary. Think over what I said about a quiet wedding. Later we could give a series of house-warming parties to include all those who would otherwise have been at the ceremony. In that way nobody would be offended. Those who'd have to come from far afield probably wouldn't make the journeys involved, and I dare say Aaron Hart will have gone back to his own country by then – '

'What do you mean?' Her question cut across his words.

He gave a shrug and wandered back to the other side of the desk, his thumbs looped in his waistcoat pockets, and he looked well satisfied with what he was saying. 'In my opinion he is not going to get Halewood, that's all.'

She stood up sharply and set both her hands on the desk, half leaning towards him. 'Why not?'

'It's come to my hearing that the bidding will be high at the auction.'

She relaxed fractionally. 'That's common knowledge. When I was at Halewood two days ago Lady Hart mentioned the surprising number of seriously interested purchasers, many of whom – to her relief – have been devoting more time to pacing about on the land in rain and mud than trailing through the house itself.'

'But you told me that Aaron isn't a rich man.'

'He isn't. But he has been given the top figure that Halewood is likely to fetch and has no qualms about not being able to meet it.'

'He *had* the top figure,' Matthew pointed out pedantically, 'but I should say that in the past few days it's soared to a much higher one.'

She froze. Frightened. Frightened for Aaron. Frightened for the house. 'Are you telling me that the railway company wants the land?'

He nodded. 'Part of it. There is an alternative siting, but to lay tracks across a section of the Halewood land would cut the distance by several miles. No mean consideration in terms of labour, steel, blasting, and tunnelling.'

'It's sacrilege!' she expostulated, horrified.

'The house won't be touched. Admittedly its views will be changed to the north and west, because the woods must be thinned out and many of the trees felled. Some of the old cottages and a farmstead will have to go, too. Whoever lives in the house will be able to see the railway from most of the windows, but there's no danger of it being turned into a signal box.'

'That's not funny!' She slammed a hand down on the desk.

'It wasn't meant to be,' he retorted, suddenly as heated as she. 'You think too much about that damned house. If I had my way I'd have it razed to the ground!'

'Such an act of vandalism could take place if it isn't kept in the Hart family!' she cried, her colour high, her eyes flashing. 'Aaron must be told of this new turn of events. Perhaps if he's forewarned – '

'What difference could it make now? Remember the auction is only four days away. If he's already scraped the barrel where could he raise any more at this late hour? The property is expected to reach a record figure, I've heard. A really great sum involving thousands and thousands of pounds.'

'So much!' she exclaimed distractedly.

'Do you want me to tell him?' Matthew's expression showed he would not be adverse to the mission.

'No!' She calmed herself with effort. 'I'll do it. It won't be easy, but it's better that it should come from me.'

'Why?' He poked his face towards her with aggressive curiosity. 'What makes you take on such an unpleasant duty when you've so much else to think about?'

Her shoulders slumped and she bowed her head. 'Because I'm the one responsible for having brought him here in the first place. It was I who raised his hopes falsely and let him imagine that one day he would be Master of Halewood.'

Matthew looked slightly shamefaced. He hadn't meant to lose his temper with her today of all days when her father lay practically at death's door in a room above. But always when he wanted to be closest to her she seemed to hold back, keeping him at a distance, even when his arms were about her. As well as her body he wanted to possess her every thought, her every feeling, sparing nothing for anyone else, and sooner or later he would do it. Surely that time would come when Halewood had passed into hands other than those of Aaron Hart and when its lands were dissected, engine smoke drifting across to hasten the decay of its stonework with soot and cinders to ruin its gardens. In his own way he could destroy Halewood and he could do it guiltlessly in the name of progress.

'I'll be going now,' he said, picking up his hat.

'Yes,' she answered vaguely. 'We must talk again. Another time.'

She walked with him to the front door. He would have kissed her, but her face was averted from him. He stepped into the porch and clapped his tall hat on his head.

'I hope you father will be better soon. I'll look in again tomorrow evening. When he can have visitors I'd like to see him.'

144

'Of course. You shall be the first.' She was already closing the door.

She went into the drawing-room. The game of chess was no longer in progress. Melissa had seated herself at the harp in the adjoining music room and was plucking the strings in a gentle, romantic little tune. She looked exceedingly pretty in her graceful pose, only the heaviness about her eyes an indication that all was not as well with her as she wanted it to appear, but the lamplight was flattering and made a golden aura of her hair. Aaron, listening from the large wing-chair by the fire, chin in hand, did not notice Delia approach, but he turned his head quickly when she sat down on the sociable nearby and he gave her a warm glance and a smile. When the last sweet notes of the music faded away they both applauded Melissa.

'Thank you,' he said. 'I enjoyed that immensely.'

'I only hope I'm not disturbing Uncle Charles,' Melissa said a trifle shortly, showing Delia that she resented her intrusion, 'but I couldn't concentrate on chess this evening.'

'No, I'm sure you're not,' Delia replied. 'He wouldn't be able to hear the music upstairs. I'm afraid I'm the one to disturb you.' She made a little placating gesture with her hands. 'I'm sorry, but I have to ask you to let me speak to Aaron alone. It is an important matter.'

Melissa sighed somewhat petulantly, but she rose from her seat at the harp. 'I had intended to retire early anyway. Good night.'

When she had left them on their own Aaron's mouth twisted in amusement, his eyes twinkling. 'Melissa has been uncommonly civil to me this evening. I can't begin to fathom the reason. Until now she's taken a vixenish delight in goading me about my American accent, my way of expressing myself, and anything else American that she can find fault with.'

Incredulously Delia considered what he had said,

although she was careful not to show it. Surely Melissa wasn't setting her sights on Aaron! Was she so determined not to return to her home and parents that she was prepared to try to ensnare the very next man who seemed suitable as a husband? Were Melissa's feelings even more shallow than she herself had suspected? Delia drew in her breath and released it again. This was not the time to think about Melissa. She had a much more serious matter to deal with.

'I have bad news,' she began. Hastily she shook her head when she saw he believed she was referring to the condition of the patient upstairs. 'It's to do with Halewood.'

'Yes?' His eyes narrowed at her.

'Matthew just told me. The railway company have expressed an interest in the land. It will make the price soar at the auction.'

The bones of his face showed white, but not a muscle twitched. He spoke quietly and levelly. 'Then I must find the extra money somehow.'

'But where?' she exclaimed. 'I have a little money of my own and you're welcome to it, but it will be no more than a drop in the ocean.'

'Your offer touches me, my darling, but I'll not accept it. I must consult a banker in the morning and also visit Mr Radleigh. Time is against me. Had I known that such a catastrophe was likely to occur I could have pressed for a greater loan before leaving Boston, but Radleigh assured me that he had quoted a figure that was above anything the property was likely to fetch.'

She reached out and rested her hand on his sleeve. 'When the sale was just of an ancient house and a good spread of land you had only to compete with those seeking the prestige of such a dwelling-place, the men who've made money out of Lancashire's coal and railways and cotton mills – but now the auction will attract a wider field. Matthew says the price will soar by thousands. The speculators are moving in.'

'Dear God!' he exclaimed hoarsely, leaning forward to let his elbows drop to his knees, his head falling into his hands. 'Thousands! Now! When it was almost mine!'

She moved swiftly across to him and his arms received her, drawing her on to his knees, and they sat enfolded in each other's embrace, she comforting him as earlier that day he had comforted her. They had no need for words. The understanding between them was absolute. They spoke only in lovers' touches of the brushed cheek, the caressing hand, the soft balm of lips in travelling kisses over the face, the gentle pressure of arms, and the sensuous snugness of bodies moulded together.

'You may find someone willing to give you a loan to bridge the gap,' she said hopefully, stroking a strand of hair back from his forehead. 'If only Papa were well I'm sure he'd speak on your behalf to someone – '

'Oh, I haven't lost Halewood yet,' he answered with determination. 'If it's humanly possible I'll raise the money somewhere, but it will make a pauper of me for years to come.' He looked into her face, compressing his lips in a wry smile. 'How will you like living on bread and cheese at Halewood and wearing patched gowns?'

She knew he was exaggerating the outcome of his poverty, but she answered him seriously. 'If fate allows me to become your wife I ask for nothing more in this life.'

His hand slid up the back of her neck under her hair to cup her head, bringing her forward to meet his kiss and she gave up her mouth to his in its loving passion.

A long, sweet sigh escaped her when she slid from his knees. She turned to face her flushed reflection in the gilt-framed looking-glass that hung on the wall above a rosewood cabinet, and put up her hands to tidy her hair. He came and looped his arms about her waist, standing behind her as he put his face against hers, meeting her reflected eyes in the looking-glass.

'Did you speak to Matthew about us while he was here?' he asked.

'I tried, but then he told me about Halewood and that put an end to it.'

'He must learn the truth of the matter. I've never associated with any man yet under false colours and I'm sure that Matthew is the same. I'll have it out with him myself without further delay.'

'No!' She swung round within the circle of his arms and took his face between her hands. 'Please be patient! I thought this evening the right moment had come for me to break it to him, but he swept it aside. I believe that in his heart he knows that I've drifted from him – he admitted it in so many words – but as yet he can't bring himself to accept it. Somehow I must bring him face to face with the realization that we could no longer be happy together. Tomorrow I must write to all who were coming to the wedding to tell them that, due to my father's illness, it will not take place. That's as far as I can go until Matthew has taken back the ring.'

'Make it soon,' he implored, tightening his arms about her and she saw by the tautness of his face that he was desperately afraid of losing her and would know no peace of mind until she was his. Some of his fear touched her, and it was to hide the fact that she was also afraid that fate might yet tear them apart that she now kissed him until they were lost again in their own private wonder of each other.

She wrote the letters on her writing-box at her father's bedside, letting Nurse Baker free of her duties for a while. He knew she was there, for he had whispered her name once, but he slept most of the time, drugged by laudanum. She had no heart for the task in hand, not because she was not overwhelmingly thankful to be released from a set marriage date, but because it was hard to concentrate on anything but the suffering of her father, and time and time again she held the pen idly in her hand, watching him anxiously, until she forced herself to continue.

Aaron had gone to consult the two sources from which he hoped to gain guidance on the speedy raising of funds, but she could see no hope for him. She thought of him as part of Halewood, part of Lancashire, but in the sight of others he was an alien with an unfamiliar accent, who had nothing to offer for collateral security on this side of the Atlantic Ocean and no time to obtain proof of backing from the other side of it. The auction was the day after tomorrow. Already the hours were running out against him.

Although they had not talked about it she knew he would not stay in England unless he was the owner of Halewood. He had nothing else to hold him here and he would never be able to endure living under an English sky while another occupied the house that should have been his. She realized she would have to go with him to Boston and start a new life completely – as the wife of an American citizen. Adapting to new ways and new customs would be easy compared with another aim to which she would be dedicated, for she must be all in all to him, driving away the memory of Halewood and what might have been, filling his life with love and companionship until at last his thoughts no longer slid away from her back to a great house on a hill around which the wind never ceased to moan.

But as yet such plans were only dreams. She took up her pen again and the scratch of the nib and the breathing of the patient became the only sounds in the quiet room.

The last letter was written. She closed her writing-box as Nurse Baker returned, bringing a small glass of egg-wine and a spoon to feed the patient. 'There's someone asking to see you downstairs, Miss Gilmore,' she said. 'I told the housemaid that I'd pass on the message.'

Delia left the sickroom. She expected to find one of her father's friends or another of his loyal patients waiting to enquire after him. But it was an office boy from Mr Radleigh's chambers who stood in the hall, hat in hand.

'Morning, Miss Gilmore. I've to tell you that Mr 'Art 'as gone to Preston on Mr Radleigh's advice. 'E said as you'd know why. 'E don't expect to be back until late tonight or p'raps tomorrow. It all depends.'

'Thank you,' she said, hoping desperately that Aaron had not gone on a wild-goose chase that would end in more disappointment and fresh hopes dashed. After the boy had gone, she fetched her bonnet and coat and went herself to post the letters, feeling a need for a little exercise.

The snow had turned grey in the streets, but there was the promise of more in the sharp air, which stung the colour into her cheeks, invigorating her after the long hours in the sickroom. She did not turn for home again after reaching the letter-box, but continued on to the market-place. There she searched among the stalls to find some little gifts for Roland, which would help to keep him amused on the long journey to Italy with his mother. She would take them to him tomorrow when she went to say good-bye to Berenice, who was planning to depart some time in the early afternoon. Berenice would be expecting her, for she had sent a note with a servant the previous day, telling of her father's illness, and by return had come calves-foot jelly, caudle, a beef-tea custard, and several other invalid delicacies.

Delia had soon collected a number of toys. There were puzzles and card-games, books of adventure stories, a monkey-on-a-stick, a box of tin soldiers, another of coloured chalks, and a number of drawing-books. She bought a cheap straw bag to carry everything home. Melissa met her in the hall, her expression sullen.

'Why didn't you tell me you were going out? I'd have gone with you.'

'I'm sorry,' Delia said sincerely, putting the bag of toys down on a chair and untying her bonnet strings. 'I should have asked you.'

'When will Aaron be coming back from seeing the lawyer?' Melissa picked the monkey-on-a-stick out of the bag and almost absently set it turning somersaults. 'He's been gone ages. I was thinking of walking to meet him.'

'He's left there – and journeyed out of Penghyll. Mr Radleigh's office boy brought a message.' She told Melissa what it had been. Melissa had heard at breakfast from Aaron about the railway company's causing such a turn of events, there being no secret about it, and he had discussed it with both her and Delia. She had commiserated with him on such ill fortune, showing an exceptional concern and looking quite dewy-eyed over it. Again suspicion had leapt unbidden into Delia's mind, but she had thrust it from her as being the return of an uncharitable thought that must not be allowed to rear up again.

'Shall you wait up for him?' Melissa asked, her lashes shadowing a sudden alertness in her eyes as if the monkey-on-a-stick had begun to interest her.

'No, but my bedroom is above the vestibule and I sleep so lightly that I'll hear him if he returns during the night.'

'Won't his knocking wake Uncle Charles?'

'I've thought of that. I'll see that the door is left unlocked.'

'That's a good idea.' Melissa put down the toy, a sly look on her face that she kept from Delia. It had been something of a shock at breakfast that morning to hear that Aaron had apparently lost all chance of acquiring Halewood, but after she had mulled it over she realized it was probably all for the better. He'd go back to the New World.

She did not fancy living in Boston, but beggars could not be choosers and she would have to make the best of it. At least she could expect to enjoy the comforts and luxuries of life, and in the book of prints of his city, which he had given Delia, there was evidence of its prosperity and fine proportions. As for Aaron himself, she could never love him,

151

although that was unimportant, for she had put love from her for ever, but his physical appearance was pleasing to her recently awakened sensuality and her mind dwelt on the breadth of his powerful shoulders, the horseman-trimness of his waist, and the tautness of thigh and length of leg revealed by the slender, well-cut trousers that he wore. When he behaved towards her as a husband should there would be compensations for all she had left behind, for Richard had taught her much in the brief, idyllic times they had spent in each other's arms and she had been an apt and willing pupil, delighting in sensations that had made her wonder at his power to waken such secrets from her body which previously she had not known existed.

Yes, she was resolved to wrest from life what she could to make up for all that had been taken from her. The only time she had cared for anyone more than herself had been disastrous. It would not happen again.

Later when Delia was in the sickroom Melissa went upstairs. On the landing she looked about to make sure no servant was nearby, then quickly slipped into Delia's bedroom. It did not take her long to discover the dispensary key, which was in a box on the dressing-table. Within five minutes she had been down to the dispensary, taken the blue glass bottle from the cabinet, poured some of the liquid out into one of the clean physic phials ranged on the shelf, corked it, replaced the bottle, relocked the dispensary, and returned the key to the box upstairs. Nobody had observed her. It was done.

She was shaking in every limb when she reached the safety of her own room with the phial, which she hid safely out of sight in a bonnet box. Almost in a state of exhaustion she lay down on the bed to recover from the nerve-racking suspense of her actions. Staring up at the ceiling, she recalled hearing it said that there was a small bridge between love and hate, and now she knew that to be true. She hated Richard for all that he had brought upon her and for his desertion. But she welcomed that feeling of icy hatred. It was the fount of the strength she needed in this battle for her very existence. Never again would she give way to weakness and tears as she had done on her first night at Sycamore House when she had poured out the whole story to Delia. Those days were over.

It was shortly after two o'clock in the morning when Aaron's hackney cab drew up outside the gates of Sycamore House. Wearily he stepped out and dived into his pocket to find money and pay the driver. Opening the gate, he went through at a slow and dejected pace, but he did not forget the sick man who lay behind the curtains of the only lighted window in the house and kept to the grass verge in order to avoid the scrunch of gravel.

He guessed the door would be left undone for him, but even as he reached the porch there was a click of the latch. To his astonishment the candle held by the pale figure showed the face of Melissa framed by the tumble of her golden hair. She put a finger to her lips as she admitted him.

'Shh! Come into the drawing-room.'

Silently he removed his caped coat, hat, and gloves, and followed her. When she had closed the double doors after him he spoke to her with some impatience and more than a little anxiety.

'What's the matter? Is Dr Gilmore – worse?'

'No. There's no change. I couldn't sleep, and I happened to be at the window when your cab stopped outside. I thought you might like something to eat and a hot drink.'

Such thoughtfulness from Melissa was unexpected, but he appreciated it, not knowing that she had removed to the kitchen the covered supper-tray that Delia had left ready for him. 'That's most obliging of you. It is many hours since I last ate.'

She put down the candle and went to poke up the fire, which had been kept stacked up for his homecoming. The coal fell into dancing flames, flooding the room with red-gold light, and thankfully he went across to warm his hands, for he was chilled through. It had been a long, cold journey and his mood of near-despair had done nothing to insulate as optimism and hope would have done. He saw that Melissa was wearing only a ruffled peignoir and a nightgown, and as she leaned towards the fire he looked down on the soft curve of breast and shadow. A faint bouquet came to him from her body and there was a fragrance about her hair. When a coal crashed out of the fire with a shower of sparks she drew back, seared by the heat, and the glow shone through the delicate garments that she wore. One spark alighted on the gossamer folds spread out about her on the carpet and he stepped on it swiftly with the toe of his shoe. She looked up at him, lips slightly parted, the tip of her tongue showing pink and moist in the corner of her mouth, and she put her hand on his foot.

'That could have been dangerous,' she said breathlessly.

'I think not,' he remarked drily, and he reached for the tongs. 'Move out of the way, and I'll put that piece of coal back on the fire.'

She rose in a billowing cloud of soft ruffles and moved back to stand by the sofa. 'You haven't told me yet how things went today. Did you get the loan?'

He replaced the coal and let the tongs fall with a little clatter back on the fender. 'No,' he answered, speaking more to himself than to her. 'I did not.'

She watched him throw himself back in the wing-chair, elbows over the padded arms, and his legs stretched out before him, his gaze never leaving the leaping flames.

'I'll fetch you some supper,' she said on a note of commiseration. 'In the meantime a glass of wine will help to refresh you.'

'Er – what was that? Wine? oh, yes.' He saw her take up one of the decanters on the wine-table and he waved a hand to show he would do it, bestirring himself from the chair.

'Leave that to me.'

She went soundlessly from the drawing-room. He removed the stopper from the decanter and poured the claret. Taking a deep gulp, he stood lost in his gloomy thoughts, paying little attention to what he was drinking, while his mind went over the disappointments of the day. He had to face the fact that he wasn't going to raise that extra money unless – by some miracle – something happened during this last day before the auction. He glanced at the clock. It was exactly 2.30. How odd. That was the time set for the commencement of the auction thirty-six hours hence. With a faint groan of despair he turned back to the decanter and refilled the glass once more. For the first time he noticed that it had left a slightly acrid taste on his tongue, which was strange, for Dr Gilmore kept a good cellar. He was about to lift the decanter to see if he had disturbed some sediment when the door opened and Melissa returned with a tray on which was set a cold collation.

'That was quick,' he said, going across with the intention of taking the load from her, and to his surprise he staggered slightly. Too much wine on an empty stomach. He had gone unvittled far too long. The sooner he ate the better.

She put down the tray and pulled a small table across to the winged chair. 'Sit here,' she said, patting the cushioned back. 'I'll set your supper beside you.'

He sat down rather heavily. She placed the tray on the table and picked up the folded linen napkin to spread it crackling across his knees. 'Thank you,' he said. 'Now don't let me keep you from your repose any longer – '

She sat down opposite him, leaning back in a green velvet chair. 'I don't feel tired and it's cosy in the firelight.'

He gave her a long look, but said nothing. He would have preferred to be on his own, having no need of company. Had she been Delia it would have been a different matter.

'Shall you go to the auction tomorrow?' she enquired.

155

'Naturally. I intend to go down fighting.'

'And after that? When you've seen Halewood sold beyond recall?'

He paused in his eating, his brows snapping together in a frown. 'I'm enjoying the food, but not the particular topic of conversation chosen. I'd prefer not to pursue it.'

'But you must have thought about what you will do.'

He controlled his impatience with a suppressed sigh, giving in to her tactless persistence. 'Eventually I shall return to the States. It depends on how long it takes Dr Gilmore to recover.'

'I'm not surprised to hear you won't want to stay in England, but why should your plans depend on Uncle Charles?'

He put down his fork, finding he was not as hungry as he had imagined himself to be, and he sank back in the chair, putting a hand to his brow. An amazing sense of peace and tranquillity had come upon him. It was the strangest kind of drunkenness he had ever experienced, for although he was not in the habit of being in his cups he could recall vividly the wilder days of his youth.

'It must be fairly obvious.' He noted with satisfaction that at least his words were not slurred. 'I don't intend to leave without Delia. She's more to me than a thousand Halewoods.'

A silence fell in the room, which seemed to him for no reason he could define to be particularly tense and almost palpable. Melissa rose and picked up the decanter to top up his glass again, but he shook his head and placed his palm over it. She did not return to her chair after replacing the decanter, but came instead to sink down on to her knees by his chair, and she rested hands and elbows along the arm, letting the side of her cheek lodge there as she looked up at him.

'She will marry Matthew. You'll never break the bond

between them.'

'I happen to think differently.'

'My poor Aaron, don't you see? She's enjoying having two strings to her bow. It's never happened to Delia before. Matthew had always made sure of that. She'll never go to the New World with you. She lacks any sense of adventure. I'm not like that. I'd go anywhere – do anything.'

Normally his irritation with Melissa and her ways, never far from the surface, would have erupted into anger that she should speak thus of Delia, but he seemed incapable of rousing himself from the curious mental langour that had possessed him. He knew only that he wanted to be rid of Melissa. With an effort he put both hands on the arm-ends of the chair and thrust himself to his feet where he stood reeling.

'You must have drunk an awful lot of wine.' Melissa's voice seemed to come from a distance, but her body wasn't far from him. She had entwined him in her arms, pressing herself to him. In his soporific state he had the sensation of being entrapped in scented cobwebs and he thrust up an arm to free himself, but she clutched him all the tighter. 'I'll help you to bed. You'll never get there on your own. You'd better take your shoes off first or you'll wake the household.'

Such a simple task was beyond him. She knelt and he lifted one foot and then the other for her to slip them off.

Her arms were round him again. 'Lean on me and don't make a sound. Remember Dr Gilmore. We mustn't disturb him.'

The staircase loomed high as a mountain, making him wonder if he'd ever reach the top, and the candle she held glinted on distorted picture frames and misshapen doors. With one arm about her shoulders and a hand on the banister rail he made the ascent slowly and reached the landing without mishap. In his room he stood while she helped him off with his coat. Like a pale golden moth she beat at him

157

with swift fingers, unbuttoning his waistcoat, which fell from him with a swish of silk lining, and untying his cravat. He knew himself to be asleep on his feet. His body was locked in inertia while one tiny corner of his mind struggled in vain to regain mastery. A faint coolness of air on his chest and back made him realize she had ripped his shirt from him. He gave his head a shake to clear it, but felt consciousness slipping from him. Then he reeled about and fell face downwards on the bed where he became lost in sleep.

His slumber was deep and black and soft as a velvet sea and he was being wrenched from it by some power that he wanted to resist. He threshed about, aware that he was naked, sweat streaming from every limb, his own gasping breath roaring in his ears. Somewhere in that abyss a sobbing, persistent and subdued, came and went, and now and again a whispered entreaty seared through his brain, but the words seemed to lack meaning and he could not comprehend them. Gradually his body seemed to become buoyant in those dark, warm waves, and he knew whatever danger he'd been in had passed. Quiet sleep drove out the nightmare and enfolded his limbs in rest.

He awoke to a cold, grey day and a sensation of nausea. Reaching out carefully he felt for his watch on the bedside cabinet, but it was not there. Propping himself on both elbows with the thought that it must be on the dressing-table he saw the state of his room and all the events of the previous night came flooding back to him. His clothes lay where they had fallen. The state of the bedclothes bore witness to his nightmare struggles, for they were twisted and tumbled and half on the floor. Of his shoes there was no sign and he supposed them to be still downstairs in the drawing-room. What a crazy fool he'd been to drink all that wine! He must have had more glasses than he'd realized while waiting for Melissa to bring his the supper. Perhaps it wasn't surprising, for his mind had been on the disappointments of the day,

158

the shaking heads of bankers, the blunt refusal in the voices of others, and he had drunk the wine automatically, giving it no consideration.

He was thankful that no servant had come knocking for admittance and walked into the untidy room. On any other morning shaving-water and copper-cans of streaming bath water would have been brought at 8.30, but on this occasion Delia, having discovered his return, would have given orders that he was not to be disturbed.

He put his feet to the floor. Fortunately the nausea had subsided and he felt better than he had any right to feel after imbibing with such reckless thoughtlessness. He put on his dressing-robe and looked about for his watch. It was on a chair. He picked it up, snapped it open, and saw it was almost noon. Only a little over twenty-four hours left before Halewood came under the auctioneer's hammer. At least Delia had promised to be there with him. She was such a talisman for good that he found it difficult to accept that her love-magic would not be able to counteract the forces of greedy commerce that would be ranged against him. But hard facts had to be faced. When he staked all he possessed in the world on a last throw for Halewood and if it soared out of his grasp in the tinkling of thousands more golden guineas he hoped he would accept defeat with dignity and without bitterness.

He began to pick up and fold away his scattered clothing. His complete nakedness on waking gave him some thought, and he realized he must have torn off the rest of his garments when he had been in the throes of that awful sweating that had been like the approach of death. He shuddered at the thought of it, doubting that he would ever be able to stomach the taste of claret again.

He crossed to the bed to pull it into some semblance of order. Out of the confusion of sheets as he jerked them there floated up into the air and down to the carpet at his feet a strip of torn pink ruffle. Slowly he bent and picked it up, frowning as he smoothed it in his fingers. How had it come to be in his bed? And when had it been torn? It must have occurred when he'd thrust Melissa from him. But surely that had been downstairs?

Still frowning, he put it in his pocket and went to jerk the bell-rope for his bath-water. At the same time his attention was caught by the sounds of hooves and wheels in the drive below. He went to the window in time to see Delia driving herself in her blue-painted gig out of the gates into the avenue. He guessed where she was bound. To Halewood. He watched her out of sight.

Chapter Nine

Delia looped up the reins, stuck her whip in its holder, and picking up her straw bag of toys for Roland from the seat, she alighted from the wagonette. She had chosen this day to drive through the archway into the inner courtyard and draw up by the grand entrance, which she had studiously avoided since that fateful day when Halewood had reached out as though to hold her to its mist-swathed, ice-cold breast, but this was probably her last visit and curiosity compelled her to discover whether the house knew it too. She had planned on the way to enter by the heart of it and on the steps of the massive entrance she paused deliberately on each wide breadth of stone almost with an air of challenge.

Her horse whinnied. She glanced back over her shoulder towards it and saw that it tossed its head restlessly. Slowly she scanned the great courtyard under the bleak afternoon sky. In Penghyll the snow had turned to grey slush and was fast disappearing, but here it still showed a pristine whiteness in crevices and corners. Through the archway she could see the branches of the birch tress bordering the drive, weaving black, skeletal patterns in the wind, but within the courtyard it was, as always, sheltered and still.

She shivered, more from an inward chill than from the coldness of the day. The house was watching her. Holding its breath. Every window an eye. And she in turn loving and fearing and pitying it. With a swirl of bonnet ribbons she went hastily through the porch and pulled the bell. She was admitted and went through into the great entrance hall, where trunks and boxes were stacked high in readiness for shipment to Italy and there was an air of bustle and departure with servants scurrying and footsteps echoing. Every piece of furniture, as yet still in place, had a label tied to it ready for packing and delivery to the London auction rooms.

It was a poignant moment for Delia. She was to say good-bye to both Berenice and the house. Nobody she knew would be the purchaser of Halewood, but should it be someone with whom she was on nodding acquaintance she would never want to cross the house's threshold with all links severed. How would Halewood fare in stranger hands? It would not tolerate violation of its boundaries and new vengeance would be wreaked on whoever was foolhardy enough to take up residence under its roof. Looking about her at the wonderful proportions of the hall and the rooms beyond, which she could see through open doors, she was terribly afraid that future inhabitants, driven out by the house's hostility, would leave it to collapse in ruins, a blind and empty shell against the sky, deserted and avoided by all.

'Where's Lady Hart?' she asked a passing footman.

'In the yellow drawing-room, I believe, miss.'

Berenice was standing at the window when Delia entered and she turned with hands outstretched. 'How is your dear father?' she exclaimed at once, taking Delia's hands in hers in a gesture of concern and commiseration.

'He is a little better. Dr Pomfret believes that the attack, alarming and terrible though it was, hasn't done the damage that he had at first feared. He says he considers it a grave warning that the time has come for my father to retire and live a quiet life.'

'That won't suit Dr Gilmore!'

'I agree, but I hope to console him with the thought that he'll at last have time to finish writing his book on the history of this district, which he has been researching for many years.'

'You're quite sure that he's getting the best of medical attention? Should you have a second opinion as to the treatment he should be receiving?'

Delia reassured her. 'I've heard my father praise Dr Pomfret's medical skill many times. I have no doubts on that score at all.'

'I'm thankful to hear it. I've had another hamper prepared with delicacies for him. Can you take it home with you?'

'Yes, indeed. That's most kind.' They sat down in neighbouring chairs. 'I told him you had sent him the caudle among other things when I fed him a few spoonfuls of it.'

'The poor gentleman!' Berenice raised clasped hands from her lap and let them fall again. She was in a travelling costume of brown grenadine trimmed with bands of velvet, ready for her early evening departure. There was a pallor in her face and her cheeks seemed to have taken on a deeper hollowness. It was as though she had sunk into a state of ailing that was to know no lifting up or brief returns to better spells. At the present time she looked as if she lacked stamina to survive the long journey to Italy, but she would be travelling with a small retinue of servants, including her lady's maid, who would take good care of her. Delia hoped the sea would be kind on the voyage from Liverpool and then at least Berenice could rest after all the upheaval of leaving Halewood.

'It's many weeks now since I first composed that letter to Aaron telling him about the forthcoming sale of Halewood,' Delia said, deciding to tell her of the railway company's interest without further delay, 'but his journey to England to purchase it has all been in vain on that score.'

Her listener showed no surprise, but lifted a languid hand. 'I know. Mr Radleigh came to see me about it. How has Mr Hart reacted to the blow?'

'What do you expect?' Delia exclaimed. 'He is quite shattered! He spent yesterday dashing from place to place trying to raise a last-minute loan. I've not seen him yet today, because he arrived home in the early hours of the morning and was sleeping when I left, but Melissa heard him come in and had a few words with him. He had no success.'

'How disappointing for him.' Placidly. Almost uninterestedly.

Delia bit her lip. She could not expect Berenice to be moved by Aaron's plight as she was. After all, Berenice, although she probably did not need it, was to become many thousands of pounds richer by this new development. What was more, she did not care what happened to Halewood or who lived in it, but nevertheless Delia found it hard not to make some retort. Berenice must have seen this, for she said, 'I have much on my own mind at this time. You must pardon me if I seem detached, but I've already talked at great lengths with my lawyer about the sale of Halewood and as far as I'm concerned there's an end to it. You think me heartless? Forgive me. Don't let it taint this time of farewell between us when we've been such good friends. I know how much I'll miss your company and all the news that you entertained me with from the town, the market, and your own circle of acquaintances.'

Reminded of the market Delia opened the straw bag which was full of differently shaped little packets, each toy wrapped individually in brightly coloured paper. 'I've some surprise parcels for Roland. There's one for every day of the journey and I've marked them with the dates for opening. There's a special one for when you both arrive at the villa in Florence. I hope it will amuse him and take away any homesickness.'

'What is it? May I ask?'

'It's a railway locomotive with a little spirit stove in the boiler that puffs smoke, and two carriages – an open one for passengers and another for goods.'

'What a splendid gift!' Berenice peeped into the bag. 'Such a collection! How thoughtful of you.'

'Has Roland become reconciled to leaving Halewood?'

Berenice let the bag's handle slip from her fingers, her expression wearied. 'There have been scenes and tantrums for days. One morning he locked himself in the stable loft and refused to come out. Now that the day of leaving has arrived at last he has lapsed into a kind of quiet despair, packing together his own small treasures. I've allowed him to take a sixteenth-century ivory chess set that he's always liked, and that seems to have consoled him enormously.'

'I'll find him before I leave and bid him farewell. Perhaps I can encourage him to write to me. I'll want to keep in touch.'

'Berenice's mouth showed a faint smile. 'You know my dislike of putting pen to paper, but even if Roland cannot be persuaded to correspond you shall have word from me sometimes.'

'I look forward to that. I hope to send good tidings of Papa's complete recovery. After that there may be other news to confide, but it's too early to talk of it.'

Berenice tilted her head more in emphasis than enquiry. 'You want to break off your betrothal to Matthew,' she said.

Delia's eyes widened. 'How did you know that?'

'I could tell you had fallen in love the first time you came to see me after Mr Hart's arrival. It wasn't anything you said. It was more what you didn't say. I could tell it troubled you to talk about him, and there was a new awareness about you. It showed in your eyes, the tilt of your head, in your whole attitude.'

'That was very observant of you,' Delia admitted tremulously.

'Is that surprising? I spend so many hours on my own that I've become observant of all things. Until I came to Halewood I was unaware that truly to observe life one must

165

draw back from it. That knowledge at least I take with me from this hostile house. Not much to learn from the years I've spent here, but it is a kernel of comfort for all the time that is left to me.'

'I wish you good fortune in Italy with all my heart,' Delia said, rising. 'I mustn't stay any longer. As soon as I've seen Roland I must get back home. I don't like to leave Papa for any length of time.'

Berenice rose from her chair. 'I thank you for coming. There's one last thing I want you to do for me.'

'Gladly. What is it?'

Berenice went across to the escritoire and opened it. She took from an inner drawer one of the smaller notices of the sale by auction of Halewood, which had been printed for distribution.

'You will remember that I talked about getting these leaflets printed to help advertise the sale still wider and Mr Radleigh dealt with the matter for me. He also had bigger posters with bolder lettering pasted up over those already in position.'

'Yes. I think you saw I wasn't keen that it should be done. To me the more widely it was advertised, the more chance there was of Aaron having to go to a higher figure to get it, and I knew how much he wanted to restore the house throughout and the vast expense that would involve him in. But it wasn't for me to persuade you against your action. You had every right to try to get the highest price for Halewood and Aaron would have been the first to agree with me. Never did I dream then that the railway company would come upon the scene.'

Berenice looked down at the leaflet which she held at opposite corners between the thumb and forefinger of each hand. 'I had my reasons for wanting Mr Radleigh to handle the reprinting for me. I had need of his advice on it, because there was something I wanted altered, although I said

166

nothing to you about it.'

Delia was puzzled. She could not remember noticing any errors, but there must have been a mistake in the original, potted description of the house somewhere.

Berenice handed the leaflet to her. 'Read it. Read it well. Remember what the first posters said, and keep what you notice until the time is right – and you will know when that will be without my telling you. Only then may you inform Mr Hart.'

In complete bewilderment Delia took the leaflet. She scanned it quickly. At first she noticed nothing different. But when she read it again, dissecting every line, she came across the time of the auction. On the earlier notices it had read *2.30 p.m.* Now it read *2.30 o'clock*. Almost in disbelief at what it meant she raised her head and looked at Berenice.

'It's the only way it could be done,' Berenice said, answering Delia's unspoken question. 'As you know, Sir Harry had written in his will that the estate must be sold by public auction, no matter if it was in my lifetime or after.'

'You're almost giving Halewood to Aaron,' Delia exclaimed emotionally. 'At two-thirty in the morning there'll be nobody else there!'

'That's why you must not let anyone else know about it. Mr Radleigh thought it best to keep even Mr Hart in the dark until the last moment lest his lack of concern give rise to any questions or queries. Even the Assembly Rooms have been hired from today in order that only those directly involved in the coup shall be present in the building.'

'I can't thank you enough! It's the most wonderful news I've ever heard! Although he's faced the loss of Halewood with fortitude I know him well enough to comprehend that without it life could never be the same for him again.'

'Not even with your love to fill the void?'

Delia shook her head dismissively. 'No matter how much I demonstrated my love for him I could never have made him forget Halewood.'

'Then let us be thankful that matters have been arranged as they are.'

'You should have been the one to tell him,' Delia declared generously, 'instead of leaving that happy task to me. I could have brought him with me. Didn't you think of that?'

A look of utter desolation swept over Berenice's face. 'I thought of it. But I can't allow myself to see him again.'

Delia caught her breath sharply, understanding. Berenice was in love with Aaron. She must have known she loved him during their first meeting. From that moment she had decided to give him Halewood. It was an unselfish token of her love, which could never be fulfilled in any other way.

'Does he mean that much to you?' Delia enquired huskily.

Berenice answered brokenly, her eyes heavy and glistening with tears. 'I glimpsed him first from the windows of my apartments. I looked down and watched him step out of his carriage. As he stood there studying the house, I saw his face and knew that the only man I'd longed for all my life was about to cross my path too late. Insurmountable barriers, kinship through marriage being one of them, stood between us. Yet I contrived a way to see him again when he was in the portrait gallery, deliberately passing where I could look in on him. Had that been all, I might have spared myself some of the pangs I've endured since, but fate brought him into the very room where I was sitting and it was my point of no return.'

'Is that why you came to the Penghyll Ball?'

'I wanted to dance with him once. To feel his arms about me once.' Berenice made an almost girlish movement with her hands, at once both timorous and vulnerable. 'Such was my passion for him that I put from my mind all caution from your father not to overtax my strength in any exercise. If that waltz shortened my life by ten years I care not.'

'Have you never loved before?' It struck Delia how quiet

168

and sad were their voices in that exquisite, sun-coloured room with the grey day pressing against the windows.

Berenice gave her a glance that was worn out with despair. 'I've known many men. Some have been gentler with me than others, and some have loved me, but I've never been able to love any one of them. My heart was born that day when Aaron came to Halewood.'

'He'll always remember you as the donor of this house,' Delia said, deeply moved. 'In that way you'll have a special place in his life.'

'But it is you who must ensure that no disaster comes to him through my gift.' Her appeal was throbbing and urgent, and she took hold of Delia by the shoulders, giving her a little shake to emphasize the importance of her entreaty. 'Use your love to protect him. I thought to slip free of Halewood, but it has played its old tricks on me. I'm doomed to unhappiness like the rest of the Harts who've lived on Howling Hill. Until the end of my days I shall yearn for a man who never loved me.'

'I'll do everything I can,' Delia promised fervently.

'Now we must say good-bye.' Berenice kissed her affectionately on the cheek. 'I've kept you from your father far too long.' She reached out and took up a sealed letter from where it lay on top of the escritoire. 'I've written a note of appreciation for all the care he has bestowed on me during my time as his patient. Please read it to him when you are able. It carries all my kindest regards.'

'I'll do that. May the city of Florence bring you solace with its beauty and Roland prove a comfort to you.'

Berenice inclined her head with dignity, her smile wan. 'I trust so. Farewell.'

Delia dipped a curtsey. In respect. In gratitude. In tribute. Quickly she left the room. Choked with pity for Aaron's benefactress she folded the sale leaflet and letter away in her reticule and hurried in search of Roland. To have loved and lost Aaron was a particular hell she could fully comprehend and identify with. Pray God it never happened to her!

As always after even the shortest absence, she went first to the sickroom on her return. Melissa was at the bedside reading a copy of *Lady's Magazine*, which she lowered to speak in a whisper.

'Uncle Charles is asleep. Have you been at Halewood all this time?'

Delia nodded, crossing to look down into her father's face. His colour was much better and he breathed easily. There was no doubt he had improved since yesterday when he had first asked her how long he had been ill and expressed concern that her wedding had been postponed. She knew he was not out of the wood yet, but the light through the trees shone bright and clear, lifting a new hope in her. Was it possible that the dark clouds that had gathered over her recently were to be dispelled one by one, advanced by her father's recovery?

'Aaron is out,' Melissa remarked, still whispering. 'He doesn't know when he'll be back.'

The information thudded home. Delia spoke on a note of startled dismay. 'Where has he gone?'

'He didn't say.' Melissa's face held a curious expression that was a blend of triumph and mockery. 'He wasn't very talkative at luncheon. I think he must have drunk a great deal of wine over his supper last night and was still suffering the after-effects at midday.'

'But he didn't give any hint of what time he expected to return?' Delia demanded agitatedly.

'I heard him tell Ellen that he wouldn't be in to dine, but there was no need for a supper-tray to be left. It's my guess he's gone hunting down the real old dyed-in-the-wool money-lenders. Why shouldn't he when all else has failed?'

'Oh, no!' Delia gave a soft groan. 'That means he could

170

have travelled far afield again. He might be as late – or later! – coming home as he was last night.' She gave Melissa a distracted glance. 'About two o'clock, didn't you say?'

'Er – I think so. Why are you worried about his coming home late? The auction isn't until tomorrow afternoon.'

Delia was brought up sharply to the realization that she had brought upon herself the very queries and questions that Berenice had wanted avoided. She must cover up quickly and not forget again. 'You're right. There's plenty of time left. Hours – and hours.' She had looked at her father's watch hanging in its bedhead pocket, which she had embroidered for him while still a child in her best cross-stitch. Eight and three-quarter hours to be precise. She was foolish to worry unnecessarily. At any moment after the evening dining hour the front door could open and Aaron walk in.

She looked towards the watch again. In her mind's eye she could see the procession of vehicles with the blink of carriage-lamps through the trees that would be wending its way down the winding drive from Halewood and out through the gates. In the first carriage would be Berenice and Roland in furs and with knee-rugs. Behind would follow the other carriages bearing boxes and baggage, the two personal servants she was taking with her, and the boy's tutor. Berenice would not give the house a backward glance. Soon the glowing eyes of the lamps would be swallowed in the darkness and there would be no sound but the perpetual moaning of the wind. On the hill-top Halewoood would be waiting with a few pale, lighted windows in the servants' quarters and the rest dark, helping to shroud it in blackness against the winter sky. Its future ownership, plotted with such care by Berenice and her legal adviser, hung precariously in the balance, everything depending on Aaron's chance to return in time to attend the auction.

Delia and Melissa dined alone together. Afterwards they

went to sit by the drawing-room fire where Melissa finished reading her magazine and Delia tried to play patience, but she could give no attention to the game, her thoughts directed towards Aaron and his possible whereabouts.

'What *is* the matter with you?' Melissa demanded with an exasperated sigh when Delia went again to the window.

'I'm anxious about Aaron,' Delia replied frankly, the truth on that point being impossible to hide. 'Money-lenders are notorious for their high rates of interest. I hope he hasn't done anything foolish.'

'I doubt it,' Melissa stated casually, helping herself to another piece of Turkish Delight from the round, wooden box on her lap. She had developed an absurd craving for it. 'He'd hardly be likely to commit himself to anything that would bring him to bankruptcy. Better to let the house go now than to the bailiffs later.'

'I'll go back and sit with Papa for a while. Nurse Baker always welcomes a little extra time to herself, I'm sure.'

She was almost at the top of the flight of stairs when she heard the crunch of gravel underfoot up the drive. Aaron had come home! With an exclamation of mingled joy and relief she grabbed up her skirts and flew back down again to charge through the vestibule and fling the door open before he had time to ring the bell.

'Aaron! Thank God!'

But it was Matthew. His own smile at the sight of her faded. He had seen the light go from her eyes and the expression of intense disappointment wash over her face. She had recovered herself almost at once, but he was hurt and annoyed by her reaction and he showed it.

'I had hoped to give you a pleasant surprise,' he commented sarcastically, removing his hat as he entered, 'but you looked as if you wished me the other side of England.'

'It's not that,' she explained tensely. 'Aaron is late home. Melissa thinks he's gone to money-lenders. In any case, you

172

did tell me that you expected to be away until the end of the week.'

'Plans have changed. One of the directors, knowing I live in Penghyll, called me into his office today. I'm to accompany him to the auction tomorrow. He is to put in the railway company's own bid for Halewood. I've just had dinner with him at the Red Lion Hotel where he's staying overnight.'

That was situated not more than a stone's throw from the Assembly Rooms on the opposite side of the square. Delia's nervousness increased. If Matthew caught the faintest hint of what was afoot he'd get that director to the auction in no time at all!

They had gone into the drawing-room and he greeted Melissa, who offered him some Turkish Delight from her box. He took a pink, sugary piece and popped it in his mouth.

'Thank goodness you've come,' she said touchily. 'Delia has been like a cat on hot bricks all the evening, starting practically out of her skin at every tick of the clock. Perhaps she'll settle down now.' Although Melissa spoke criticizingly of Delia she was far from relaxed herself, even though she had gone into Aaron's room earlier to make sure he hadn't packed his bags and left, for with all chance of Halewood gone from him she felt she had to watch him closely: there was no telling what any man would do in a fit of pique or temper. After what had happened with Richard she put no faith in any man's word, and Aaron's declaration that he was in love with Delia she had taken with a pinch of salt. He probably was at the moment. Men were like that. But she sincerely believed that had Aaron been given the choice of Halewood or Delia, he would have chosen the house every time.

Delia saw that Melissa's ill-chosen remark had made Matthew look more disgruntled than before and she sought to distract him. 'I was on my way up to sit with Papa when you came. Would you like to see him?'

Dr Gilmore was awake. With the doses of laudanum cut down he was beginning to be more alert. Matthew and Delia drew up chairs to the same side of the bed in order to spare him the exertion of looking one way and then the other.

'It's good to know you're making progress, sir,' Matthew said conventionally.

'I'm feeling much better,' the doctor answered weakly. 'The pain has gone.'

'I'm very pleased to hear it.'

'The attack was no surprise to me. It had been coming for some time.'

Delia widened her eyes. 'That's the first I've heard about it.'

'The surprise was that I should survive it. That's why I wanted to see you wed, my dear.' He showed distress. 'Now I've been the cause of your marriage being postponed.'

Matthew answered him. 'But not for long, sir. You'll soon be on your feet again.'

To Delia's relief Matthew left the subject of their marriage and went on to tell Dr Gilmore what he had been doing, holding his interest. Delia could see it was doing her father good to have a visitor.

'Lady Hart sent you a letter,' she said when the conversation had turned to Berenice's departure after Dr Gilmore had enquired after her.

'I'd like you to read it,' he said, pleased, 'if Matthew doesn't mind.'

Matthew smiled. 'Not at all, sir.' Then seeing Delia was about to rise, he added: 'Where is it? Can I fetch it for you?'

'Would you? It's in my velvet reticule on the dressing-table in my room.'

He brought it to her, dropping it by its cords into her hands. She stretched the gathers to take out the letter. As she did so it became caught up with the sale leaflet, which fluttered to the floor.

'What's this?' Matthew reached down by his chair and picked it up. The black lettering stood out. His voice took on a bitter note. 'You're actually carrying one of these around with you, I see.'

She held out her hand for it, but in his irritation at what he considered to be her obsession with the house he pretended not to notice, reading it slowly through. Turning to Berenice's letter Delia opened it for her fa her, telling herself that the notice was no different in any way from those pasted about the town for all to see, and there was nothing uncommon about *a.m.* and *p.m.* being omitted on daytime events. There were some people who might be pedantic about it, but there was no reason for Matthew or anyone else to question the time of the auction. As far as she knew there had never been one held in the middle of the night in Penghyll or anywhere else, and it wouldn't occur to anyone – unless their suspicions were inadvertently aroused – that Halewood was to change hands in the dark hours. Provided, of course, that Aaron returned in time.

Dr Gilmore listened to the letter and asked her to acknowledge it for him. He would have liked them to stay longer talking, but Nurse Baker came in and signalled to Delia that she thought it had been long enough.

As they went out of the room, Delia pretended to have forgotten that Matthew still held the leaflet, but she could tell he had not finished with the matter and was intent on worrying her with it, being in a mood that was all too familiar to her, and her heart sank. Even in their childhood days when something she had said or done had irritated him, he had refused to let the matter rest, harping on about it until eventually she had snapped into temper or dissolved into tears. The pattern still continued on a more sophisticated plane. If she showed anger, he would welcome the excuse to quarrel. If she became distressed, he would immediately be contrite and seek with a loving embrace to make amends. But she was wearied with such petty niggling and all patience with him had fled.

'Where did you get the leaflet?' he persisted as they stepped from the last stair to cross the hall.

'I picked it up at Halewood today,' she answered in what she hoped was a casual tone. 'They were all over the place.' That was true. She had noticed several stacks of them.

'You can't see or read enough of the blasted place, can you!'

She turned on him, eyes flashing. 'No, I can't! I'd live and die there if I could.'

'Well, there's no chance of that. I wouldn't make a home for us in that morgue if it were given to me free!'

She bit back the retort that sprang to her lips and deliberately let her anger drain from her. Bickering with Matthew was a foolish waste of time for both of them. In addition there was the danger that he might goad her into making some slip that would set his mind on the auction in such a way that there'd be no diverting him until the truth was out.

'You'd best leave, Matthew,' she said calmly. 'I don't want to quarrel and I can see that will happen if we continue any kind of discussion at the present time.'

Unnoticed Melissa had come to the open drawing-room door and she pouted prettily. 'I don't want you to go, Matthew. If we're to sit up half the night waiting for Aaron to come back, you can at least help us to pass the time in a game of cards.'

Delia felt herself go pale. 'I said nothing about sitting up.'

'But you will, won't you?' Melissa challenged. 'You'd never be able to sleep not knowing whether or not he's managed to get the loot from the money-lenders. I intend to sit up anyway. I find it all quite exciting.'

'I'll play cards with you,' Matthew stated heavily, seizing

on the opportunity to thwart Delia's desire for him to be gone, and he strolled towards Melissa, crumpling up the leaflet in his hand at the same time. 'I agree with you. It will be interesting to hear if Hart is going to put up a fight at the auction tomorrow or not. What shall we play? Cribbage? *Ecarté*?'

'I don't wish to take part,' Delia said, knowing that she would not be able to concentrate on a single card.

'Then let's play piquet,' Melissa suggested to him.

'Very well.' To Delia's relief he hurled the crumpled leaflet into the fire before starting to unfold the leaves of the card-table. At least temporarily the auction had been put out of his mind.

As the two of them settled down to play Delia put a silver dish of bon-bons on the table for them. 'A glass of wine, Matthew?'

'Thank you,' he replied with icy politeness. 'If you please.'

She opened the cabinet doors to take out the crystal decanter needed, but to her amazement it was empty and had been washed clean. At the table Melissa spoke up.

'I told you I thought Aaron had been drinking a lot last night.'

Delia said nothing, but she went from the room to get her household keys and fetch a bottle and decant it. She was surprised that whichever servant it was who cleared up Aaron's supper-tray that morning had forgotten to tell her that more claret was needed. And it was odd that the washed-out bottle should have been replaced in the cabinet. Dr Gilmore did not allow the servants to go to it except when specially instructed. Having had experience of drunken servants in his time, they were banned also from his cellar. On her way back with the replenished decanter in her hand, she lingered by the hall window to watch the lamps of the carriages going past, hoping that each one might stop to let Aaron alight, but she was doomed to disappointment.

Melissa and Matthew enjoyed their card-playing, both fiercely competitive. The French clock on the mantel struck each hour with a delicate chime. Delia, making a pretence of reading, heard midnight come and go, and then one o'clock rang out. She had formed a plan in her mind. At two o'clock she would announce she could sit up no longer. But instead of going to bed she would slip out of the back door and go to the auction to bid on Aaron's behalf. She had no idea what reserve price Berenice would have put on the property, but she was certain it would be within easy range of the figure that had been bandied about as the most likely sum the house would fetch. With this resolution made she became a little easier in her mind.

'Ring for more coals to be put on the fire,' Melissa said, looking over her shoulder at Delia. 'If we're sitting up until dawn it will get cold.' She and Matthew had switched to backgammon some time earlier and the game was in full swing.

'The servants will have gone to bed long ago,' Delia said, putting down her book and seeing the fire had reduced to white-gold embers, 'but there's coal in the scuttle.'

'I'll do it.' Matthew went across to take up the tongs and lift the coal from the bucket-shaped copper scuttle. As he did so Delia saw that the crumpled leaflet had not burnt as she had supposed, but must have lodged at the side of the grate and rolled out again when she had been attending to the decanter. Holding her breath she watched Matthew hook it up out of a corner by the fender with the tongs and instead of throwing it at once on to the embers he looked at the singed paper for a fraction longer than seemed necessary. The paper had uncurled slightly with the heat. *2.30 o'clock* was the scrap of lettering revealed.

Then she relaxed, trembling, as he cast it on to the embers where it immediately burst into flame. He heaped on the coals and, returning to his chair, took up the dice to shake it

178

as if there had been no interruption in the game.

'I'm sitting here no longer,' she said at last, closing her book with a snap. It was almost two o'clock. 'If you like I'll make some tea and then you must excuse me.'

Melissa hid a deep yawn behind her hand. She had had almost no sleep the night before and her intense tiredness was affecting her playing. She had lost the previous game and it was obvious she was going to lose the one in progress.

'I'd like a cup of tea,' she said sleepily, 'and then I'll go to bed too.'

'That leaves me no choice but to go home,' Matthew said cheerily, very much alert and on his mettle, 'but I'll enjoy that tea first.'

In the kitchen Delia set the kettle on the hob. Cook had made some oven-bottom cakes and Delia popped them in the range oven to heat, ready to be split and spread thickly with butter. She was getting cups and saucers out of a cupboard when the clop of hooves came to a halt at the gate. Aaron! Swiftly she put her head into the hall to make sure the others had not heard the vehicle stop, but they were arguing noisily and with laughter, intent on the final stages of the game. Back into the kitchen she went and across to shoot back the bolt of the kitchen door and dart out into the freezing night. The lawn sparkled with frost in the moonlight and she took a short cut across it, the grass crackling under her racing feet. The cabby was leaning down from the driver's seat to take the fare from Aaron when she arrived breathless at the gate.

'Aaron! Get back in the cab and go at once to the Assembly Rooms!' she gasped, giving him no time to speak. He had turned to her, surprised and startled by her sudden appearance, and she leaned over the gate to snatch at his collar and bring his ear close to her mouth, not risking the cabby overhearing her urgent whisper. 'The auction is to take place at half-past two! Berenice arranged it for you. It's been kept a secret. You'll be the only bidder.'

179

'Come with me!' He made a quick move to open the gate for her, but she stayed his hand.

'I can't! Not yet. But I'll follow and be there with you as soon as I can. I'll explain then.'

He kissed her warmly and swiftly. With a swish of coat-tails he was back in the cab. Delia was already rushing back to the house when he thumped with his cane as a signal for the cabby to proceed with all haste to the destination given.

Swiftly she bolted the door again. The kettle was steaming and she warmed the pot and made the tea. She had buttered the cakes when Matthew came into the kitchen to carry the tray for her.

'Who won the game?' she asked, handing it to him.

'I did.' His gaze was hard on her. 'It went badly against me for a while. It happens that way sometimes. But, as always, I was determined to win in the end.'

It was a barb directed at herself, but she chose to ignore it, holding the door to enable him to walk through with the tray. In the drawing-room Melissa exclaimed at the cakes and took one. She bit into it with her small, white teeth.

'Mm! Aren't you going to have one, Delia?' she asked incredulously, buttery-lipped.

Delia shook her head. 'I'm going upstairs now. Good night.'

Matthew followed her out in the hall and caught her by the wrist, but she remained with her back towards him, stiff and unresponsive, impatient at the unwanted delay.

'Is there anything you should tell me, Delia?'

She froze. Did he mean that he understood she wanted to end their betrothal – or did he suspect that something was amiss about the auction? She dared say nothing in reply that might give the latter away. Not turning, afraid her face would reveal her confusion, she answered him briefly.

'Nothing that can't wait until our next meeting. The hour is too late. Good night again, Matthew.'

He released her wrist. She was aware that he remained where he was, watching her go up to her room. As soon as she had closed the door behind her she opened it a fraction again and listened. She heard him go back into the drawing-room, but if he drank the tea he must have downed it in a gulp, for he left soon afterwards. It was not long before Melissa came slowly from the drawing-room to mount the stairs, dragging up one foot and then the other, yawning as she went. By that time Delia, clad in her warmest coat and the Spanish shawl draped over her head, had reached the kitchen. Waiting there in the darkness she heard the boards creak overhead as Melissa entered the guest-room to go to bed.

Swiftly Delia unbolted the kitchen door for the second time and once again she sped across the lawn. Out through the gate she went and away down the avenue in the direction of the market square, her footsteps echoing. A canopy of stars hung over the sleeping town and underfoot the thawing slush had frozen with the night-fall temperature to form a thin and treacherous coat of ice, which made running hazardous. She was forced to slow her pace after twice narrowly saving herself from falling by clutching first at a wall and then at a fence, snagging and tearing her gloves.

Several times she glanced nervously over her shoulder as she hurried along. She had never been out on her own late at night without male escort before and never on foot. Once she stopped, her heart thumping, convinced that she had heard a footfall somewhere behind her, but there was no one to be seen. On she went again. Never had she realized from the comfort of a carriage how singularly dark and ill-lit the streets were for pedestrians. Then she did see someone, but this was a drunken man ahead of her, who was reeling unsteadily from side to side and constantly missing his footing on the icy ground, tumbling down with grunts and groans. She kept to the opposite side of the street, thankful for the first time for the black shadows, and slipped past without his seeing her.

She reached the market square. It appeared deserted. A few lights shone in the hotel and others in some upper windows above the shops, but not a glimmer showed from the Assembly Rooms where the auction was to be held in the large hall at the rear of the building. Then she did hear the scrape of a sole on cobble and knew she was being followed. It was not her imagination! Unhappily she recalled the garrotter who had never been caught after strangling one of the market traders less than three months before, and there were other cases of attack and rape that until now had been reports in the newspaper to be shuddered over from a distance. But no longer! Danger stalked her!

Bunching up handfuls of her skirt to lift the hems she leapt forward and ran full pelt in a direct line across the square towards the Assembly Rooms. The man behind her knew he had been discovered and no longer made any attempt at concealment. His footsteps came pounding after her. Her breath rasped in her chest, for she had used a fast pace since leaving home, and her scarred leg, which always gave her trouble if used too violently, shivered with weakness. She had only one thought in her head and that was to reach the doors of the Assembly Rooms. Aaron would have set someone in the entrance hall to see her in. She dared not scream or shout for help, for she would bring half the inhabitants of the square prying into why she was about at such an hour.

Barely able to believe her good fortune, she reached the wide steps of the Assembly Rooms, and a sob of relief escaped her as she charged up them. But her attacker was on her. He whirled her about and she threw up her arms in defence to ward him off, knocking his hat from his head, and even as the involuntary scream rose in her throat she recognized him with a different kind of horror. It was Matthew!

'What the devil do you think you're about?' he stormed, his nostrils flaring, his whole face livid with rage. 'First making out you were going to bed, and then creeping through the streets like a draggle-tail!'

'You've spied on me!' she expostulated furiously. 'And frightened me! I thought – oh, I don't know what I thought I was so frightened!'

He clamped her to him in his temper, his iron grasp crushing the flesh of her arms through the thickness of her dress and coat-sleeves. His face jerked towards the doors of the Assembly Rooms and then back to her. 'Why did you run in this direction? What brought you to this dark, shut-up place when you'd no idea who it was on your heels? Whom were you expecting to meet – or to rescue you?'

A single, booming stroke from the church clock resounded hollowly over the town roofs. Half-past two! The auction would be starting! At all cost she must keep Matthew from suspecting what was afoot or he could still leap in there and ruin everything. For all she knew he might in such an unusual contingency be able to take upon himself the power to bid and be commended for it. But it was too late to say anything. Comprehension was dawning in his face.

'I believe I'm getting it! I was able to tell all the evening you weren't yourself. I've known you too many years to be deceived. You were particularly agitated when I picked up that Halewood sale pamphlet. I couldn't think why. Something lay at the back of it all that was different from any other tiff we've had about the house, but I couldn't puzzle out what it might be. I thought about it again when I picked up the pamphlet out of the fender and threw it back on the fire. It worried me. All those hours playing cards and backgammon never took my mind away from trying to guess what it was. In the end I thought to ask you outright and to clear the air between us. But oh, no! You couldn't come out with whatever it was! That's when it came to me you were sheltering Hart in some way and for some reason that you didn't want me to know about.'

'But how was it you followed me?' She had to keep him talking. With any luck he could be on a wrong tack, imagining she had planned a secret *rendezvous* with Aaron for a reason other than that of the auction.

'I saw your footsteps across the frosty grass when I left the house. It told me you had been out once, and I remembered thinking I'd heard a carriage stop outside when you were getting the tea, but then when Hart didn't come in I told myself I'd been mistaken. Now I knew you had stopped him coming in. I waited under the trees and watched your bedroom window. Your lamp was on only for a minute or two. As I'd expected, it wasn't long before you came out of the side door.' He looked again towards the entrance doors of the Assembly Rooms and his hold on her relaxed. 'I don't think that place is as shut up as it looks. You were going to meet Hart in it. The auction! Two-thirty o'clock that pamphlet said. I was staring at the solution to the whole thing and didn't know it.'

He released her and would have made for the doors, but knowing only that she had to stop him she grabbed his coat and hung on with all her strength.

'No, Matthew! No! Let Aaron have Halewood!'

His inexorable young face did not change expression. 'Never!' he ground out bitterly. 'If he gets Halewood he'll get you too! I have it in my power to prevent that happening and I intend to use it.'

He tried to thrust her from him, but she would not release her hold, dragging on him with all her weight, and when he grabbed her wrists, intending to snatch her grip away, she lurched towards him. She had not intended it, but her leg had given way at last under her, throwing her off balance, and the sudden impact of her body against his caused him to miss his footing on the icy step. As though jerked by a rope his head thudded back against the stone column behind him and he pitched forward down the steps, taking her with him.

184

It all happened in a matter of seconds and even as she cried out she found herself lying with him in a tangle of legs, petticoats, shawl, arms, and coat-tails. His tall hat, which she had knocked from his head at the first moment of onslaught, lay on the cobbles some little distance away.

He had broken the impact of the fall for her, for she had tumbled across him, and she struggled up to a sitting position, scooping her hair back out of her eyes. 'Oh, Matthew,' she moaned tragically, 'I never wanted anything like this to happen. I do love Aaron and I had no idea you had guessed. I've been trying to find a way to tell you –'

Her voice trailed away and her eyes dilated with an awful terror. He was lying sprawled half down the steps with his head resting on the cobbles, his eyes closed. Frantically she called his name, springing up to lean over him and cup her hands under his head. Blood seeped into her palms.

In the hall of the Assembly Rooms Aaron sat alone in the third row of over a hundred seats that had been set out in readiness for the expected bidders for the property of Halewood. On the rostrum stood the auctioneer and back by the wall his clerk waited with all the necessary papers. Mr Radleigh, who was present, seated at a side table with his spectacles on his nose, had had the two men brought from London, telling them nothing until they had arrived at the hall.

The auctioneer cleared his throat after giving details of the property for sale. 'Now who will start the bidding?' he questioned as though every chair held an eager buyer. 'Let us open it – at one guinea.'

Aaron straightened in his chair, scarcely able to believe what he had heard. A token sum of one guinea! Berenice had been munificent indeed! How he wished Delia was here! He had paced the floor waiting for her. Slowly he raised his catalogue.

'Thank you, sir! Any advance on one guinea? Going,

going, gone!' The gavel crashed down. 'Sold to the gentleman in the third row.'

The clerk went through the formality of scribbling down
his name while the auctioneer proceeded with the next part
of the sale, which to Aaron was totally unexpected, and it
was a nod from the lawyer that had kept him in his chair.

'Now the fine contents of Halewood Hall. Do I hear a
guinea from you again, sir?' asked the auctioneer.

Aaron put up his catalogue. The gavel was lifted again
while the final call was made. Down it crashed once more.
Everything was his. The house, the paintings, furniture,
tapestries and silver, the carriages and blood horses, the
land, the livestock, and all the outlying farm property. But
where was the girl who was to be his wife and mistress of it
all?

He sprang up to go in search of her, accepted Mr Radleigh's handshake of congratulation, and was almost at the
doors leading into the corridor when they swung open and
Delia rushed in. Her face was drained of all colour, her hair
dishevelled, and frozen slush was melting on her coat. He
thought she must have run to get there and taken a few falls
on the way. Her distress he took for her failing to arrive
before the auction was over.

'Halewood is ours, Delia, my love!'

She scarcely seemed to hear him. 'It's Matthew! He's
badly hurt. He's lying outside.'

He did not stop to ask questions, but was ahead of her out
through the door, leaving her to summon up the others'
assistance as she followed him. As he rushed to help the
injured man, not knowing what he would find, he knew with
a despairing flash of insight that fate had cleaved Delia
asunder from him in some totally unexpected way. His
triumph in the possession of Halewood had been short-lived.
Had its curse already fallen on him?

186

Chapter Ten

At first Matthew lay in a coma. When at last he recovered
consciousness he was incoherent, not knowing anyone,
unaware that he lay in a darkened sickroom in his grandparents' house, a delicate and dangerous operation having
been performed on his head to remove a clot of blood.
Christmas came and went. His fever had long since passed
and the bandages about his head were no more than a
protection over the healed scar when he eventually opened
his eyes with recognition of his surroundings. Delia was at
his bedside and she dropped the tatting that she had worked
on to while away the hours, leaning over him.

'What's that noise?' he whispered. It was almost as
though he had been wrenched from the lost depths that had
held him by yet another distant boom beyond the town,
which rattled the windows and shook the ground.

She answered him in a voice shaky with joy that he had
come back to the world. 'It's the blasting for the new railway
line. The company settled without further delay for their
second choice of route for the tracks.'

'I should be there.' His murmur was agitated.

'No, no,' she said soothingly. 'Time enough when you're
well again.'

He looked at her, confused and puzzled and distraught. 'I
thought I'd lost you.'

'Why should you think that?' she asked tremulously.

'I've been calling for you all the time, but you never came!'
There was no point in telling him he had only babbled her

name occasionally and never once had he cried out as he imagined he had done, but with a wrenching pang she wondered what terrible anguish he had endured whilst floating up and down again on waves of near-consciousness. 'I was here, Matthew. I've spent hours every day at your bedside.'

'Don't leave me again.' He would have attempted to raise himself up to reach an arm to her, but she restrained him quickly, knowing he must not move, and sat on the edge of the bed, exerting a little pressure with her hands on both his shoulders.

'You mustn't worry about that or anything else,' she said placatingly, but he was not to be distracted.

'Promise me!' He was restless and disturbed, a very real fear of retreating back in that abyss without her showing in his eyes, and he strove to lift himself towards her.

'I'll be with you for as long as you want me,' she cried, frantic with concern.

He relaxed, his lids drooping with exhaustion, and gave a long sigh. 'That's for evermore.'

She saw that he slept. There was a faint smile on his lips and she touched them with her finger-tips, tenderly, but as she would have touched a frightened fawn or child or any other helpless creature that had looked to her for succour and solace, but her own face was wan and hollow-eyed. She knew to what she had committed herself.

Rising soundlessly from the bed she went to find his grandparents and give them the glad tidings that their beloved grandson had spoken lucidly at last. Both of them were true Northerners inclined to understatement and not given to displays of emotion, but on this occasion they embraced her and each other with tears of thankfulness.

Matthew spoke again several times that afternoon, but he was content and placid and there was no further talk of his earlier fears. Delia knew she had set his mind at rest.

When she walked home in the gathering dusk, passing the street lamp-lighter going about his task, her thoughts dwelt on all that had happened since Matthew had first been carried from the market square and laid in that bed. Aaron had settled into Halewood, but she had not yet visited him there, having no time to spare, although they had seen each other when he had called in at Sycamore House at regular intervals. Her father had made excellent progress and was now allowed to sit in a chair in his bedroom where he spent most of the day reading. He could even walk slowly with a stick, but realized he must accept enforced retirement, aware that he would never be the same man again. Fortunately he was not low-spirited and was determined to make life as full as his capabilities allowed.

Melissa had used the excuse of wanting to do what she could to help during his convalesence in order to stay on at Sycamore House and avoid returning to London where Uncle Henry had won his by-election. No objection was raised by her parents, and Delia believed them to be relieved not to have to set eyes on their daughter again for an indefinite period, forgiveness being out of the question.

Delia had been quite glad of her cousin's company, for she had made an effort at first to be helpful, although that helpfulness had waned considerably as soon as her continued sojourn in Penghyll had been assured. Recently she had lapsed into a state of ennui, which she declared was a delayed reaction to all she had been through, and Delia did not question it.

Having reached the market square, Delia followed the pavement past the Red Lion Hotel, not looking at the Assembly Rooms on the far side where the sight of the flight of steps evoked painful memories. There had been practically a riot when those who had hoped to purchase Halewood discovered that the auction had already taken place, but there had been nothing any of them could do about it and after more angry discussion they had dispersed. Nearly all were outsiders and no local ill-feeling remained to fester against Aaron; on the contrary, it was considered only right that a Hart should be residing at Halewood and whatever misfortunes should befall him there were only part and parcel of his birthright and he had to take the rough with the smooth as his predecessors had before him.

It had started to rain by the time she reached the gate of Sycamore House and she was glad to get indoors. On a salver in the hall was a letter from Italy and she recognized the writing. She took it with her up to her father's room where a cosy fire glowed and the curtains were closed against the dismal evening. Dr Gilmore woke from dozing in his chair when she entered.

'The most wonderful thing happened today!' she announced, kissing him on the cheek. 'Matthew recovered consciousness completely and spoke to me. In fact he talked quite a lot. Dr Pomfret called shortly before I left and seemed extremely satisfied.'

Her father expressed his pleasure, smiling at her happy face. 'Nobody could have been more patient and attentive at his bedside than you've been during these worrying weeks. You've probably done more to help him than you'll ever know.'

A slight frown creased her brow. 'You're quite wrong. I've done nothing. He had no awareness of my presence there at all. He told me.'

Seeing that she was distressed by this knowledge Dr Gilmore nodded towards the letter she held. 'Is that from Lady Hart by any chance?'

'It is indeed! A letter at last. I'll read it to you.' She smiled as she opened it. 'It's as short as the one I received from Roland by the look of it.'

It was a brief note, but where Roland had merely listed the reasons why he hated Italy and wished he were home in

England, Berenice wrote of her delight in the villa that she had made her home. It was everything she had hoped it would be. Unfortunately Roland was being naughty and difficult. As an extreme measure she had allowed his tutor to cane him, but it had done no good at all, and she wouldn't let it occur again. She sent her regards to Dr Gilmore and would Delia be so kind as to tell Mr Hart she had received his letter of thanks for donating Halewood to him, for she would not be acknowledging it and considered the correspondence closed. She remained, affectionately, Berenice Hart.

'Hmm.' Dr Gilmore gave a reflective nod. 'Lady Hart was generous beyond all count in ensuring that Halewood became the property of Mr Hart, but in my opinion she had no liking for the young man. That remark about the correspondence being at an end amounts to a very noticeable snub.'

Delia, folding the letter up again, made no comment. Poor Berenice. The very reverse was the reason why she could not bear to receive any more letters from him. 'I'll write tomorrow and tell her about Matthew. She'll be glad to know he's on the road to recovery.'

'You must not look for a speedy return to health,' he advised seriously. 'I fear it may be many months yet before you stand at the altar with Matthew. Dr Pomfret will keep Matthew lying in that darkened room for some time to come. It's too early yet to tell whether any real damage has been done to the brain. That he must have continued absolute quiet goes without saying, and no upsets of any kind.'

'I realize that.' Her head was bowed, her attitude grave.

He put out a hand and lifted her face upwards to him. 'Matthew is never going to need you more than he needs you now. You must give no more time to me. Nurse Baker will stay on for as long as she's needed and after that you shall employ a suitable housekeeper. Your duty is only to the man to whom you are betrothed. Nobody else.'

191

'I know.' Her voice was barely audible. He withdrew his touch and her chin sank to her breast. She was aware that he had no real idea of the conflict of loyalty and love she was enduring, but she could not talk to him about it. With hands motionless in her lap she sat very still with shoulders dipped, lost in thought. When the doorbell rang in the depths of the house she did not stir, nor yet when one of the servants went to answer it. Only when Aaron's voice sounded did she sit up with a start.

'Aaron has come with those books from Halewood's library that he promised you.' She sprang to her feet, putting her hands instinctively to her hair as if it might have been disarrayed by the very turmoil of her thoughts. 'I'll go and meet him.'

He had already reached the landing and carried three enormous vellum-bound tomes in his arms. 'Look at these vast volumes on Halewood's history that I've found for your father to peruse.' He gave a laugh and lifted them slightly. 'Do you think his reading table will be strong enough to hold them?'

She faced him in the lamplight, her bottle-green gown dark against the crimson wallpaper and carpet, her face ivory-pale. 'Matthew knew me today for the first time.'

His expression mirrored his immense exuberance at the news. 'That's wonderful! Splendid! He's going to be all right again.'

She was quite motionless. 'Nobody can be sure about that yet.'

'But he will be.' He shoved his load of books on to the bow-fronted chest of drawers that stood near at hand. 'It was only a crack on the head after all. That happens to lots of people. I was out for two days myself once when I was thrown from a horse.'

'There's a great difference between you and Matthew.'

He screwed up his eyes speculatively at her, black brows

drawing together, and he stayed by the chest of drawers about a yard from her. He had become accustomed to her withdrawing from him since the night of the auction, her melting tenderness quickly suppressed, her mouth half surrendering and then closing defensively, but he had been patient, understanding that Matthew had come between them in an entirely new way, and knowing that until the unfortunate man was well again that was how it would be. But this evening there was something different in her whole attitude. As if the whole of her being was one despairing cry. Not in physical yearning, which made her breath sob and her flesh leap under his touch, but in a complete rejection of him.

'Yes?' he questioned, warily.

'Nobody else caused you to be thrown from a horse, but I brought about Matthew's fall.'

'It was an accident. You can't hold yourself responsible.'

'But I do. I'm the one who made him lose his footing. However one looks at it, I pushed him down those steps. I alone am the reason why he's been lying sick. Whatever ill-effects he still may suffer can only be laid at my door.'

'He has nobody but himself to blame! If he hadn't spied on you, followed you – '

'That's beside the point. None of that brought about his injury. It was the fall and only the fall. Had I not panicked and struggled with him it wouldn't have happened. I should have reasoned with him somehow.'

'This is hindsight. Mere supposition. You took the only course that seemed open to you at the time. Why do you speak of it as though it occurred through some selfish whim of your own? You sought to stop him going into that auction for my sake.'

Her cheeks were hollow. 'I nearly killed Matthew for you.'

He caught in his breath sharply and lifted his hands in appeal. 'Don't torture yourself. Matthew didn't die and he's not going to die. He'll recover and take up his life again.'

'And I must help him do that.'

He refused to accept the significance of her words and made a swift, impatient gesture. 'Yes. Naturally. A few more weeks —'

'Longer than that.'

His mouth felt dry. 'How long?'

The effort of answering seemed almost beyond her. Her lips hardly moved. 'For as long as he wants me. I told him that today.'

He stared at her. Shock went through him like a deadly current. She whom he loved beyond all measure, whose body he looked upon as the perfect complement of his own, whose being gave him the entire reason for his existence, had with a few words severed herself apart from him to a point of no return. He tried to speak, but no sound came, every muscle of his throat seemingly paralysed.

She half-extended her arms, her hands curled upwards from the wrists in an attitude of abject sorrow and defensiveness. 'Don't look at me like that,' she implored in a heart-torn whisper.

He found his voice. 'You can't mean that this is the end of all that lies between us.'

'I do.' She was barely audible. 'Nothing can make me change my mind. Nothing at all. This is how it has to be.'

His face was haggard. Suddenly, out of the unbearable hurt, the unendurable sense of loss, came a great gush of searing anger. It was a white-hot rage directed against the cruel capriciousness of fate, but he made her his target.

'So this is how little you loved me.' He did not shout, his low-spoken words the more devastating because of it. 'You did not care. Your heart was never mine. All along Matthew has come first with you. It's he whom you've loved all the time!'

He wanted her to deny it. To cry some protest. To show

some sign. But she only stood as though all power to move had deserted her, an awful look of desolation on her face. Her silence was infectious. It choked into him and he hurled himself about and ran down the stairs to snatch up his hat and his cape, which he threw over his arm. As he wrenched open the vestibule door he stopped and looked up over his shoulder. His eyes blazed at her. In fury and in love and in despair. Then the vestibule door crashed after him and there followed the more resounding thud of the front door. Outside hooves leapt and slithered on the gravel as a whip had cut home, and went galloping away into the night.

She moved stiffly and went to the books he had left behind. *The History of Halewood* in three volumes. Stunned with grief she lowered her head and put her cheek against the top volume, encircling the pile with her arms.

It was the creak of a landing floorboard that made her raise her head. Melissa had come from the guest-room in outdoor clothes. Her face showed that she had overheard all that had passed between them.

'You may not want him, but I do!' she declared, her voice vibrant and high-pitched. Seeing Delia's incredulous expression she gave a shaky little laugh, which revealed her extreme nervousness. 'I'm going to make myself mistress of Halewood. Even my father will approve of that!'

She darted down the stairs, her skirts swooping out as she swung round the bend of them to traverse the rest of the flight. When she reached the vestibule door she paused as Aaron had done, but her eyes had a very different look in them. Delia had seen it only once before, and that had been in the eyes of a man in the gaming room at a party. All had gathered round to watch the card-play. He had staked far more than he could afford to lose on the hand he held.

'Be magnanimous!' Melissa cried imploringly to her on a shrill note of desperation. 'You're the only friend I ever had. God alone knows what Halewood will do to me!'

She had gone. Delia, unable to comprehend why Melissa should imagine Aaron would turn to her, knew a new sense of foreboding to add to her agony, but she was given no time to remain there on her own as she would have wished. Her father was ringing the little hand-bell by his chair, no doubt getting impatient to see Aaron and thinking he was a long time coming to see him. Picking up the heavy volumes she went in to him.

Dr Gilmore exclaimed at the size of the books. 'They're too heavy for you! Put them down quickly – yes, over there on the table. That's it. I declare you've exhausted yourself. You're quite pale.' Then he looked towards the door she had left open, and back at her. 'Where's Mr Hart?'

'He was in a hurry,' she managed to say, running her shaking finger-tips along the gilded edges of the pages. 'These are splendidly bound books. I'll have to fetch the larger reading stand up from the study. The one you've been using will be top-heavy.'

'Would you read the opening chapter of the first one to me, my dear?'

It was the last thing she felt like doing, but she could not refuse him. 'Yes. Of course.' She took her place beside him, the book heavy on her lap, and opened it at the first page. Quietly she began to read, but her eyes and tongue seemed to be acting independently of her mind, which was following Melissa, who was herself in the wake of Aaron, on a fateful journey through the rain to the distant black outline of Halewood on the hill.

The chapter seemed endless, and when she came to the last line of it she looked up and saw that her father had dropped off to sleep. Not knowing how she had been able to make sense of the words, she leaned her head back against the chair in utter exhaustion, one hand resting on the book, the other falling limply to her side. Her eyes were deep, dark pools in her white face, her gaze distant and unfocused, her heart yearning towards the man who could never be hers.

At Halewood Aaron stood silhouetted against the huge fire of blazing logs on the hearth in the long hall, feet set apart, hands clasped behind his back, head thrust slightly forward. All the old angers, sorrows, lost-love pangs, and immeasurable miseries that had permeated the walls over the centuries seemed to have seeped out and gathered into his frame. The weight was heavy on him and when a footman announced there was a young lady to see him no hope flared, for every fibre of his being would have known and thrown off the shackles if by some miracle Delia had come to retract her rejection of him.

'Miss Barton, sir.'

Aaron turned slowly and leaned an arm along the stone mantel, one foot coming to rest on the hearth, as she entered. He gave her no welcome, his cold stare designed to show his resentment at her intrusion, which increased when he saw that she had left bonnet and coat with the footman, obviously intending to make herself at home. That her outward composure hid an inner anxiety of desperate proportions he did not suspect.

'Good evening, Aaron.' She walked towards him. She had a graceful walk and covering the length of the hall between them gave her a chance to show herself off to advantage, the shot-silk gown she had chosen with care to wear changed colour from rose to gold with every rippling gather, its neck high and modest, the sleeves long and tight.

'I'm in no mood for social chit-chat,' he stated bluntly. 'If there's some purpose for this visit please state it and be gone.'

She seated herself in a chair where the firelight danced over her face. 'I have kept my own counsel, wanting to be sure before I mentioned the matter to you, but I can't believe you haven't been somewhat prepared for the possible outcome of that night when I let you late into Sycamore House.'

197

He threw up his hands in exasperation. 'What the devil are you talking about?'

'Have the looks I've given you, the chance remarks I've let fall, meant nothing to you?'

He was completely baffled, and angry with it. 'Have you come for some belated and additional apology for my drinking more than I should have done on that occasion? If you have, I think you could have chosen a better time. I recall apologizing next morning, and as I said to you then, it's not my habit to imbibe inordinately and the lack of food for more than fourteen hours had had unprecedented results. I'm sorry again for any embarrassment I might have caused you. There! Does that suffice?'

'It wasn't an apology I wanted. I've come for more than that.'

He dug fists into his hips, elbows jutting, strained almost beyond endurance by the unwanted interview. 'What, pray?'

'I want your name for – our child, which was conceived that night.'

He thought at first he had not heard correctly. But even as she had spoken her nerve had given way, her apparent composure had disssolved, and she pressed shaking fingertips against her mouth, her eyes quite terrified of him. Had she shown bravado or hostility or arrogance he might have doubted that she was speaking the truth, but to him her helplessness and fright rang completely true. He was aghast and put a hand to his head, trying to remember the events of that night, but as always everything eluded him. He could see himself staggering to the foot of the stairs holding on to Melissa for support, but beyond that – nothing. Except that she had wept. Continually. And cried out to him. Had he believed himself to be holding Delia in his arms? Frantic to possess her, had the wine so clouded his senses as to create the illusion that it was not Melissa he was compelling into surrender?

He paced to and fro. 'We must talk about this. Tell me everything.'

Sheer fright that she would fail to convince him continued to lend a note of authenticity to all she said. Truth and lies blended together. She made it impossible for him to doubt her. No innocent girl, such as he believed her to be, strictly brought up and carefully chaperoned, could have made up the details she was divulging to him. She took care to remind him in an indirect way that she had gone nowhere without Delia in her first days at Sycamore House and that he himself had escorted her to the Penghyll Ball. In no way could he connect her with other male company. Again she congratulated herself that inadvertently she had ensured that no word of Richard's impact on her life had ever reached him.

She could tell he remembered nothing of that night she had plotted with care. Her own experience of the drug which she had added to the claret had not played her false. True, there had been a terrible couple of hours when she'd been afraid he had taken too much of it and would die, but it had worked better than she had dared hope. Now was the time to deal the last stroke.

She stood up and faced him squarely. 'What's done can't be undone. You'd not see the heir to Halewood born out of wedlock!'

He looked at her with loathing, unable for the moment to say anything. As a man of honour he accepted that there was only one course open to him. As a man in love with another girl, no matter that he had lost her, he was repelled by the sordid events in which he had become embroiled and the prospect of a marriage precipitated by them was abhorrent to him in every way.

At last he spoke.

'You're right,' he said bitterly, 'but the marriage of convenience in which we'll both be unwilling partners shall be no more than a civilized and legal arrangement. Should you find it intolerable to continue living under this roof after the baby is born you'll be free to go and live elsewhere. I'll make no claims on you. You shall have the house of your choice and a settlement for life.'

'And the child?'

'The heir to Halewood remains here. There'll be no further contact between the two of you ever again.'

She was willing to agree to anything, enervated by the ordeal she had been through, sustained only by triumph. 'Let's be married tomorrow. There's not a day to waste. I can't lace myself indefinitely. I'm not going back to Sycamore House. Send for my baggage. I left everything packed.'

His face was set in hardness. 'What of your parents? Should I not go to London to see your father – '

'No!' She fluttered her hands in protest. 'Suppose he insisted on some delay? You must do everything to salvage my reputation!'

He sighed. 'Whatever you say. Whether we can be married as quickly as tomorrow I've no idea, but I'll do all I can. Now I'll see that your boxes are sent for and summon a servant to show you to a suite of rooms.'

He left her alone in the long hall. She hugged her arms in jubilation. She had done it! She had guaranteed a future for Richard's baby! She had averted disgrace and humiliation! She was free of her hateful father! In fact, when the next six months were over she would have freedom beyond her wildest dreams! She wouldn't have to stay in this cold, draughty house a moment longer than was necessary. And what a cold place it was! How eerie the moaning of the wind in the chimney!

She shivered, rubbing her arms instead of hugging them, and she drew nearer to the blazing fire. As she did so, a great gust of wind blew down with a sudden roar, puffing out smoke, scattering the hot ash on to her skirt, singeing countless tiny holes and causing a small flame to flicker near the hem. She gave a shriek and extinguished it before it took any hold, but she was severly shaken and she drew back to a safe distance. How odd that gust had been, and totally without warning. Almost as if the very house had struck out at her in hatred.

She gulped. That was nonsense. She mustn't let her imagination run away with her. Many a time she didn't believe a word of the old tales about Halewood, but that had been easy to say when she'd been far from it.

On the hearth the huge logs were spitting and crackling, roused by the gust of wind into a kind of fury, leaping up high in showers of dancing sparks, but instead of the warmth radiating towards her she felt colder than ever. It was as though she stood entrapped in the eye of a circling draught.

Panic rose in her. 'Aaron!' she cried frantically. He would be a shield between her and the house. He'd let no harm come to her. She sobbed his name again and broke into a run back down the length of the hall in the direction of the archway, intent on finding him. But she tripped and fell, crashing down on a vast spread of carpet, which slid into folds under her. She lay there gasping, telling herself that she must have caught her toe in the fringe, but it was as though she had been given a violent push in the back so great was the force with which she had fallen. No! No! To think such thoughts was inviting madness!

She was getting to her feet again when Aaron returned and he rushed to help her up. 'What happened?'

'I was running – and I fell over the edge of the carpet,' she explained shakily.

'Running?' he echoed with a grim anger. 'There'll be no more running or hurrying or any other kind of stupid behaviour that might harm the baby you're carrying. You'll take the greatest care at all times. Understand?'

'Yes,' she said meekly, lowering her lashes to hide the

malevolent satisfaction in her eyes. He had given her a weapon to use against him if need be. If his concern for the unborn child was to be so all-embracing she'd only have to threaten some harm to it to get anything she wanted from him.

'You'll be shown to your rooms now,' he said, walking with her to the archway. By the foot of the stairs a maidservant waited in a bobbing white cap and streamers. 'I must write a letter to Delia explaining why you're staying and what is to take place.'

'You'll not find her unprepared,' she answered. Turning to take the way indicated, she did not care what he wrote. Nobody suspected that she had been pregnant when she'd come to Penghyll. She hadn't known herself at first, although there had been some indication. It was hard not to laugh out loud at the way she had fooled everybody. Little did Aaron know that, far from seducing her he had not laid a finger on her, except to try to thrust her from him in one last effort to be free of her before the drug had finally overtaken him.

Following the maidservant she noticed how the wind beat ceaselessly against the house, rattling windows as she passed them, swirling curtains in a draught, and always keeping up an endless moan that rose and fell perpetually. No wonder the house had an icy atmosphere that the heat of fires could not banish.

Suddenly a howl, more eerie than anything she had ever heard before, seemed to rise up against all sides of the house. She came to a standstill, a nervous hand to her throat. 'What's that?'

'Nobbut t'wind, miss. It allus gives newcomers a bit of a start, but you'll get used to it.'

Melissa shivered, hurrying after the maidservant again to let no distance fall between them. 'Why should it do that? I've never heard such a dismal sound.'

The cap-streamers flicked out as the girl glanced back

over her shoulder. 'They say it's summat to do with how the current of air cuts through t'fells from t'south and meets another blowing from t'sea. That's how this hilltop where Halewood stands got its name. Howling Hill. Have you never heard that?'

'Yes – but I didn't realize it was so bad.'

'Oh, it's extra noisy this evening.' The clicking heels came to a halt and double doors were opened into a pretty, lilac drawing-room. 'It happens like that now and then. It's supposed to mean there's no good afoot. That's th'old tale anyroad.'

Melissa looked about at the room. There was the sparkle of crystal lustres on chandelier and wall-sconces reflected in exquisite Florentine looking-glasses. But she returned her attention to the maidservant, who was stooping down to add more coal to the fire. 'Doesn't it frighten you?'

'No, miss. Why should it?' The girl straightened up pertly and smoothed down her apron. 'I ain't a Hart. T'curse only falls on t'family, and on them that become family when they marry into it.'

Melissa clasped her hands together. 'Do you believe that there is a curse?'

'Course I do. So does my Grandma. She remembers tales of what happened to th'Harts at Halewood that her grandma told her. So it goes far back.'

'Tragedies happen in all families.'

'I know, but it's summat special what happens to th'Harts. It's allus to do wi' love, miss. Nowt ever goes right for a Hart that weds and lives i' this house. I like weddings, but it's to be hoped as t'new master of Halewood stays a bachelor for his own heart's sake, but that's hardly to be expected wi' his fine looks.' The girl's voice trailed away, something in her listener's face telling her she had let her wagging tongue run away with her. 'I meant nowt disrespectful, miss.'

203

'I hope not!' Melissa's mouth was very tight. 'I'm here to marry Mr Hart.'

Crimson flooded the maidservant's face. 'Beg pardon, miss. I wasn't gossiping. Only answering t'questions you asked me.'

'Show me the rest of the suite,' Melissa demanded irritably. The maidservant sprang with alacrity to open more doors, thankful she had said no more than she had done.

It was a little over an hour later when Aaron's letter was delivered into Delia's hands. Ellen brought it to her in the drawing-room where she was sitting in the firelight, the lamps unlit.

'There's two Halewood grooms come to fetch Miss Melissa's boxes out to a carriage.' Ellen informed her. 'One of them says she'll be staying up at t'big house.'

Delia's head jerked and her back straightened as if she had been pulled upright by a puppet's string. 'Then show them where her baggage is and let it be carried out.'

Left alone, Delia slipped from the chair and sank to her knees where she sat back on her heels by the brass fender. With nerveless fingers she opened the letter and held it to the firelight and read it through. A numbness came upon her as the words leapt out in the fine black ink.

Delia, my beloved,

Had I harboured any doubt about the existance of the evil curse of Halewood it would have been doubly dispelled this night. After your dismissal of me a second calamity befell to snap the last lingering thread of hope I would have been foolish enought to cherish yet, and it causes my hand to tremble as I write. It pains me beyond measure to have to tell you that Melissa is with child by me, and we are to be married without delay. I make no excuses for myself. The blame is entirely mine. I fell into my cups in your father's house when I arrived late home after a long and fruitless journeying after a loan to secure the purchase of Halewood at auction. In my drunkenness I knew nothing and forced Melissa to submit to me. By my action I brought humiliation to an innocent girl and offended against the gracious hospitality your father extended to me. My sense of shame knows no bounds. Most bitter of all is the knowledge of the irreparable harm I have done to that sweet and tender emotion that bound us together, whether you wished it or no. I cannot ask for forgiveness. That would be impertinent. I only ask that you do not harden your heart against me, but know that I have loved you and love you still.   *Aaron.*

The letter drifted from her shaking fingers and she dropped her face into her hands, racked by an anguish that made her moan softly over and over again. She stayed there until the fire died down and shadows took possession of the room. Somehow she knew that, at Haleewoood, Aaron also sat alone, reaching out in his despair to her in the midst of his suffering as she did to him.

Chapter Eleven

Delia stopped to look in the milliner's window. Although spring was still far away it was a joy to look upon the pretty straw bonnet that had been put on display. Yellow silk roses clustered under the brim and the ribbons were striped in the same colour. When she had more time she would go in one day and try it on, but Matthew was expecting her and he did not like her to be late.

Her thoughts dwelt on him. He was a difficult invalid, but that was natural in a man who had never been ill before in his life. Some days he was plagued by terrible headaches and then the opiate given on Dr Pomfret's instructions caused him to sleep for hours at a time, but on other occasions he appeared to be quite well and almost recovered.

She stepped off the pavement and the crossing-sweeper sprang in front of her to clear mud and dung out of her path with his broom. When she handed him a coin on the other side of the street a commotion caught her attention. A young woman coming from a draper's shop to get back into her waiting carriage had collapsed in a faint. It was Melissa!

Delia ran to her, thrusting her way through the people who were gathering, and reached her side at the same time as the groom who had leapt down from the back of the Halewood carriage.

'Lift her up!' Delia instructed, 'Lay her on the carriage seat, and then drive back to Halewood.'

The second groom had come to help him and Delia sprang into the vehicle ahead of them to clear a space, for the seats were covered with dresses and bonnet-boxes, showing that Melissa had been on a spending spree. The shopkeeper had come with smelling-salts, which Delia accepted, and when she spotted the shop-boy standing uncertainly with a pile of packed purchases that he had been bringing out to the carriage she beckoned him forward and took them from him.

Quickly she dived into her reticule. 'Here's a sixpence,' she said, taking it out. 'Get your master's permission to go at once to Number twenty-three, Holly Place. Tell Mr Matthew Shaw that Mrs Melissa Hart is indisposed and Miss Gilmore will be accompanying her to Halewood.'

Melissa was laid on the seat and a few seconds later the carriage rolled forward. Delia loosened her collar and waved the smelling-salts under her nose. It took effect instantly and as soon as Melissa opened her eyes and saw her she burst into tears and sat up to throw her arms about her neck.

'Hush! Hush!' Delia said with concern. Melissa's storm of weeping was completely abandoned. Great snorting sobs and gushing tears and strangled cries.

'I'm so unhappy! Why haven't you been to see me?'

Delia bit her lip. 'I couldn't come. You know why. You heard all that Aaron and I said to each other on the night you went to Halewood to tell him about the baby. I have to forget him. He's your husband – '

'Husband!' Melissa almost spat the word, an angry self-pity drying up her tears, leaving some still sliding down her cheeks. 'He denies me nothing but his company!' It irked her that she could have clothes, trinkets, and any kind of food she fancied without a word of protest from him, foiling her original intention to use the well-being of the baby she carried as a threat to get her own way, and in truth it was not his company she wanted, being a little afraid that she might make a slip of the tongue that would give her away, but loneliness was lying heavy on her garrulous tongue and it relieved her to set all her troubles at his door. 'I hardly ever

207

see him. He never comes near me if he can help it! All he thinks about is Halewood. Do you know, the other day I found him in his shirt-sleeves helping the labourers to shift some stone in the restoration work. I eat alone. I sleep alone! I pass the endless hours with nothing to do and no one to talk to.'

'You could invite people to Halewood,' Delia pointed out, 'and surely invitations have been coming to you both since the announcement that your marriage had taken place was in the newspapers. I'm not your only friend in this neighbourhood.'

'Yes, you are! I told you that evening I left for Halewood. The others are only acquaintances. But it's more than that.' She frowned sullenly. 'Aaron has forbidden me to lace myself, and I'll not have those hateful girls and their mothers staring at my waistline and working out the months behind my back!' She set her hands on her waist as she spoke and eased herself uncomfortably. 'I laced myself this morning in case I met anyone I knew. I loathe looking plump.'

'But when the baby is born –'

Melissa tilted her chin defiantly. 'Seven months! I'll tell everyone it came at seven months!' Then she groaned in weary exasperation. 'Aaron is like a madman about the baby, but only because he wants an heir for Halewood. He's made up his mind it will be a boy. I don't care either way. I detest children. I don't want this one – and don't you dare say I'll feel differently when it's born, because I shan't. I've detested it since the moment I began to realize I must be pregnant, and it's to blame for all the misery I'm going through, both physical and mental.'

'The baby is innocent!' Delia protested, 'You mustn't blame –'

Melissa interrupted her ferociously. 'It's there! Inside me. A horrible lump that's going to get bigger and bigger! That's its crime. And I have to go through all the dreadful business

208

of childbirth, which I find too frightening to think about.'
She uttered a despairing sigh. 'How I wish babies came
floating down on angels' wings as we were taught in the
nursery and the schoolroom.'

Delia raised her eyebrows. 'Actually I was never taught
that. Being a doctor's daughter I saw too much of the
patients to be brought up in ignorance. The first home I
remember was in the market square above the surgery.'

Melissa made a fastidious little grimace. 'That was the
dreary time before Uncle Charles had any rich patients,
wasn't it? Mama mentioned it once. A poky place by all
accounts.'

'We had happy times there. My mother was alive then.'

'I forgot. So she was.'

'At least neither your mother nor your father had anything
to complain about in the size of Halewood when they visited
you after you let them know you were married. Aunt Rachel
was overwhelmed and Uncle Henry – even though he'd
arrived in a towering rage – had nothing but praise for the
house and approval of the match when they came back to
Sycamore House afterwards.'

Melissa's face tightened. 'Halewood hates me!' she said
quietly. Too quietly as if the very words held menace.

'Why do you say that?'

Melissa clutched Delia's hands. 'It's true. It's true. I'm
made to feel an intruder there. Some force of resentment is
working against me. Halewood despises me and wants me
gone. I know it!'

'But there's no reason for that,' Delia insisted placatingly.

'You don't know! I – ' Melissa clamped her lips together,
biting off what she had been about to say.

'Yes?' Delia prompted with a puzzled frown.

Melissa realized how nearly she had given herself away.
She avoided Delia's gaze, looking aside through the carriage
window where the outskirts of the town had given way to the

209

countryside. 'It's a tormented house,' she said soberly. 'I only wish I'd never had cause to set foot inside it, but don't let's talk about it any more.'

When the carriage passed through the gates it was a deeply emotional moment for Delia. She looked towards Halewood with pain and love. The pale morning sunshine lay like a transparent veil over the old house and the window panes were molten gold. To her surprise the coach-driver did not sweep towards the grand entrance through the inner courtyard, but drew up at the side door that she had usually used in the past.

'I prefer this entrance,' Melissa said in explanation, preparing to get out. 'I never feel able to breathe in the courtyard, and it's always so exceptionally cold there.'

Delia made no attempt to get out after her. 'I'll borrow the carriage to return to town if you don't mind, and I think you should take off those stays and lie down.'

'No! You mustn't go!' Melissa grabbed at her. 'I insist you come in for a cup of tea. Oh, please! You won't see Aaron. He went riding off early this morning.'

And so Delia went with Melissa into the house. It seemed to breathe a welcome over her and she touched an ancient chest in passing, rested her fingers on a vase, brushed a chair, and set her hand on a door jamb. Talking to the house with touch. Letting it know she'd missed it.

She stayed no more than half an hour. When she reached Matthew he spurned her greeting and looked at her with cold and angry eyes from where he lay on his pillows.

'How often do you go to Halewood?' he demanded testily.

'This was the first time since Berenice left.'

'I don't believe you.'

Knowing that the last thing she must do was to get annoyed or argue with him, she answered him with her usual calm mien. 'I've no time to go visiting — and I don't want to. I only went today because Melissa fainted and I didn't think

210

she should go home on her own. Have you forgotten that Aaron and Melissa are married?'

He did not always recall what he had been told, but in this case he did remember. 'That's not to say you and Aaron don't want to go on seeing each other.'

She sighed inwardly. He was in one of his old goading moods and she would have to put up with it. 'I don't want to see him,' she said truthfully, for it was a special anguish she had so far avoided and hoped to continue to avoid, 'and I'm sure he doesn't want to see me. Melissa is going to have a baby. She told me that Aaron thinks of nothing else but Halewood and his future heir.'

Matthew's too brilliant gaze did not leave her. 'If you were having my child,' he said carefully, 'I'd think of you first and the house and baby afterwards. Why did he marry her when he doesn't love her?'

She turned her stricken face from him and rubbed her palms unhappily together in her lap. 'Circumstances brought their marriage about. That's all I can tell you.'

He caught his breath incredulously. 'Don't tell me he got her in the family way!'

The euphemism made Delia shudder. She clapped her hands over her ears to shut out the sound of his laughter. It was the first time he had laughed since the accident and she had never dreamt that the sound she had longed to hear again would be the cause of gouging anew her very deep and personal agony.

Matthew continued to make good progress as the weeks went by. Gradually his headaches grew less violent and as time went on there were longer spells between them. His forgetfulness ebbed and he began to look forward to when he could return to work. His colleagues in the railway company called often to see him, reporting on the progress of the new line, which he was impatient to see and chatted about to Delia. His first walk of any distance was with her to view the

211

new terminus that was being built in the town, a grand edifice of pillared gateways, elaborate brickwork and chimneys, and pie-edged platform roofs supported by iron columns ornamented with pineapples, oak leaves, lilies, strawberries, and chestnuts.

The coming of the railway to the area had brought a new population to flood the town. The railway navigators, or navvies, as everyone called them, were everywhere in their distinctive dress of square-tailed coats of velveteen, canvas shirts, waistcoats that were often of rainbow colours, and moleskin trousers. On their heads they sported at rakish angles white felt hats or sealskin caps. Wild and rough and illiterate, some had moved into lodging houses in the poorer parts of town, but most of them were housed in huts erected in the working area where the land was being gouged by spade and shovel, accompanied by the constant rumble of wagons, barrows, and tip-trucks, the clang of hammer, clink of chisel, and thud of pickaxe. A motley collection of women, whom the navvies had brought with them or had attracted from local sources, cooked for them in the open air, washed their clothes, suffered their battering, and joined them in their drunkenness. Fights and brawls in the town inns had become daily and nightly affairs, although vast quantities of cheap beer formed part of the men's remuneration for their labours, and they frequently worked in a drunken state. Delia had glimpsed some of the huts from a distance, but they were best avoided and fortunately as yet she had had no cause to follow any of the routes out of town that would take her into their vicinity. In all the weeks that had made up the passing months she had done little more than walk or ride between Matthew's home and her own.

It sometimes seemed to her that he no longer talked of anything but the railway. He never discussed when they should set a wedding date, although he did once express concern over the house at Fellfoot, hoping that it was not getting damp. She had been able to reassure him, having given a key to a local woman who lit fires and looked after it, and after that he did not mention it again. She realized he wanted to take up the threads of his life fully before their marriage took place, making sure that he would be the competent breadwinner and once more in the peak of health, and she was thankful that he should feel that way, being in need herself of a chance to recuperate after looking after invalids, first her father and then Matthew, although she had a new responsibility in Melissa, who made continuous demands on her time and patience.

Melissa had become a frequent visitor at Sycamore House. At times she arrived in tears, wallowing in self-pity, at others in an ill temper, and always gloomy. She was ailing in her pregnancy and her earlier nervousness had developed into an almost hysterical fear that she would die in childbirth if not before.

'The house wants me dead,' she moaned on the day she arrived with a bunch of daffodils that she had picked for Delia in the gardens of Halewood. 'It plays its awful tricks on me all the time. I trip on stairs. My bedroom windows fly open at night and the wind sweeps in cold enough to give me pneumonia. I've never dared go through the portrait gallery since the day one of those heavy pictures fell from the wall and missed me by inches.'

There was no questioning Melissa's genuine fear, but Delia refused to accept that the house would deal out physical harm. She knew through her own experience, as well as Berenice's sensitiveness towards its atmosphere, that it was able to communicate through a receptive mind, which could drive a nervous or frightened person towards some perilous action, such as when she herself rushed straight into a half-hidden man-trap, but that was the limit of its powers.

'You must take more care on the stairs,' she advised, 'and hold on to the banister rail. Then you won't trip. Tell the housekeeper that you want new catches fitted on your windows – I expect the old ones are worn. You can also give orders for a handyman to check all the hangings of the paintings and looking-glasses throughout the house, because I don't suppose they've been seen to for years.'

'You think I'm letting my imagination run away with me,' Melissa cried, clutching at Delia's hand. 'But I'm not! You must be with me when the baby is born, otherwise I'll be at. Halewood's mercy. The baby and I will have little chance of survival.'

'Now that is nonsense,' Delia said firmly. 'Halewood has done no harm to any brought-to-bed mother or newly-born child in all its history. I know, because I've read right through three huge volumes about the house that Aaron lent to Papa. Entirely natural causes have been responsible for tragedies of childbirth that have inevitably occurred in the past, and none of it need worry you. You'll be having the best medical attention. Be sensible! The house will welcome an heir.'

'But this baby isn't – ' Melissa bit deep into her lower lip until it showed white, her eyes enormous and tragic and brimming with tears.

Delia felt all colour drain from her face, some sixth sense telling her what Melissa had been about to blurt out, and she grabbed her by the shoulders. 'Go on! Finish what you were about to say!'

Melissa swallowed, and she spoke faintly. 'It isn't a true Hart. Aaron isn't the father.'

Delia shook her wildly. 'Then who is?'

'Richard Dibley.'

'How can you be sure?'

'For the simple reason that Aaron never touched me. I only pretended he had. You see, Richard never knew I was pregnant. I'd discovered my condition by the time of our planned elopement. That was why it was a double shock

214

when he jilted me. Oh, Delia. I had to save my skin some-how! Please understand. Aaron was an obvious choice.'

Anger blazed within Delia. A searing, white-hot anger such as she had never known before. She struck Melissa hard across the face and sprang to her feet from the sofa where they had been sitting. 'You despicable little cheat!'

'Don't turn from me!' Melissa became frantic, falling to her knees at Delia's feet and clutching at her skirts in the same childish way as once before when she had appealed to her out of misery. 'I had to do it! Papa would have turned me out. I was desperate!'

The whole story came tumbling from her. When she dis-closed how she had stolen the drug Delia stared down at her in horror. 'You could have killed him!'

'I know that now. I really thought he was going to die. I cried, "Don't die! Don't die" to him over and over again!'

Delia took a step back from her, dragging her skirts free. 'Yet you didn't summon help!'

'I was panic-stricken! I couldn't think!' Melissa shuffled forward on her knees. 'I'm not like you. You're practical and level-headed and capable. I'm none of those things. For mercy's sake, don't desert me now or Halewood will murder me for my deceit. Please! Oh, please!'

She collapsed in a snivelling huddle. Pity and anger and contempt blended together in Delia as she looked down at her, but also came the thought that Melissa could well harm herself and her baby through terror of Halewood if no help-ing hand was held out to her.

'What of Aaron?' she asked coldly. 'Do you intend to confess to him as you have to me?'

Melissa raised a startled, piteous face. 'I can't! I daren't! I never meant to tell you, but somehow it slipped out and I'm not sorry it did, because you can't repeat anything I've told you to anybody. It's all part of the secret about Richard, which you promised to keep silent about. But now you know why I need you to protect me from Halewood.'

Delia stooped to help the girl to her feet. 'Why do you imagine I have special powers?' she enquired uncompromisingly.

'Because you love the house! We all know that. I've said many times I want you to be there when the baby is born. Now I've told you the reason you won't desert me, will you? Say you won't!'

'I won't desert you,' Delia said in the same cool tones. She remained straight-backed and unbending while Melissa hugged her gratefully, for she was thinking with compassion of Aaron, her heart aching for him.

She had seen him only twice since it had all ended between them, but neither time had he seen her. Once he had been engaged in conversation with two other gentlemen on the steps of the Red Lion Hotel and she had been quick to lose herself among the shoppers in the crowded market, and the second time had been shortly after Matthew had returned to work in an advisory capacity, giving her time to herself again, and Aaron had ridden by on a glossy black mare, not knowing she had spotted him through the lace curtains of the dressmaker's establishment, and she had scattered pins from her half-fitted gown to dart across and watch him out of sight.

He had called on her father any number of times, but always during the day when she had been with Matthew, and recently he must have heard that Matthew was back at work, for he never came without sending a messenger to ask if it would be convenient, which gave her the chance to be out of his way if she wished it. And she did.

From the start she had known as he had that it was best that they should avoid each other's company. People she met, assuming she was in continued close communication with him since he had stayed in her home, questioned her inquisitively, much as they had done about Berenice in the past, wanting to know why the new Master of Halewood and his wife had not only done no entertaining yet, but had politely declined all invitations except those he accepted on his own to entirely male gatherings, for dinner, cards, or billiards. All knew that Melissa was expecting a baby, for no secret had been made of that, and those among the girls with whom she was acquainted, married or single, who had looked forward to gossipy sessions over the Halewood teacups, were huffy when she was not at home when they called. Servants' gossip had leaked out and they were curious to know if the haughty Melissa, whom few had really liked, was further gone in her time than she should be, for it opened up the most intriguing speculation about what had been going on beforehand. Delia parried their probing questions as adroitly as she had parried all others in the past, not caring when they became disgruntled and at times almost rude.

The final stages in the completion of the railway branch line coincided with the remaining weeks of Melissa's pregnancy. The last balustrades and green-painted seats and marble-topped refreshment counters were being set in place in Penghyll terminus. There was to be a grand opening and Matthew and Delia were to be among the special guests invited to enjoy a train ride to the first halt and back in the company of railway directors, local dignitaries and their wives, and other people of importance.

He drove her along part of the route when he went to check on some final work being carried out at a certain point. He was in high good humour. Gradually he had reinstated himself with the railway company and that morning he had been informed of another, much more important line that was to be laid down, for which he was to be entirely responsible.

'It's more than I'd dared hope for,' he confided cheerfully. 'One of my chief worries during that long convalescence was

217

that I'd be forgotten by the people who matter and stepped over by fellows with less qualified experience than myself. My! Isn't it a grand day!' He grinned appreciatively up at the sun.

It was indeed a grand day. The soft May sunshine was warm in their faces and was held as though reflected in the golden tip of celandine, cowslip, and dandelion which showed amid the meadow-grass. The earth about the track itself lay raw and open, a running scar that vanished through a tunnel in the distance and was lost amid the hills beyond. The lane they were following led on to Fellfoot and he had suggested they go on there and take a look at Wistaria Lodge.

'It's time now to forget all that has happened over the past months,' he had said. 'We must settle our wedding plans.'

It was near the tunnel that he drew up. Saying he would not be long, he went clambering down the embankment to where a gang of navvies was at work. Waiting for him in the gig she wondered how she would feel re-entering the house with him where once she had looked to a contented future as his wife, never dreaming that a passionate love such as she had never imagined possible was to twist and turn her life about, leaving her bereft and with a loneliness of spirit that nothing could ever abate.

The screeching of quarrelling made her turn her head. Away on the opposite side of the track were some of the mud and brick shanties that housed the navvies and she could see a couple of women almost coming to blows over a clothes-line strung between two of the ramshackle buildings. The shanties presented a sorry sight, the litter of the past months strewn about, and one was a burnt-out shell where a drunken brawl among the men sharing the hut had led to a fire in which several of them had lost their lives. Not only had the navvies made a nuisance of themselves on drinking randies in Penghyll, but their fighting with each other had led to the inflicting of terrible injuries and even to murder. Matthew had told her that the men had taken a dislike to the Penghyll line, for it had taken its toll in a record number of accidents and once there had been a near-riot when part of the tunnel being excavated had caved in and buried three men.

'Now we can go on.' Matthew had returned and he sprang back up into the seat beside her and took the reins. 'It's a good thing the line is almost ready. I'm not sorry I've had nothing much to do with it.'

'More trouble?' she enquired.

'It's the mood of the navvies. They've put in a claim for a compensation bonus and they'll never get it. They must stick to their original work contracts and there's an end to it.'

She could tell his earlier good humour had begun to spiral down. At first she assumed it was due to the troubles he had mentioned, but gradually as they came to Fellfoot and turned into the lane where Wistaria Lodge lay she realized it was more than that. It was she who was first down from the gig to go through the gate and he followed on slower footsteps to cast his gaze over the house as if it no longer appealed to him in any way. Yet its charm had increased since it had been painted and the flower-beds were full of colour around a lawn as neat as a newly-ironed green silk handkerchief. The gardener had done his work well.

Inside the house Matthew wandered a little aimlessly from room to room while she took a look at the furniture being protected by dust-sheets to make sure there was no bloom of damp. He came back into the dark-beamed living-room where she was and made a helpless, half-angry gesture with his hands.

'Maybe we shouldn't start our married life in this place.' He looked strained and not far from despair. 'We could sell it easily enough and buy something else outside Manchester. It would suit me to be nearer the centre of things.

She knew what lay behind it all. He was making a final

effort to convince himself and her that a new beginning amid new surroundings with nothing of the past tagging on to them would enable them to pick up the threads again as if all that had happened between them had never been. The time had come at last for her to sever cleanly the worn-out bond that held them. Until now he had refused to acknowledge even to himself that nothing could be the same again, but his words had given him away.

'Do you really think it would make any difference?' she challenged gently.

He ran his fingers through his hair and slumped down on a window-seat. 'I know it wouldn't,' he said simply. 'You stopped loving me long ago.'

She went and sat beside him. 'I never stopped loving you in the way I've always loved you, but it was never enough for marriage. I was wrong to imagine it could be. The blame is entirely mine.'

'No. I should have known. I *did* know when I saw the expression on your face at the steps of the Assembly Rooms when you implored me not go in to the auction. All you felt for Aaron Hart was in your eyes. Afterwards I told myself I'd imagined it. It had all happened in the heat of the moment. When I heard he had married Melissa I truly believed for a while that I'd been mistaken about the whole thing. But it's no good. It's all a sham. No matter whether you still care for Aaron Hart or not, you've resigned yourself to life without him, I know that, but what's left isn't enough for either of us. We can't build a marriage on ruins. Other people might be able to, but we can't.' He put an arm about her shoulder and hugged her to him, bringing her head to rest against his neck. 'We've meant too much to each other.'

They sat in silence there together, not moving, drawing comfort from each other's nearness as they had done so often in the past. When at last they stirred he put a hand against her cheek.

'If ever you should have a change of heart –' he began.

She shook her head and took his hand in both of hers to press a kiss against his knuckles. 'It's over. We have friendship left. That will be just as it's always been. Let's be thankful that without any bitterness or animosity we have salvaged that which has brought so much joy to our lives.'

'Dear Deli,' he said, using his first childhood name for her.

She looked down and drew the pearl and ruby ring from her finger to place it in the palm of his hand. It was done. Their betrothment was at an end.

They talked quietly on the way back to Penghyll. He said he would be leaving at the end of the week. She asked what time she should be ready for the grand opening of the branch line, for neither saw any reason to cancel the outing together. She left the choice of which agent was to sell the house to him, but it was decided she should dispose of the furniture. It all seemed very simple and straightforward. Only when he left her at the gate did the full impact of it all seem to hit him. He looked completely stricken and turned from her without another word.

The grand opening of the railway brought people from miles around crowding into Penghyll from the early hours of the morning. Extra stalls were set up in the market square and trade was brisk from first light. Hundreds of navvies, many of whom had been on an all-night randy, roistered drunkenly among the ordinary sightseers, many having returned from new working sites to join in the celebrations and to lend their support to a fiery show of shouted compensation demands that broke out amid scuffles here and there. In the midst of banners and bunting and with whistle and steam, the high-funnelled, red-painted locomotive chuffed slowly out of the terminus on its maiden run, its five first-class carriages with the plump, upholstered seats full of the invited passengers. One third-class carriage had been coupled up next to the guard's van, more to display the new comfort provided for the humbler traveller in the wider bench seats and adequate roofing to keep out rain and engine sparks than to give a ride to the minor railway officials and town clerks who had taken their places in it.

It was the first time Delia had been on a train and she enjoyed the ride tremendously, thrilled at the sensation of being carried along at more than twenty miles an hour. Matthew, who had secured her a window-seat with her back to the engine to avoid the danger of any soot or cinders flying into her eyes, leant forward from where he sat opposite her to tell her points of interest and to answer questions she put to him.

At the halt, everyone got out as if they had been in the train all day instead of a distance of no more than ten miles and refreshment awaited them in glasses of lemonade under a canopy of bunting, where they were watched by more spectators who had come from the neighbouring farms to stare both at the hissing locomotive and the fortunate passengers.

That evening there was a civil dinner attended by all those who had been on the train and other local personages. To Delia's delight her father felt able to attend the dinner, but she thought it best to take him home when the speeches were over and before the entertainment. Matthew had collected them and he escorted them home again in his own carriage, being concerned for their safety, for there had been a great deal of trouble with the navvies all day and in spite of the extra police on duty, they were still surging about the town, singing and shouting, smashing windows, and picking fights with innocent passers-by and with each other.

'Thank you for the wonderful time I've had today,' Delia said when Matthew had helped her father to the doorstep. 'Are you sure you won't come in?'

He shook his head. 'I'm leaving for Manchester early tomorrow morning and I've still some packing to do.' He gave her a serious little smile. 'Good-bye, Delia.'

'Good-bye, Matthew.'

Indoors her father was already going slowly upstairs to bed. Nurse Baker had left long since, but her sister, Mrs Wallace, had more than filled her place, combining the duties of housekeeper and part-time nurse in a way that made Dr Gilmore feel independent while she unobtrusively watched over him to make sure that all was well. She was at his side on the stairs now, a tray with his medicines, pills, and night-cap of hot milk in her hand, but in reality she was there to make sure he did not totter or fall.

In her own room Delia had removed her ear-rings and the cameo on its black ribbon from about her throat when there came a thunderous knocking on the door combined with a wild jingling of the bell. She swept out on to the landing, and looking down from where she stood by the balustrade she saw Aaron come rushing in when Ellen cautiously opened the door.

He saw her at once. 'Please come! Just as you are. Melissa is crying out for you.'

She guessed immediately the reason why she was needed. 'Is the midwife with her?' she asked quickly.

'Yes. And Dr Pomfret is on his way, but it's been the devil's own task to get a message through to anyone. Those crazy navvies are everywhere, turning over vehicles and blocking the roads. I sent transport for you three hours ago, but the coachman and groom were pulled from it and beaten up, the horses cut loose, and the carriage upturned into the river. I came for you myself as soon as a farmhand brought word to Halewood of what had taken place.'

'I'll get my cloak!'

She snatched it up from where it still lay on a bedroom chair and rushed downstairs, telling Ellen to let her father and Mrs Wallace know where she had goen. Then she was out into the night with Aaron, who had brought a phaeton with four horses, which stood steaming in the moonlight.

'Did you meet any of the navvies on the road?' she asked as they went bowling down the drive and out into the avenue.

'Only a few stragglers, because I came into Penghyll near the old church, avoiding the market square and the centre of town. We'll leave by the same route.' He dived into his pocket and put a hard metal object into her hands. 'Here. Take this. Just in case there's any real trouble and I have my work cut out handling the horses.'

It was a gentleman's pocket pistol such as her father had carried in the days he had attended the poor and destitute in the Liverpool slums where it was not safe for any reasonably dressed person to walk alone and which he had still carried when he had gone far afield on his own. She had never fired a pistol, but she knew the feel of holding a weapon through handling a pair of antique duelling pistols which were kept in the study.

'I hope I don't have to use it,' she said unhappily.

'Showing it should be enough,' he assured her, 'and if the worst comes to the worst fire into the air.'

The phaeton went rattling down the narrow side streets, the wheels bouncing on the cobbles, but when the church loomed dark against the starry sky and the lane they were making for was no more than two hundred yards from them a mob of navvies with flaring torches came swarming round the corner. At the sight of the approaching carriage a great roar went up and they began to run to meet it, waving staves and pieces of fencing. A bottle came rippling through the air with an opal gleam and it struck one of the leading horses, which shied and wheeled, frightening and confusing the other three.

'Hold on!' Aaron instructed grimly. 'We're going through!'

The whip cracked over the horses' heads and they thundered forward. Ahead the navvies scattered out of their direct path, but the boldest hurled themselves at the bridles and the shafts, the dragging of their burly weight having an immediate effect on the nervous animals, and other willing hands came forward to help. Aaron half-rose in his seat and turned his whip on the navvies, causing two or three to drop away with howls of pain. Delia felt a jerking hold on her skirt and screamed, a red-bearded navvy having grabbed at her as he clung to the side of the phaeton. The whip flashed out across her and there was the rip of taffeta as the man fell back with a yell, but another brutal-faced navvy had taken his place, his huge ham fist locked about her ankle. With a powerful jerk he would have brought her crashing down from the seat if she had not been clinging to the back of it, and she screamed again.

'Fire!' Aaron roared at her.

Even as she made a move to obey him she was snatched at again, and this time her grasp on the seat-back was weakened, for she had removed the hook of her elbow to prepare to fire. Down to the floor of the phaeton she tumbled in a sea of taffeta and hoops and petticoats, the pistol jerking out of her grasp as her wrist suffered a painful blow. Again the whip lashed for her protection, striking away those tearing at her skirts, and with a sob she saw the pistol sliding towards Aaron's foot. He must have realized what it was, for instinctively he raised his heel and clamped it down again on the weapon to hold it fast. With a sob she reached for it, giving his ankle a little thrust as a signal for him to release it, and with a trembling hand she aimed for the stars.

The deafening report had the desired effect. Scared and unnerved, the navvies dropped their hold on the phaeton, released the dragging grasp on the harnesses of the wild-eyed horses, and gave vent with the foulest curses while they hurled the bludgeons that they carried. Pieces of fencing, blocks of wood, broken flagons, rocks and stones and lumps of earth all crashed and thumped and thudded against the hood of the phaeton and back of it, but pursuit was impossible and the road ahead was open to escape. The noisy clatter of the horses' racing hooves on the cobbles changed to a rhythmic thud on the hard mud of the lane, and the outskirts of the town soon began to fall away behind.

'Did the wretches do you any harm?' Aaron enquired anxiously, helping her regain the seat beside him.

'No,' she answered breathlessly, giving a shaky little laugh. 'I've suffered a bruise or two and my gown is torn, but nothing more. What of you?'

'I'm all right. What a mob! Had the thick-headed authorities listened to the genuine grievance that some of the unfortunate injured presented to them – and done something about it – all this rioting in the town tonight would never had happened. Instead the trouble-makers and all those ready enough to fight have taken up the cause with drink and violence and intimidation, and no good can come of that either.'

They reached the open countryside and he eased the pressure on the horses, although he kept them at the fastest pace possible for safety along the rutted lane.

'What a way to bring you to Halewood,' he remarked wryly. 'After months of not catching as much as a glimpse of you I snatch you from your home and bundle you through mob-infested streets to enable you to carry out an enforced promise to Melissa, who swears she'll not survive the malevolence of Halewood without your protection.'

'I'm glad you fetched me. If my being with her gives her peace of mind, that isn't much for me to do for my own kin. She is my cousin after all. Unfortunately she is sadly afraid of childbirth and she has added her own terror of Halewood to it. Are you harbouring some objection to my being there?'

He shrugged. 'None at all. Indeed, if you're to be the talisman that Melissa confidently expects you to be I can look forward to the arrival of a strong and healthy son.'

She glanced out of the corner of her eye at him. His profile was illumined by the glow of the phaeton's lamps. 'Why have you made up your mind that it will be a boy?'

He turned his face towards her, and she saw clearly the sad and bitter look in his eyes. 'It has to be,' he said grimly. 'It's my only chance of a legitimate heir.'

When they arrived at Halewood she was surprised that he did not take her to Berenice's former apartments, which by tradition were always occupied by the mistresses of Halewood. Instead, he took her to the lilac suite and escorted her into the bedroom where Melissa lay tossing on the draped four-poster bed, alternately sobbing and shrieking. Dr Pomfret had not arrived and the midwife looked annoyed and harrassed. When Melissa saw Delia she struggled up against the pillows and gave a long, appealing cry.

'I thought you'd never get here! Oh, Delia! Don't let me die! Don't let me die!'

Delia went to her and smoothed her tumbled hair back from her pain-shadowed eyes. 'You're not going to die,' she said calmly. 'Everything will be fine. Dr Pomfret will soon arrive, and if he should be delayed we have the most capable midwife with us who knows exactly what to do.'

The bedroom door closed. Aaron had gone. Delia thought it was to find out if the doctor's carriage could be seen coming up the drive.

But Dr Pomfret did not come that night, being kept busy with casualties in the town, several of them cases of life and death. After a hard and difficult labour Melissa gave birth to a puny little girl with pale yellow hair.

'I don't want to see it!' she cried with distaste, turning her face away when the midwife would have shown her the baby wrapped in a shawl and ready to place in her arms. 'Take it away. Put it in the nursery. Get a wet-nurse. Never bring the wretched creature near me again.'

The midwife clamped her lips together in shock and disapproval. Holding the baby to her she stalked from the room in the direction of the nursery, which was at the far end of the wing.

Melissa lifted her head from the pillows and glared at Delia, who stood at the foot of the bed. 'You make sure the wretched woman doesn't disobey me, or I won't be responsible for my actions towards that baby!' Her head fell back again. 'Oh, God! What I suffered! Never again. No, never again!' Delia's silence acted like a barb to her and once more she raised her head, keeping a need to sleep at bay a little longer, her lips parting in a vindictive grimace. 'What are you standing there for? Go and tell your beloved Aaron that he has a daughter!'

Delia found him in a chair in the library, one long leg resting on a footstool before the ashes of a fire on the hearth. She could tell he had not slept. He did not look towards her when she entered, but he knew it was her. With a single listless movement of his hand he indicated that she should sit down.

She sank down in a cushioned chair and leaned back in exhaustion, her wrists hanging limply over the ends of the wooden arms. A few untidy wisps of hair hung down by her cheeks and the torn fold of her wide skirt draped on the floor.

'Melissa has come through the birth remarkably well,' she said, wondering why he had not asked her at once about the baby. 'She was about to go to sleep when I left her.'

He made no comment.

'It's a girl,' she said.

He showed no surprise or disappointment. 'It doesn't matter either way,' he said heavily. 'The child isn't mine.'

Delia gasped. 'How do you know?' she asked.

'It was something Melissa cried out when you arrived last night that gave it away. It was as if a door had been flung wide for me. I knew then that it had been more than an empty stomach and a few glasses of claret, however potent, that had induced that state of intoxication I fell into on the night she and I were alone together. She must have obtained some tasteless potion from your father's dispensary and added it to the decanter, her plan laid with truly devilish cunning, although how she knew which drug to select I've no idea. If she picked at random I'm fortunate to be alive!'

'You had an overdose of sleeping draught that my father had prescribed for her on one occasion.'

He gave her a hard, sharp glance. 'When did you discover that?'

'She confessed to me after you'd married her and it was far too late to change anything. I couldn't tell you then, Aaron.'

He gave her a weary half-smile. 'Don't worry. I understand. You were in an intolerable positon. I'll not ask you who fathered her child. Melissa herself shall tell me.' Thoughtfully he rubbed his chin, which rasped unshaven against his fingers, his gaze going back unseeingly to the ashes. 'When I heard her cry out to you not to let her die I recalled in a flash her calling to me in a similar way. "Don't die! she had begged many times over like a monotonous prayer. I remember believing I was about to die, never having felt more ill in my life. There are other small points, too. Mere snatches. Nothing very definite, but enough to know without a shadow of doubt that Melissa caught me in a trap of lies and deceit that would never have worked if I'd had my mind less on the possibility of losing Halewood and more on the suspicious and uncharacteristic kindness she was showing me.' He raised his foot and kicked away the stool almost in belated self-impatience at his folly.

'You'd had a long and exhausting day,' she reminded him.

He rolled his head round to look at her again. 'Do you remember my telling you once that I didn't look for happiness in the possession of Halewood? At the time I'd thought to find a rich compensation in a loving union. I'd even hoped such a special love as ours would be strong enough to break the curse that falls on every Hart who becomes master of Halewood. What a crazy thought that was! The curse is as dark and old as Time.' He gave the deepest of sighs. 'There's no breaking it. I know that now.'

She had been listening in love and sorrow. She believed, as he had done, that if she had come to Halewood as his bride their passion for each other would have been strong enough to conquer that ancient curse and destroy it. But it had laid hold on him as soon as he became earmarked as the house's next master. They had been defeated from the start.

Yet she could not hate Halewood for parting them, because never once had she felt there was anything evil or malevolent in the stones and mortar of the beautiful old house itself. It was held as firmly in the grip of the curse as all the unfortunate Harts who had ever lived in it. Then from whence came the tainting? Where lay the source if not in the house itself? Could it be from the land on which Halewood stood? But that was surely an entirely fanciful idea! Nevertheless it was one to give some thought to later on.

She stood up. 'I'd like to go home now. I'll come back later in the day and see Melissa. She's in good hands. There's nothing more I can do.'

'I thank you for coming.' He had risen to walk to the library door with her, but his attention had been caught by her left hand and he raised it, looking gravely and questioningly from her bare third finger to her strained and tired face. 'Is it ended then?'

'Yes,' she said quietly. 'It's over.'

She withdrew her fingers and moved away. He reached in front of her to open the door, but kept his hand on the knob without turning it. Against her will she lifted her head slightly and their eyes met and held. His gaze on her was dark and sad.

'I'll not be here when you return later. I made up my mind during the night to go away for a while. I've seen nothing of the rest of Europe and this seems the right time to take a vacation.'

She nodded wordlessly. It was as well. Perhaps when he returned he would find himself able to forgive Melissa.

Still he did not open the door. 'There's a certain favour I'd like to ask of you.'

'What is it?'

'I've no idea yet what Melissa will decide to do. It was agreed between us that if she wished to leave me after the baby was born she was free to go, but I was to keep the child. It's possible that she will still want me to hold to this arrangement. I have nothing against the unfortunate infant. It is a Hart by name if not by lineage. If Melissa leaves her here and I'm still abroad, will you visit Halewood sometimes and make sure that the nurse is suitable and the little girl well treated?'

'I'll do that gladly,' she said, touched by his generosity of spirit. He opened the door for her. 'Farewell, Aaron.'

He did not answer her, all the pain of parting in his face. It echoed her own torment. She hurried from him. The morning sun shone on her bedraggled evening finery and threw the shadow of her hoop-skirted figure across the hall floor. He could still see it when she had gone from his sight. Then even her shadow was there no more.

Melissa stayed exactly a month at Halewood after the birth of her baby. Not knowing when Aaron would return, his travel plans having been fluid, she wanted to be gone and not meet him again. She had made up her mind to reside in Paris. With her untouched inheritance and the adequate allowance she was to receive from Aaron, who had kept his word on their bargain in spite of discovering the truth, she would be able to live comfortably. It also put the Channel between herself and her parents, whom she had not invited to the christening, a private affair with Delia and Dr Gilmore standing as godparents, and she had composed a tale to

231

relate in her new surroundings of Aaron's unspeakable cruelty that had forced her to leave him and her child, which she considered would give her a highly romantic aura in the eyes of any of her London acquaintances who chose to visit her in Paris as well as to all the new people she would meet.

She came down the great staircase of Halewood for the last time, wearing a striped travelling costume, violets trimming her bonnet. Delia, waiting to say good-bye, wondered how she could leave so blithely, not even going along to the nursery to take a final look at the child whom she would probably never see again. Emma was the infant's name. It had been Delia's choice, for Melissa would come to no decision, proclaiming a complete lack of interest right to the door of the church on the day of the baptism.

'Well, I don't think I've forgotten anything.' Melissa gave a cursory glance towards the trunks and hat-boxes being carried out to the waiting transport by a small army of servants. 'I've taken nothing that belongs to Halewood, needless to say. I want no reminders of this hateful house! If ever you're in Paris come and visit me. I'd like to hear from you if you feel like writing to me, but never mention Halewood to me, or anyone in it. I've shaken its dust from my skirt-hems for ever!'

She went sweeping out through the great porch. Defiantly she was leaving by the grand entrance and her carriage waited at the foot of the wide steps to transport her to Penghyll railway terminus where she was to set off by train on the long journey to her destination in France. Before getting into the carriage she looked about her for the last time at the inner courtyard and gave a merry little laugh that rang with triumph. She had used the house for her own ends and won through. Its curse had failed to touch her. She was free!

The groom shut the door of the carriage as she seated herself. Her grey-gloved hand gave a little wave to Delia standing in the shadow of the porch. With a jingle of harness and clop of hooves she was carried away from Halewood and down the winding drive to the gates. Seven miles away in the darkness of the tunnel on the Penghyll branch line several drunken navvies with an unappeased compensation grudge against the railway company were dragging a heavy tree-trunk on to the tracks.

Chapter Twelve

On the gallery in the library at Halewood Delia moved the ladder along and climbed up again to search among the books on the top shelf. Below her on a table were several old and dusty volumes in which she had inserted slips of paper for reference, beside them her own notes written in a neat, close hand.

'Ah!' She had found another book to help her in her research. It was a wordy historical account of the Viking invasions of north-west England and she sat down on top of the ladder to glance through it eagerly.

Three months had passed since Melissa and twenty other people had been killed in the appalling train crash that had occurred in the branch line tunnel. Aaron's whereabouts had not been known and by the time he was contacted in Milan the funeral was over, and Delia had written to him that it was pointless to cut short his travels and return. He had been grateful for her handling of everything for him, but she had had Mr Radleigh to turn to for advice and felt she had done little enough in her own way.

The bright spot in Delia's life was Emma, and she had come to love her dearly. She was a plain baby with none of her mother's pretty features, but she had an engaging smile and a gurgling laugh, which enchanted Delia, who would pick her up and cuddle her whenever opportunity allowed. The nurse in charge of her had strict rules for the nursery, but there were times when Delia waived them aside to give Emma extra hours of loving warmth and contact, which she felt took priority over feeding and sleeping by the clock.

When not with Emma she was always in the library. Instead of occasional visits to Halewood as Aaron had visualized to check that all was well, Delia came daily. It had been a few chance remarks from her father that had started her researching extensively into the origins of the Halewood curse. He had made them the day after Melissa's funeral.

'She's not the only mistress of Halewood to meet death tragically. The first wife of Raoul Hart, who built the house, was crushed by some falling masonry before it was even completed, as you will remember from reading those three volumes of Halewood's history that Mr Hart loaned me. I often think it's no wonder that sorrow and tragedy haunt that house. It should never have been built on top of Howling Hill in the first place.'

'Why not?' she had enquired curiously.

'For the simple reason that Heaven alone knows what violence was done in earlier centuries for possession of the most strategic spot in the whole of this district. From it the view is open as far as the eye can see. Whoever held Howling Hill could claim mastery over all the surrounding countryside, which must have grown good crops with the right husbandry even in primitive times.'

'That surely means you share my belief that it's not the house itself that is responsible for all the sorrow that has befallen the Hart family there,' she had pursued eagerly, her face alight. 'I've considered the possibility that in some strange way the curse might be centred in the very ground on which Halewood stands. That's your opinion too, is it?'

He had held up a hand, smiling. 'Now don't jump to conclusions. I'm not saying I believe anything. But I have a healthy respect for the effect of the power of suggestion on the mind. If generations of Harts and their nameless ancestors before them have passed down the superstitious fear that whoever owns the house – or in earlier times whatever primitive dwelling places, fortified and later unfortified, that stood on that site in the past – it is bound to have created a tendency towards depression, anxiety, and other dark moods of the mind, which in turn will affect the lives of all concerned. Inevitably, in many cases, with tragic or disastrous results.'

'Do you mean that it was the precarious position of the chieftain or leader – first one and then another slain in succession as rival bands fought for possession of the hilltop – that gave rise to the original superstition that ill luck always ruled the one who held Howling Hill?'

He had nodded. 'In all the reading I have done on folklore in Lancashire and other parts of Britain I have always attempted to sift out the possible source of any legend that has particularly interested me. The Halewood curse is one of them for which I have a perfectly logical explanation. Had the house been built on any other site there would have been no old, dark tales lingering on to throw a shadow over all who lived in it. It only needed that unfortunate, fatal accident to Raoul Hart's wife, which was doubtless caused by some workman's carelessness on the scaffolding, to stir up local memories of the ill-fated hill and talk of other domestic tragedies remembered from the dwelling that was being replaced by Halewood. The seal would be set on the curse. Those old beliefs linger yet.'

The discussion had continued. The next morning she had begun her work in the library, believing that her father's theory was the solid basis on which to base her investigations, but not wholly accepting that it was an explanation to cover everything. She realized with interest that she was not the first one to have set about an investigation into the past, although in an entirely different way. Alice Hart, who had gone to the stake as a witch, had '*by wicked and diverse means summoned up a she-devil out of Howleing Hill and did converse with the same, which name was Gyda and deade these many years.*' But

236

that had been only one of the numerous crimes listed against Alice by the witch-finder who had brought her to justice, and although Delia read a full account of her trial there was no further mention of the unknown Gyda. Delia had careful notes, but she was forced to leave that section of Halewood's chronicles for lack of more information.

Nevertheless, there remained at the back of her mind the conviction that when Alice had not been casting spells over cattle and decocting magic potions and behaving in an unseemly manner with a local coven she had been just as interested in the old curse and had sought to find out about it through weird, primeval methods of her own.

Delia looked up from the book she was scanning through. A visitor must have called. It did happen sometimes that somebody came to see Aaron, not knowing he was still absent. She could hear voices in the hall. A certain vibration of excitement reached her and her heart leapt and pounded. Aaron was home!

She darted down from the ladder, hastily patted a stray wisp of hair into place, smoothed down the folds of her skirt, and went quickly into the hall to meet him. He was not alone.

With his back towards her he was saying something about the grand staircase to the young lady and two gentlemen of about his own age who were with him. By their accents she could tell they were fellow countrymen and by the amount of travel-labelled baggage being brought in by the servants it looked as though they had come to stay for a while. The young lady, whom Aaron had addressed as Isobel, noticed Delia first and cast an enquiring glance in her direction. She was a tall, slim girl with a bright, intelligent face, her hair thick and dark beneath a becoming leghorn hat.

Aaron must have guessed immediately at whom she looked. Delia saw his shoulders straighten slightly, almost as if he steeled himself, and after a second or two of apparent hesitation he turned round slowly towards her. He had deliberately composed his face against any revelation of expression, for it gave nothing away, and his eyes had narrowed to bring the thick black lashes mingling together.

'Welcome home,' she said faintly. Disappointment hacked at her. She had expected him to be subdued by returning a widower to Halewood. No man of compassion such as she knew him to be could have remained indifferent to the tragic end of Melissa, no matter that she had played him false. But she had thought when they met again to see her own deep and quiet joy in their reunion reflected in his face. Instead there was nothing to be fathomed in his features that she loved, nothing to embrace her in that mere glint of guarded eye.

'Thank you, Delia.' He spoke quite formally. 'I've brought three compatriots of mine home to show them the beauty of the Lancashire countryside. They were under the impression that it was all mills and coal-mines. Allow me to present Miss Isobel Mitchell, her brother, Mr Theodore Mitchell, and an old schoolfriend of mine, Mr Oscar Wasilewski.'

The introductions over, they converged into one of the drawing-rooms, Isobel admiring all she saw. Delia soon heard that Aaron had run into Oscar in Venice and through him he had met the Mitchells, after which the four of them had travelled on together. It did not take Delia long to see that Isobel was much attracted to Aaron and sought to hold his attention.

'Halewood is everything you promised me it would be,' she said to him in her deep attractive voice, her eyes sparkling.

'I'm gratified to know I've not disappointed you,' he replied easily.

Refreshment was served. Afterwards the guests were shown to their rooms and Delia and Aaron were left alone together. He opened and glanced through some of the letters that had been stacked up for his return while she informed him on various matters, which he questioned her about at the same time. When she talked fondly of Emma, he put the letters aside and shoved his hands into his pockets, going across to stand and look out of the window at the spread of lawn and garden, the distant woods, and the fair hills beyond.

'How often have you been coming to Halewood to see the child?' he asked.

'Every day, but also I – '

'I'm afraid it can't continue.'

She thought she had not heard aright. 'What do you mean?'

He continued to gaze out at the view. 'It's not that I don't want you to take an interest in Melissa's daughter. It's natural and right that you should, being related through the mother to the child, and I appreciate all you've done. But it's more than that, Delia.' Now he did turn to face her, clearly and directly, his features steeled into a mask she could not read. 'I wouldn't willingly hurt you in any way. I'd give my life first before letting that happen if there were any choice, but I have to tell you. I reached a decision while I was away. We must no longer see each other except – considering that we live in the same district – when circumstances make it impossible to avoid a meeting.'

'There's someone else!' she gasped, pale-lipped, not knowing how to endure what he said.

His gaze did not falter. 'There's no one else.'

'You're lying to me!' she cried accusingly. An unbearable agony of spirit consumed her and found an outlet in anger. 'It's Isobel! You've met her and brought her home to Halewood and you don't dare to tell me. You're taking the coward's way. Pretending! Shamming! Making me a fool! I saw how she looked at you! She's ready to fall at your feet. But perhaps she's already done so. Venice is a romantic place for lovers, I'm told.'

'Delia!' He thundered her name at her, but there was no stopping her tirade. She knew she had lost him. It had been there in the inexorable tone of his voice. There was no going back. All the longing and loving, the yearning and the adoring and the endless heartache broke through in an undammed flood, her helpless fury a raft to which she clung for survival.

'You care nothing for me! You don't know what it is to love anything but Halewood! I feel sorry for Isobel or anyone else you marry. She'll take second place all her life. And as for myself I agree with you. We must no longer see each other. My only regret is that we ever met!'

She spun about and ran blindly from him back to the library. There she shot all her things from the table into the woven bag that was hers. Then throwing her shawl about her shoulders she ran from the house. From the driver's seat of her wagonette she whipped up the horse and a great gust of wind swept up the hillside as if to beat her back into the house, tearing at her hair and snatching her shawl from her to send it flying away. She did not as much as glance in its direction. She set her chin into the wind and drove at top speed down the hill and out through the gates. At the drawing-room window Aaron watched her go. He stood with hands clenched, for it was taking all his will-power not to follow her and bring her back.

It was not until she found it difficult to see ahead that she realized tears were coursing down her face, but the horse knew the way home and she let him have his head. Arriving at Sycamore House she hurled herself indoors and up to her room. Behind the locked door she lay across her bed and wept, steeped in such a well of pain and loneliness that she felt she would never know release from it again. She would love Aaron until she died. And if there was life after death her yearning would be with her through all eternity.

During the weeks that followed she lived every day as it

came, keeping busy and giving herself no rest. Then there came a day when she needed another pen in haste, and she opened the woven bag, which she had not touched since she had taken it with her from Halewood. To her dismay she saw that it contained the book she had been looking at when Aaron had arrived home. She pressed a distressed hand over her mouth, pierced anew by her excruciating heartache.

The book must be returned to him. He had had her shawl sent back to her, and she had come face to face with him the day after she had received it. She had been accompanying her father in an open carriage to visit some friends when Aaron, with Isobel Mitchell beside him, came alongside in his curricle, driving in the opposite direction. Isobel had inclined her head in a friendly manner, but Aaron's face, already taut and strained, had whitened and he raised his hat, a greeting acknowledged by Dr Gilmore. Delia, half-stunned by a wave of misery and love, had sat straight-backed and motionless, knowing herself to be as pale as Aaron, her hands shaking in her lap.

Since then she had not seen him, but she had had news of him in plenty, for he was a favourite topic of conversation among her friends and acquaintances at tea-parties, musical evenings, and other social gatherings. The three American visitors had stayed a month. He had taken them to all the historic places of interest in the county. Rumour had it that Miss Mitchell would be returning in the spring. Other wagging tongues declared he was to visit her, returning on holiday to his own land. Delia had listened and said nothing, but her heart had answered them. *This* is his land now! He *is* Halewood! He belongs nowhere else! And in love, no matter who or what has come between us, he belongs to no one else but me!

With a shuddering sigh she opened the book and looked through it as she had done once before. In her research into the origins of Halewood she had read other books about

241

Vikings and their invasions of England, Ireland, and other more distant lands, and she felt there was little she did not know about their customs and rites, their battles, and their way of life. But this book, concentrating as it did on north-west England, contained a last chapter of local sagas, and with listless fingers she turned to it.

A name jumped out from a page at her. *Gyda!* The she-devil from the past with whom Alice Hart was said to have conversed! With a rush of interest that lifted her out of the mental inertia that had settled on her over the past despairing weeks, she started on the ancient tale. It was not very long or detailed and the name of the site where the events had taken place was not mentioned, but as she read it was easy to picture the summit of Howling Hill with a square of primitive dwellings standing there. It was an account of battle with the attacker and his berserks killing the defending war-lord, and then the saga took a particularly interesting turn. The widow, Gyda, described as being exceedingly fair of face with hair the colour of the sun, had been taken to wife by the victor, but she had cursed him and his house, being an unwilling partner to the match, for he had failed to give honourable burial to her late husband, whose valour had been prodigious and skill in battle renowned far and wide.

That was all. Delia closed the book and sat deep in thought. Nothing much to go on. No proof that it had ever taken place on Howling Hill. And there was the strange reference to the victor treating the slaughtered loser as straw underfoot. Suppose Alice Hart, being an eccentric as she was, had heard the tale and imagined the whining and wailing of the wind in the chimneys of Halewood to be the voice of the still mourning Gyda wanting honour done to her long-dead love. If Alice had gone about the house talking back to that imagined voice it was no wonder that the witch-finder had seen her behaviour as more evidence to stack against her.

Delia drummed her fingers on the closed book. If only she could revisit Halewood armed with this new knowledge to continue her original investigations. And why not? She would return the book herself instead of sending it with a servant, and she would see Emma at the same time, for it was some long time since the baby had last been brought by the nurse to Sycamore House, Aaron having arranged this way of allowing her to see the little one. She stood up sharply. She would go now! Without further delay.

'Mr Hart's away, Miss Gilmore,' said the footman who opened the door of Halewood to her.

'That is of no account,' she replied, entering. 'I've come to see Emma and return a book to the library.'

'T'bairn's proper poorly, miss.'

Fear struck. 'Not well? What is the matter?'

'Measles, miss.'

Measles! Children died of measles! It happened frequently. Forgetting everything else she rushed to the nursery suite. The nursery maid was folding baby clothes and nodded towards the bedroom door.

'Little Emma's real bad, miss.' There was deep concern in the young girl's voice.

Delia went into the night nursery where additional dark curtains had been hung up to keep out the light. The nurse sat at the cot-side where Emma lay whimpering, her little face scarlet-spotted and feverish. Delia conversed with the nurse in whispers.

'How long has she been like this?'

'Two days. It's most unfortunate that Mr Hart should be abroad.'

'Where is he?'

'Gone back to Florence.'

'I never knew that he had visited Florence before. I remember he went to Rome, Venice, and Milan.'

'He saw Lady Hart on that tour of Italy. She sent Emma a little wooden doll in Italian costume, which she can have to play with when she's more of an age to appreciate it.'

Delia was completely taken aback. So Berenice's longing to see Aaron had overcome her scruples, and now he had returned to visit her again. Comprehension dawned. It suddenly came to her that it was not Isobel Mitchell who had come between them, but Berenice! Beautiful, fascinating Berenice, who had thrown aside all those grand, self-sacrificing resolutions, and after seeing him once had recalled him to her with her siren lure.

A cry from the cot distracted her from her own tormented thoughts. She leaned over Emma and gently brushed back the sweat-soaked curls, concern for the baby she loved taking over and thrusting all else from her. 'I'll stay and help look after her,' she whispered to the nurse. 'A servant shall go with a message to my home, and the housekeeper there will pack the few things I need and send them over.'

Two days later Emma died. Dr Pomfret assured Delia that together they had done all that was humanly possible to save the child, but she was plunged into deepest grief, refusing to be comforted, and she rocked in her distress, her hands covering her face and large shining tears dropping from between her fingers. Again the task fell to her to write and tell Aaron that the shadow of death has passed over Halewood once more, taking with it the child he had barely known and whom she had come to love as if the little one had been her own.

To assuage her grief to some degree she resumed with an obsessional diligence her investigation into the Halewood curse. Having established herself in the house she saw no reason to leave yet, and none, not even the housekeeper, demurred against her authority there.

One day in the portrait gallery she took a long look at Alice Hart. She was able to see every tiny detail of the woman's

244

face down to the tracery of wrinkles and a mole on the chin, since Aaron had had the glass roof cleaned, allowing it to sparkle in all its original glory and giving back the brilliance of light to the gallery that Halewood's architect had planned for it. There was no doubt that Alice had an odd, demented look about the eyes that had never been noticeable before. The poor, mad creature should have been cared for and protected instead of falling victim to a witch-finder with her own kin too afraid of her themselves to lift a finger to save her.

From the gallery Delia went on towards Berenice's old apartments, but found that the double doors into them were locked. She hailed a maidservant she spotted in the distance. 'Where is the key to open these doors?'

The maidservant came up to her, cap ribbons rippling down her back, and bobbed to her respectfully. 'The master had them locked the night the late Mrs Hart – or Miss Barton as she was then – came to Halewood for the first time. He said they were never to be opened without his permission.'

'Thank you,' Delia said, low-voiced. She knew why he had done that. By tradition those apartments were used only by the mistress of the house, and he had intended that she herself as his wife should have them for her own use, but when fate had stepped in and decreed otherwise, giving him another marriage partner whom he did not love, he had determined that no other woman should take her place there. Now they would never be occupied in Aaron's time. No matter how much Berenice loved him nothing would bring her back to Halewood.

With lowered head Delia turned away from the locked doors to the rooms where once she might have been enshrined in love as wife of the Master of Halewood. Weighed down with sorrow, she wandered on into the north wing, seekir a window other than those in the locked

245

apartments to look down on the inner courtyard, which had been her only reason for wishing to enter there, being in the vicinity.

She stopped by an embrasured window and sank down on the cushioned seat to open it and look out. Below, lay the wide steps of the entrance and beyond, the green sward of the courtyard. She had been giving much consideration to her eerie experience that had taken place there on her first ever visit to Halewood, and as she gazed down she wondered again if the secret key to all the house's suffering lay therein. The grassy sward was virtually the same since those ancient days when the Viking settlers had built their dwellings to form four sides of a square as a better protection for themselves and their animals against attack. Much in the shape of the present house, which itself formed a quadrangle. Was it on the green sward that Gyda's warrior had fallen in battle? She thought over again the mention in the book of the victor treating the dead hero like straw underfoot.

Had he – ? Was it possible that – ? Such a simple explanation had presented itself to her that she hardly dared believe she had stumbled on it. Suppose the dead hero had been laid there in a grave in the heart of the conquered settlement where every day the victor would stride across the place where he lay. To Gyda the brutal revenge would be beyond measure. Without an honourable burial her love could never take his rightful place in the halls of Valhalla. To others it would be a grim tale to tell and pass down, word spreading that the hill was an ill place on which to live, but the site had continued to attract men to it by its very magnificence of view and lushness of setting until at last Raoul Hart had built his fine mansion and caught the echoing note of doom when his wife had been crushed by the falling masonry.

Delia closed the window. She knew what she must do. It was a simple rite she had to perform, but she would have to choose the right moment for it. All she could hope for was that by going through with it she would remove once and for all that deep-rooted belief in the curse from Aaron, and thus lift it from the house itself.

As the days went by she made careful preparations. She was thankful for something to keep her mind from Aaron and Berenice. Finally all was ready. She had only to wait for a misty night when she would be unobserved.

It came at last. All day the mist had been settling on the hill and excitement and fear blended together within her as she watched the hours tick away. She had to wait until midnight to make sure all the servants were abed in their quarters, which were situated away from the courtyard. Then, warmly wrapped in a thick shawl against the cold night, she slipped out of the house with a lantern and basket in her hands.

She left the basket where she could find it again and began the heavy work. First she carried bales of straw from the stable and made a boat-shaped stack of them in the centre of the sward. On them she piled twigs and sticks and branches, which she gathered from the woods during the past week and hidden in a convenient place, and finally a wheelbarrow full of logs, which had been destined for the hearths of Halewood, were added to the pile. It left one last thing to do. From the basket she took a loaf of bread, some fruit, a bottle of wine, a coat of Aaron's, and some silver threepenny bits in a purse, and she laid it all on the pile. The long-dead warlord should have had horses and dogs and a waggon to take his spirit on its last journey, and perhaps a slave or two to wait on him, but he had been given the essentials in the symbolic trappings of clothing, food, drink, and wealth, and she had stacked the fuel into the shape of a longboat.

She thrust a light into the pyre. Flames grasped at the straw and swept high in a matter of seconds. A noise of crackling, snapping, and spitting broke the silence of the mist-grey night, and the heat soon forced her to stand back, the fire burning fiercely with a roar, sparks drifting on the dancing smoke like thousands of firework stars. She and the whole of the inner courtyard were bathed in a red-gold light, the mullioned panes reflecting the brilliance like watching eyes.

A sense of exhilaration filled her. The smoke was rising higher and higher, a sight that would have gladdened Gyda's heart for it was a good omen. She could even see the mist clearing about it, showing a glimpse of the stars. It was then that she realized that the wind was rising and the fire could get out of hand! If it swept across the grass and bridged the flagged path that bordered the sward Halewood itself could go up in flames!

Yet she could not bring herself to raise the alarm and douse the cleansing fire, knowing that unless this deed were done, carried through to the end, a sickness of mind would continue to haunt all generations of Harts to come. Better to let Halewood go as the ultimate sacrifice than that the curse should continue to bring despair into their lives.

Aaron, sighting the golden flick of flames from his carriage window, leaned out to yell at the coachman that Halewood was on fire and to whip up the horses. His companion on the carriage seat beside him, worn out by the long journey from Florence, did not stir and remained fast asleep. Aaron let down the window with a slapping of its leather strap and the wind blew into his face, tumbling his hair, as he strained his eyes impatiently through the darkness in the direction of his home, thumping an exasperated fist against the frame when a copse of trees or tall bushes momentarily blocked his view. There was a short delay at the gates, but the old lodge-keeper employed in the past had been retired with his wife to a cottage on the estate and it was only a matter of half a minute before the new man came running in his nightshirt, roused by the combined shouts of coachman and groom, and swung the huge gates wide. With a crack of the whip the horses and carriage went racing through.

It came to a hoof-slithering halt by the archway into the inner courtyard as the first stable-hands appeared, pulling on fustian jackets as they came, roused not by the fire, but the sound of their master's returning carriage, and their faces mirrored their alarm at the flickering glow. Aaron, hurling himself out of the carriage, saw in astonishment that Delia was sitting on the sward by what appeared to be an oval-shaped bonfire, which was already dying down and he saw immediately that any danger from it was past. At the sight of him she sprang to her feet and came running to bar his way with outstretched arms, the golden brilliance of the fire behind her creating a soft nimbus about her head.

'Don't let anyone put it out!' she implored frantically, her hair tumbled and untidy, smuts begriming her face. 'It's the end of the curse that has plagued this house since its foundations were laid. I'll tell you everything if you will give me time, but let the fire die naturally. Then it will be over. For ever!'

He did not question her, but turned to reassure his servants. 'There's nothing to concern yourselves about. No, the hand-pump isn't needed. See to the horses and baggage.'

Delia, watching with relief as he took charge, looked beyond him to the carriage and her eyes widened in a stare at the sight of the sleepy, tousle-headed boy who came stumbling out of it. She recognized him instantly, although he had grown since she had last seen him.

'Roland!' she exclaimed, running forward. 'What are you doing here?'

He grinned at the sight of her and gave a shout, rushing to meet her and throw his arms about her. 'I've come home to England! But only for a little while. Mama wrote to Mr Hart and asked him if he would fetch me away from Italy and

249

arrange my education in America. I'm going to a fine school in Boston run by a friend of Mr Hart and will spend my holidays either with Mama in Florence or with a family living near the school that has boys around my age. And I'm never going to see another tutor again!'

Delia, hugging him to her, looked at Aaron over the boy's head. 'Whatever made her reach such a decision?'

He gave her a steady look. 'I've much to tell you, but it must wait for the moment.'

Taking the boy by the shoulders, he drew him away from Delia and propelled him towards the housekeeper, who had stopped to dress in her best black before coming out of the house. 'Go with Mrs Bridger, Roland. She will take care of you and give you some food and see you to bed.'

The boy was taken off. Aaron put his fingers around Delia's wrist and drew her with him to the fire. There she told him the whole story of what she had done and the reason why. He listened, but made no comment. With a sinking heart she wondered if it had all been in vain and he was no more released from his belief in the curse now than he would ever be.

'How was Berenice?' she enquired swiftly, unable to bear his silence.

'I didn't see her.' He bent down to pick up a piece of smouldering wood that had rolled with a flurry of sparks out of the fire and he tossed it back into the flames. 'She avoided a meeting as assiduously this time as she did on my previous visit to Florence.'

He brushed his hands together, freeing them of the dusty ash, and turned to her, standing dark against the fire's glow. 'When I was in Florence the first time while touring Italy I called at her villa, but I was told that she was not at home, although I had presented my card and there could have been no mistake over my identity, as I was later to discover for certain. I was disappointed not to see her, being much

250

depressed at the time. News had reached me the previous week in Milan of Melissa's death, which had come to me as further proof of Halewood's ability to destroy or make wretched those bearing the name of Hart. I had hoped to talk over Halewood with someone who had lived in it longer than I, and when she would not see me I wrote from the hotel where I was staying to ask if I might call at a time more convenient to her. On the eve of my departure for Rome she sent me a gift for Emma. Nothing more. Not long after that I happened to meet Oscar and the Mitchells, and their company was balm to my loneliness. I was desperate to come home to you. I could think of nothing but taking you in my arms and loving you and never being separated from you again, but I knew that could never be. I had resigned myself to never marrying again. I could never ask you to share my name and the terrible ill fortunes that Halewood would be certain to bring down on you as on myself and all the other Harts. I loved you too much to risk any harm coming to you, and it was for that reason alone I forced myself to surrender you.'

She was deeply moved. 'I didn't understand.'

'I invited Oscar and the Mitchells back with me for purely selfish reasons, although they weren't aware of it. I didn't want to be alone in those first few weeks after my return to Halewood when I would have told you why it had to end between us. I put it into words very badly, but I was wild with distress at what I was doing and knew if it wasn't done then I'd never have the strength to send you from me again.'

'My dearest Aaron,' she whispered, as much to herself as to him.

'I'd have left Halewood with you, and everything to do with it if I'd felt that was the answer, but I'd had proof that it was pointless to make such an attempt in Melissa's tragic death and in my own father's yearning misery for Halewood that ruined my mother's life, quite apart from all the other

251

incidents in the Harts' history which bear that out.'

There was Berenice, too, she thought. Doomed to a love that could never be fulfilled. But he knew nothing of that. 'What took you to Florence this time?' she asked. 'Nobody in the house knew you were going to bring back Roland with you.'

'I didn't know myself. I received a letter from Berenice out of the blue. She said it was vital to her that I come to Florence without delay. I left for Italy that same morning. I was only glad that there appeared to be some mission I could carry out for her in return for all her benevolence towards me. But even then, as I told you, I didn't see her. An Italian lawyer acted as her spokesman. She has an inflammatory condition of the lungs, an illness of long standing that has recently taken a rapid turn for the worst. Your father must have known the serious state of her health and that her days were numbered even before she left Halewood. I fear that by now time will have run out for her, but she didn't want Roland to leave Italy thinking that he would never see her again. It was her last wish that I find Roland a good home as far as possible from Halewood, which she still feared, and to act as his guardian. She had nobody else to whom she could turn.'

Delia bowed her head, deeply saddened by the news he had brought her and distressed to know how greatly she had misjudged Berenice, who even in the face of death had not swerved from that original, heart-breaking resolution she had made. Aaron, seeing her sorrow, put his arms about her in a gentle embrace, and how long she stayed with her face pressed against his neck she did not know, but when she drew away at last she saw that dawn had broken and the first golden rays of the sun were touching the chimneys of Halewood. It was going to be a fine, bright day. Some of its first warmth touched her and with it came a surge of hope and conviction.

'Notice how mild the air has become!' she exclaimed

252

breathlessly, stepping away from him and letting her shawl slip from her shoulders. 'The chill has gone from the court-yard. There's nothing to fear any more!'

He made no comment, having stepped over the edge of the fire to check that the white-gold ashes and last flickering flames were safe to leave, and she could not see his face fully. But when he turned back to her and took her by the hand she could tell there was no need for words. His eyes told her he was at peace within himself. Even as Halewood itself, held in thrall for ten centuries, would be at peace, no longer torn by the strife and torment it had known in the past. In tranquil-lity and repose the house would shelter and protect with its marvellous, ancient walls all those who lived in it throughout the years to come. Thankfulness overcame her and when she leaned blissfully against him he cupped her head with his other hand, holding her to his shoulder while he led her up the steps to the great entrance. In the porch he brought her to a standstill and they stood facing each other within the framework of its richly carved pillars. His gaze on her was very serious and loving.

'I'm proposing to you, Delia. I've loved you and wanted you for my own since our first moment of meeting, as you have known only too well. Marry me, my darling. It seems to me I've waited a thousand years for this time of asking you to be my wife.'

She smiled at him, lashes drooping in her happiness. 'Yes. Oh, yes, Aaron! I love you with all my heart!'

He crushed her to him and devoured her mouth with all the pent-up passion for her that had possessed him since he had first set eyes on her. When he released her it was only to stoop and sweep her up into his arms, holding her to him.

'I'm carrying you over the threshold.' A wide smile curled his mouth. 'It's not usual before the wedding ceremony, but I'll do it again then. I want Halewood to know I've brought you home to it at last!'

Her arms were about his neck and they kissed with a deep and intimate joy as he carried her into the great house.